# TANSEN

The name of the legendary Tansen, one of the nine jewels of Emperor Akbar's court, is synonymous with the grandeur of Hindustani classical music. He is renowned for his rendering of the *dhrupad* and *dhamar* and for composing the majestic ragas *Mian ki Todi* and *Mian ki Malhar*. In this historical novel, Tansen comes to life with incidents of his *guru bhakti*, his quest for music, his loves and his family and as chief court musician, which are interwoven into a rich drama with several imaginery figures. Altogether, it becomes a delightful journey into the life and times of one of the country's greatest musicians.

GIRISH CHATURVEDI, born in 1937, grew up in a family of distinguished Hindi litterateurs and showed literary promise at an early age. In 1958, he joined Akashvani and retired as its Director (National Service) in 1995. He has scripted T.V. serials like *Gautama Buddha* and *Sambhavami Yuge Yuge* and authored *Tansen, Yeh Muhalewale* (novels), *Yamuna Se Yamuna Tak* (Essays and Reminiscences), *Sandesa Ansuan Ko* (Khand Kavya—Brij Bhasha). The Uttar Pradesh Government bestowed the Shridhar Pathak Puruskar on him. He has been awarded the Nehru Fellowship (1995), for his project on *Braj ki Lok Sanskriti*.

TANSEN

OTHER LOTUS TITLES

| | |
|---|---|
| ASHISH KHOKAR | *Baba Allauddin Khan* |
| A.S. PAINTAL | *Ustad Amir Khan* |
| DHANANAJAYA SINGH | *The House of Marwar* |
| GANESH SAILI | *Glorious Garhwal* |
| IRADJ AMINI | *Koh-i-noor* |
| JAIWANT PAUL | *'By My Sword and Shield'* |
| JYOTI JAFA | *Nurjahan* |
| KHUSHWANT SINGH | *Kipling's India* |
| LALI CHATTERJEE | *Muonic Rhapsody and Other Encounters* |
| L.K. PANDIT | *Krishna Rao Shankar Pandit* |
| MANJARI SINHA | *Ustad Bade Ghulam Ali Khan* |
| MUSHIRUL HASAN | *India Partitioned: The Other Face of Freedom*, 2 vols |
| P. LAL | *The Bhagavad Gita* |
| RUSKIN BOND | *Ruskin Bond's Green Book* |
| V. S. NARAVANE | *Best Stories from the Indian Classics* |

FORTHCOMING TITLES

| | |
|---|---|
| AMRITA PRITAM | *The Other Dimension* |
| JOHN LALL | *Samru Begum* |
| LAXMI SUBRAMANIAN | *Medieval Seafarers* |
| MAGGI LIDCHI-GRASSI | *The Great Golden Legend of the Mahabharata*, 2 vols |
| MANOHAR MALGONKAR | *Dropping Names* |
| NINA EPTON | *Mumtaz Mahal: Beloved Empress* |
| SHOVANA NARAYAN | *Kathak: A Journey Through the Ages* |
| SUDHIR KAKAR | *Indian Love Stories* |
| V.S. NARAVANE | *Devadas and Other Stories by Sarat Chandra* |

# Tansen

Girish Chaturvedi

Translated from Hindi by
Sarala Jag Mohan

Lotus Collection



This edition first published 1996
The Lotus Collection
An imprint of
Roli Books Pvt Ltd.
M-75, G.K. II Market
New Delhi 110 048
Phones: 6442271, 6462782, 6460886
Fax: 6467185
Also at
Varanasi, Agra, Jaipur and The Netherlands

ISBN: 81-7436-017-4
Rs. 150

Typeset in Galliard by Roli Books Pvt. Ltd., and
Printed at Pritha Offsets (P) Ltd. Ph. : 5708654-55

❖

*'Now, the tenor of Tansen's life had completely changed. No music emanated from his lips—not a single note. He was obsessed with Hussaini. And all he did was to drink in her beauty.*

*Deep at heart, Hussaini was quite perturbed about it. She was beginning to have the nagging fear, that Tansen might get alienated from music. One day, when she found Tansen in a happy mood, she said to him in an extremely soft voice, 'I wonder what has happened to you. Imagine for a long time, you haven't even sung an* alap. *Just see the layer of dust on your* tanpura . . .*'*

*Tansen listened to Hussaini's remark with head bowed. He realized that Hussaini was talking sense. He wondered how he had neglected his music all this time. He said, 'You're right, Hussaini, very right. Music is my life. It is my heartbeat.'*'

❖

## *Raga Mian Ki Malhar (Holi-dhamar)*

Oh Krishna! You have come to play Holi in the rain.
The clouds rumble like the sound of a tambourine,
Clouds of *gulal* cover the whole sky.
Lightning flashes, and a shower of colours falls.

❖

### मियाँ की मल्हार • होली- धमार

स्थायी - खेलन आये होरी; बरषा के समैं घन गरजत डप ढकार

अन्तरा - ध्यत गुलाल दामिनी दमकत रंग की परत फुहार- फुहार.

| 1 | 2 | 3 | 4 | 5 | 6 | 7 | 8 | 9 | 10 | 11 | 12 | 13 | 14 |
|---|---|---|---|---|---|---|---|---|---|---|---|---|---|
| | | | | | र | — | स | — | स | ध | ऩ | प | — |
| | | | | | खे | ऽ | ल | ऽ | न | आ | ऽ | यॅ | ऽ |
| | ऩ - | ध | (म)न | स | सा | स | रे | — | स | — | स | स | — |
| | हो | ऽऽ | री | ऽ | व | र | षा | ऽ | के | ऽ | स | मैं | ऽ |
| स | व़ | ध | नि़ | ध | न | (सं)नि | (सं)नि | सं | — | ऩ | ध | म | — |
| ध | व | ऽ | ऽ | ऽ | ग | र | ज | व | ऽ | ड | प | ड | ऽ |
| प | ग़ | म | रे | स | | | | | | | | | |
| का | ऽ | ऽ | ऽ | र | | | | | | | | | |
| अन्तरा | | | | | | | | | | प | नि़ | ध | न |
| | | | | | | | | | | ध | रा | ऽ | गु |
| सां | - | सं | सं | - | सं | — | रें | — | सां | स | ध | न | प |
| ला | ऽ | ल | दा | ऽ | मि | ऽ | नी | ऽ | द | म | क | ऽ | त |
| म | प | प़ | ध | रें | सं | ध | ध़ | प | म | प | ग़ | म | प |
| र | ग | को | ऽ | प | र | त | ऽ | ऽ | फु | हा | ऽ | र | फु |
| प | ग | म | रे | स | | | | | | | | | |
| हा | ऽ | ऽ | ऽ | र | | | | | | | | | |

# Preface

Indian classical music has a tradition spanning several centuries. In the *bhakti* period, singers expressed their devotion and worshipped their deities through this music, which in due course, evolved into distinct musical lineages or *gharanas.*

The name of Tansen is inextricably linked to classical music, indeed as life is to breath. Tansen raised Hindustani music to celestial heights. He was no doubt a maestro in rendering the *dhrupad* and *dhamar*, but the various ragas he composed, like *Mian Ki Todi* and *Mian ki Malhar* speak of his deep knowledge of music.

*Tansen* is a historical novel. Extensive research went into piecing together the incidents related to Tansen. Of course, a writer always resorts to imagination to develop the story. In this novel too, the imaginary characters of Tani, Kafia, and Dawan Khan have been introduced into the story.

The reputed singer, Asha Bhosle, inspired me to write this novel. She had planned to make a T.V. serial on Tansen and she asked me to write the script. But I felt this job would be made easier if I first wrote a novel on him. To the best of my knowledge this is the first novel on Tansen to be published in English. I am grateful to Roli Books for publishing this English translation. Very little is written about poets, artists and musicians. However, I wrote this novel on Tansen, hoping that through it, lovers of literature and music all over the world would be able to know something about one of the greatest Indian musicians.

GIRISH CHATURVEDI

Tansen, the Emperor of Music

# 1

Spring had set in. A cool breeze carrying with it the fragrance of flowers came from the mountains. A cuckoo perched on a mango tree was warbling sweetly while its young cooed on the next branch. The mustard fields looked joyful. The roses, *champakas*, *chameli*, *rajanigandha*, *palash* and *kareel* had opened their crimson lips. It seemed that nature was singing a lovely poem, filling the air with an intoxicating joy and excitement. The red orb of the sun rose above the horizon spreading light everywhere.

Behat village, three *kos* from Gwalior, was eagerly waiting to welcome a newly married couple. Makrand Pandey was returning after his wedding at Antri, followed by the bearers carrying the palanquin of his bride, Parvati. They had walked along the forest roads throughout the night. At dawn they rested the palanquin under a shady tree and some members of the marriage party performed their morning ablutions. The forest was so dense, that the rays of the sun could not penetrate it. It was all quiet, but for the occasional sounds of the wild animals.

Makrand had a drink of water and waited for his companions. A sword hung at his waist. He estimated that they would still have to walk about ten *kos* and it would be night by the time they reached their village. All kinds of thoughts crossed Makrand's mind. He thought about his future married life, about his worship at the Shiva temple with Parvati by his side and about how he would give a grand feast for the villagers.

Makrand was lost in his thoughts when suddenly, he heard the roar of a lion. Nervous at first, he gradually recovered from his fear. He took out his sword and looked around. Throughout the journey his newly-wed bride has been sitting silently in the palanquin. Her heart sank when she heard the roar of the lion and saw Makrand's naked sword. She drew apart the palanquin curtains and said hesitantly, 'What will happen if the lion comes? Your life will be saved if you climb up the tree.'

'And what about you?'

'I don't know how to climb a tree.'

'Parvati, do you think your husband is such a weakling that he would climb up the tree leaving you alone?' Makrand remarked. 'I've held your hand with the sacred fire as a witness. Your safety is my responsibility. I cannot forget my duty.'

The lion's roar now appeared to be closer. Parvati drew Makrand towards the palanquin, urging him to come inside. But Makrand did not oblige. He waited for the lion. After a while, the lion's growl was heard no more. It had probably returned to the jungle. Both of them heaved a sigh of relief. Now that they were alone, Makrand said, 'Parvati, marriage is a social bond. More than that, it is a union of the minds. We have to steer our lives' ship together. All my happiness will be yours and we shall share our misfortunes.'

Parvati looked very beautiful as she raised her dark eyelashes and for the first time looked into his eyes. She felt happy at heart. Then, slowly lowering them she said, 'Be assured, you will always find me by your side. I am fortunate to have found a husband who is exactly how I had imagined him to be.'

Parvati came back to the palanquin since the members of the wedding party had returned. With folded hands she thanked God for such a brave husband.

The bearers lifted the palanquin and moved on. The sun's rays filtered through the forest, lighting up patches. Herds of deer, wild buffaloes, jackals, wild cats and *langoors* on the trees, all ran helter-skelter.

The wedding party proceeded towards Behat. After walking for about an hour, the jungle became sparse. Now the wedding party went along a dusty path. About a *kos* away from the village, the wedding party sat down to rest under the shade of a tree. The bride was given *besan laddoos* and water for breakfast.

After a while, a group of some twenty men arrived on the scene. Some had swords hanging from their waists and some carried lances and axes. One of the men had a harmonium hanging from the neck and another a *dholak*. In reply to Makrand's question, a man with a big mustache and a beard said that they were going to Mathura on a pilgrimage.

Soon the pilgrims started singing devotional songs. Their melodious voices reverberated in the jungle. But as the singing stopped, the bandits disguised as pilgrims starting looting the wedding party. A bloody fight ensued. Makrand also displayed his courage and swordsmanship. People on both the sides were wounded. The bandits fled leaving behind their loot and as the sun set the wounded members of the wedding party somehow reached Behat.

The evening shadows began to darken. Stars started appearing in the sky. Parvati's palanquin was lowered in front of the house. The village women ran to receive her. They welcomed her with mellifluous songs. Parvati was made to sit on a comfortable seat. Everyone was happy that a woman had come to light the lamp in Moti Pandey's house. But Makrand felt sad at that moment with the thought of his parents. How happy they would have been to see his wife!

Makrand's father, Moti Pandey had been the village zamindar. He was a very noble man and everyone in the village respected him. But, a plague in the village took away both Moti Pandey and his wife prematurely. Fifteen year old Makrand, somehow survived. There was no one to support him.

Makrand had a *pucca* house and fields, which he inherited from the zamindar's estate. He studied in the small village school. Every morning, after his bath, he would go to the Shiva temple on the outskirts of the village and sing *bhajans* after making offerings to the Lord. He never asked himself why he went to the temple. His father had taken him everyday and so, he continued going. What man learns in childhood remains with him till the last moment. Makrand too, had grown up in the same way.

The moon was shedding a lovely light all across the sky. The twinkling stars looked like embroidered dots on a sari. The month of *phalgun* had set in and the breeze brought rapturous joy to body and mind. Far in the distance, the shepherds sang the *phaag* accompanied by drums, cymbals and *bela*.

Makrand enjoyed the *phaag* immensely. Beautiful like a rose-bud, with her intoxicating eyes and the red tinge on her lips—Parvati on her first night waited patiently for Makrand in their room. Her large eyes searched for him through the door. And then, she saw him coming towards the room. Parvati's heart skipped a beat as she waited eagerly to be with her beloved.

The light of a lamp filled the room. When Makrand entered the room, Parvati touched his feet. Makrand sat on the nuptial bed and asked, 'How do you find me, Parvati?'

Parvati lowered her eyes and replied, 'Very nice.'

Makrand said, 'Parvati, I've wandered life's alleys alone. My parents died prematurely and I have been alone ever since. But now you've come. With you, I shall sail through life. Also I have great faith in Mahadev. Will you come with me to the temple everyday?'

Parvati agreed.

It was already late, for it was the first glorious night of love. Makrand did not realize when he fell asleep. He slept peacefully for he had Parvati in his arms and sleep in his eyes. The two hearts rested as one.

# 2

The aurora of the dawn started diminishing. The sky turned red as the sun rose. Birds twittered on the trees as they emerged from their nests. Flocks of parrots flew across the blue sky. The farmers with ploughs on their shoulders proceeded to their fields singing *bhajans.*

The sun's rays scattered over the ramparts of the fort, on the rocky terrain of Gwalior. Pigeons cooed on its turrets. *Langoors* swung on the branches of the trees, occasionally plucking and eating the leaves. There was a palace inside the fort, where the peacocks danced and herds of deer leapt about joyfully on the green grass.

Outside the palace the horsemen guarded the fort with bared swords. Down below, the horsemen and infantry waited with elephants and drums for the king, Man Singh Tomar, who was about to go hunting. Their swords, lances, spears and arrows glittered in the sunlight. Soon, the youthful Man Singh Tomar came down the fort, riding a beautiful elephant. Cries of victory for the king filled the air. He appeared magnificent with his bushy eyebrows, black mustaches, and his turban was decorated with precious pearls and jewels. Raja Man Singh Tomar gave the signal, by raising his hand. Soon the hunting party began its march towards the dense jungles of Shivpuri to the sound of the trumpets and the beating of the drum.

The whole day the convoy marched and reached Shivpuri at sunset. The jungle was dense, thickly grown with *peepul*, banyan, pine, teak, rosewood and *jamun* trees. There was a beautiful lake in the jungle which was visited by wild animals at night to drink water. *Machans* had already been erected in the jungle and tents were pitched for the soldiers after clearing the ground. Raja Man Singh was tired after the long journey. He got down from the elephant, drank water from the gold jug with the spout and later settled down for dinner.

He was still washing his hands after dinner, when drums started beating to lead the animals towards the hunters. In the dense jungle and dark night, two drum-beaters, sitting on the edge of a culvert, were puffing away at the hubble-bubble. Beyond the culvert, a lion emerged from the dense jungle and jumped to the other side. The drum-beaters could not see anything in the dark and the lion landed on their heads. The weight of the lion pushed their heads down to their torsos. On hearing their cries, the people nearby rushed to the scene.

Raja Man Singh Tomar was informed and he reached the spot ready with his sword. While he was still talking, the enraged lion appeared from the bush and attacked the king. The king ducked and with a single blow, struck the waist of the lion. But his paws had attacked the king's left arm and blood dripped from it. The news of the king's injury spread like fire. The royal physician applied herbal ointment and bandaged the arm. The following day, the king's convoy carrying the dead lion returned to Gwalior joyous and happy.

After trudging all day the convoy reached Gwalior. Darkness had descended, and people had lit lamps in their houses. The torches were lit on the fort. Rani Mriganayani was restless as she waited in her palace. Several lamps were lit in the chamber, which was filled with the fragrance of burning incense. The queen was deep in thought. She clapped her hands, when a maid appeared and bowed to her. 'Any information, Pallavi,' she asked.

'No, Maharani!'

'What could have happened? The Maharaja had said he would definitely return by evening. Go to the minister and find out if there has been any message from the Maharaja.'

After Pallavi left, the queen started peeping through the spy-holes of the palace. Soon, she saw the Maharaja's convoy approaching the fort. Mriganayani's eyes flashed with joy. The palace inmates looked curiously at the hunted lion tied to a staff, which the kingsmen were carrying.

A little later, the king entered Mriganayani's chamber. She greeted him very happily but was stunned to see the bandage on his arm, for even now, the wound was bleeding a little. 'What happened to you, Maharaj? Why this bandage? Why?' she asked impatiently.

'Oh, it's nothing, my dear. The lion accidentally struck me with his paw. The royal physician has applied some ointment. The wound will heal in a few days.'

'But Maharaj, I'm really frightened by the blood oozing from your arm. What would I have done, if something untoward had happened?' she cried and her eyes were filled with tears.

The king drew her close and said, 'You're a brave woman. You shouldn't be scared of seeing blood. Our hands are always smeared with blood. When we cut off the heads of our enemies in the battlefield, we see blood spurting like fountains. Then with raised swords we dance the *tandava* on the enemies dead bodies. Blood alone, brings glory to us. In blood lies our victory, Mriganayani!'

Mriganayani's breath mingled with the breath of the king. Their minds were in ecstasy. The flowers in the garden smiled and the two united as they lay on the bed. . . .

Mriganayani woke up in the morning. She combed her hair, changed her dress and adorned herself after applying a lotion of saffron, musk and sandal. The chamber-maid had left fresh flowers, which she tied in her braid. Then with her eyes sparkling with collyrium, she waited for the king to wake up.

Raja Man Singh Tomar woke up a few moments later. He was groaning in pain. Mriganayani was in a terrible panic. 'Is the wound paining more Maharaj? Shall I call the royal physician?'

'No, Mriganayani. I enjoy being in pain. It makes music flow from my heart. And now give me my *veena*.'

'But what about your wounded arm?'

'I shall play the *veena* with one hand. I want to sing.'

Mriganayani got up. Handing over the *veena* to him, she asked, 'Maharaj, is this music born out of pain?'

'Yes, Mriganayani. According to me music comes out of tears. When a child cries at birth, there is rhythm even in that crying—there is a tune, a certain tone. There are modulations. Musical notes can be heard even in the waves of the sea. There is intoxicating music even in the blowing wind; in the chirping of birds and cries of animals—there is music in everything, Mriganayani.'

'What is the benefit of this music, Maharaj?' Mriganayani asked affectionately.

The king replied seriously, 'Music is the most beautiful expression of one's mind. It is the great means to reach God. Music is the power of the word, Mriganayani. It can make a crying person laugh and a laughing person cry. Music means power, devotion, supreme joy.' With these words, the king started pulling at the strings of the *veena* with one hand.

The chamber reverberated with sweet notes. Mriganayani sat still, like a statue, listening to the music. The king started with the *alap* of a *dhrupad* and all the variations, from the roar of a lion to the delicate cooing of a cuckoo. The notes of the music sank deep into Mriganayani's heart. Her eyes closed, she was completely absorbed in this music which flowed like a river.

The king continued singing the *dhrupad*. When he finished, Mriganayani wiped the sweat of his brow with the end of her saree. The king's music had penetrated into the depths of her heart. Mriganayani, who had been fascinated by arrows and swords, was now enraptured by his music.

The king was lost in thought. Mriganayani said in a gentle voice, 'This music is so intoxicating, I forgot everything and just sat listening to your music. I even forgot about the wounds on your arm. Shall I suggest something, Maharaj?'

'Speak on, Mriganayani,' the king replied with affection.

'Maharaj, I wish you would open a music school in Gwalior.'

'Wonderful, my queen! What a beautiful suggestion! I'm really blessed to have a queen like you. Mriganayani, today itself, I will make an announcement in the royal assembly about starting a music school in Gwalior.'

It was quite late in the morning. The king changed his dress and left to go the darbar with the firm resolve of starting a music school in Gwalior. . . .

Raja Man Singh Tomar entered the *darbar* and sat on his beautiful throne. His arm still ached. Occasionally, he would stroke it with the other hand. The courtiers noticed the king wincing with pain. 'Maharaj, it seems that your wound is very painful. With your permission, let the *darbar* end for today,' suggested the prime minister.

Raja Man Singh Tomar smiled at the prime minister's suggestion. He said, 'Not at all, let the *darbar* continue. It is not unusual for me to be wounded like this.'

Starting the proceedings, the prime minister said, 'Maharaj, our kingdom faces the constant danger of invasion. We shall have to increase our military strength. More will have to be spent from the treasury.'

The king heard the prime minister in silence. Other members in the *darbar* also spoke in support. After patiently listening to each one, the king said, 'I have listened to all of you. Now you should hear my decision. You see, I am a valiant man. I am proud of my sword. Defence of the kingdom is a matter of supreme importance. But. . .'

Silence prevailed. Breaking it, Man Singh Tomar went on, 'War and peace, blood and calm, tears and smiles are all part of life. You should definitely think of the kingdom's defence and increase the military strength. But don't let things come to such an end that the cries of war rob us of our joy altogether. Let not blood streak from our lips. Life, is like the sky in which the rainbow also shines. The rainbow, with its orange, blue, violet and red hues—that is our life. I do wish to fight against the enemies, but let there always be music on our lips. A weeping man cannot fight against the harsh realities of life. It is my wish that we should immediately establish a music school in Gwalior.'

After listening to Man Singh Tomar, the courtiers raised a joyful cry. A little later, he sent for his court singers—Nayak Bakhshu, Gurju, Bhagwan, Dallu and Dhodi. All the court musicians arrived and after making their salutations took their seats. Man Singh said to Bakhshu, 'Nayak Bakhshu, I am proud to have a great musician like you in my *darbar*. I wish to open a big music school in Gwalior where children will be given systematic training in music. Let the students be given thorough training in *dhrupad* and *dhamar* which are the very soul of our Indian music.'

Bakshu bowed his head and said, 'Maharaj, your orders will be fully obeyed. As such, Amir Khusro, the court musician of Allauddin has beautifully rendered *tals* like *jhumra*, *ada*, *chaar tal* and *soolfag*. He has made great contributions in the fields of *qavvali*, *tarana*, *geet*, *jilf*, *saajgiri*, in *sarparda* and other *ragas* as well as the *tabla* and *sitar*. With your permission, we can train the students in these aspects too.'

Man Singh Tomar thought for a while and said, 'Very well, but they should be trained first in *dhrupad* and *dhamar*. They are the very soul of our ancient tradition of music. We must preserve the purity of our music. We must imbibe the elegant and beautiful from wherever we can. You are a great musician. The reputation of our kingdom should spread all round not only on account of the strength of our sword but also the intoxication of our music. Now you all may leave and get to work on this great task.'

With this, the king dismissed the *darbar* and left for the palace.

# 3

Maharaja Man Singh Tomar, apart from being a very brave ruler, was also an art-lover. If music created waves in his heart, so did the clanging of the swords, for the flute and the gun were equally dear to him.

The music school was started with much fanfare. The king himself paid a visit one day and ordered that oil-portraits of his ancestors be hung there. Promptly, artists set about this task. The beautiful paintings of the rulers of the Tomar dynasty adorned the walls of the music school. Vir Singh Dev's portrait was put up first. He had conquered Gwalior in 1375 during the reign of Ghiasuddin. Later on, Vir Singh Dev built Lakshman Paur in the Gwalior Fort in the name of his son Lakshman.

The next was the portrait of Uddharan Dev Tomar who succeeded Vir Singh Dev. In 1402, General Iqbal Khan of Delhi invaded Gwalior with a view to plunder its rich treasures. But he had to surrender before Uddharan Dev's manoeuvres and fled after plundering the city.

The third portrait was of Maharaja Durgarendra Singh. He was another very brave ruler and had won many battles against the Sultans of Delhi and Mandavgarh. After his death, Maharaja Kirti Singh occupied the Gwalior throne. He was succeeded by Maharaj Kalyan Singh who built the Badal Mahal. Their portraits too, were put up in the music school.

Maharaja Man Singh Tomar had ascended the throne of Gwalior in 1486. One day, Gwalior was surrounded by clouds of dust raised by trotting horses. There was an uproar because Behlol Lodhi had invaded Gwalior with a huge force. Maharaja Man Singh's army were impatient to fight. The mighty army of the Gwalior kingdom trounced Behlol Lodhi's army so badly that they fled for their lives. Man Singh Tomar was ecstatic and there were celebrations to mark his victory. Then one day amidst great pomp and clamour, the music school was inaugurated.

Meantime, Sikandar Lodhi of Delhi focused his attention on Gwalior. A cruel ruler, he launched attacks on Gwalior a number of times, but every time he had to surrender on the battlefield to Man Singh Tomar's brave and well-planned resistance. Harassed under his cruel regime, many artists migrated to Gwalior and peacefully devoted themselves to their respective arts.

Though Raja Man Singh indulged in clanging the swords, he was an artist at heart. He had profound knowledge of music. On the battlefield, he was like an earthquake, a typhoon which spelt death for the enemy. But in times of peace, he gave himself up to the pursuit of music and art dominated his mind.

He had ordered, that music compositions should be in the language of the people. He revived the old tradition of devotional music. As a result, devotional songs, or songs to the glory of the Lord were accorded an important place in classical music. Not only that, such songs became popular even for auspicious occasions. Hindu gods and goddesses were praised in song everywhere. Man Singh Tomar wished that music should also give a glimpse of the pleasures of marital love. He himself talked to the musicians about *Nayika-bhed*. The rules of music were to be presented in a popular language so that all singers could benefit from them. . . .

One day, Maharaja Man Singh Tomar was sitting in his beautiful palace thinking about the enemy invasions, his own military strength, protection of Gwalior and other matters. A little later, Maharani Mriganayani entered his chamber. Man Singh Tomar was lost in his thoughts. Mriganayani asked in a gentle tone, 'Maharaj, it seems that today you're seeing a heavenly sight.'

Raja Man Singh was startled. Regaining his composure, he said, 'No, Mriganayani, I was not imagining anything heavenly. My heaven is in the kingdom of Gwalior. My heaven is in your marble-like arms. Come Mriganayani, sit down.'

Mriganayani sat near him. Well-endowed with natural charm,

her large eyes, inquired after the king's welfare. The king addressed her, 'Mriganayani, I have gone through life considering the battlefield as my bed. I have opened my eyes in the face of loud shrieks and groans which have been like lullabies. In my life, I have seen death from very close quarters. But Mriganayani. . . the king stopped mid-way.

'What is it, Maharaj? Why did you stop?'

'It's nothing, Mriganayani. I have been constantly thinking that all this bloodshed, these swords and lances serve no purpose.'

'Why?'

'Because they do not give life but take it. They spread destruction. They do not create, but destroy. Even if we win a war after shedding much blood, what happens? How much blood gets shed and how much weeping and wailing is witnessed! I consider art to be of supreme importance. Art makes man immortal. An artist never dies. With the passage of time, kings and kingdoms leave no trace behind them on the earth. I hear the notes of human creation, the sounds of ***mridanga*** and cymbals. Mriganayani, I think I should write a book about music. What do you feel?'

Mriganayani paused and said, 'Maharaj, it is a very good idea. But would the constant danger to the kingdom permit you to write a book about music?'

'Yes, Mriganayani. Music is my hunger. Music is my food. Music is my thirst. I cannot live without music. I keep on composing music even in the midst of the clanging of swords and tumult and shrieks on the battlefield.'

Then Man Singh fell silent. Mriganayani asked with a smile, 'What is the book you will write, Maharaj?'

Man Singh gave her an affectionate look and pressing her lovely cheeks with his hands he said, '*Mankauthuhal*'.

While, Man Singh Tomar worked on the musical treatise *Mankauthuhal*, his court musicians, Manju, Bakhshu, Lohand and others trained students in music. They created new ***ragas***. These ***ragas*** sung in the Gwalior ***darbar***, came to be appreciated in other kingdoms as well. Sultan Bahadur

Shah of Gujarat ordered his musicians to sing only those *ragas*.

Man Singh Tomar created the *Dhruvapad*. He innovated musical compositions to the glory of gods and goddesses, *stuti* or invocations and compositions narrating the various stages of love.

Because of his tireless efforts, the creeper of music planted by him began to flower and the whole country came under the influence of its melodies and intoxication. In course of time, it even reached the harem of Muhammad Shah Rangila. Even Akbar's courtier, Abul Fazl described the musical style as beautiful and in accordance with popular taste. . . .

It was evening. The sky over Gwalior was dark and overcast. Man Singh Tomar heard the rumbling of the clouds. Soon, there was a heavy downpour. Man Singh Tomar was particularly fascinated by the rainy season. He felt like welcoming the rain clouds with his singing.

Mriganayani came to Man Singh Tomar beautifully dressed. Her large, flashing eyes smiled with a touch of collyrium, while her pink cheeks, throbbed with youth and joy played about her crimson lips. Placing her delicate hands on the king's shoulders she asked, 'Are you enjoying the sight of these dark clouds, Maharaj?'

The king looked at her with affection and then said calmly, 'Yes, Mriganayani. It is the collyrium of those dark clouds that you have applied in your eyes today. The collyrium looks so lovely in your eyes! These dark clouds too are smiling with the collyrium of beauty. Mriganayani, the red tinge of your cheeks and the varied hues of the clouds are prompting me to sing the *Dhruvapad*. Fetch my *tanpura*! I shall greet you and these clouds by singing *Dhruvapad*.'

The rain poured from the clouds and with it nectar poured from the king's throat. He was deeply engrossed in his singing. Mriganayani sat listening to him totally entranced. What a genius the king was! He was a terrific warrior, poet and singer as well. There was no limit to his accomplishments.

After the king finished singing, he sat quietly. Mriganayani broke the silence, 'Maharaj, your music has penetrated deep into my heart. I do wish you will keep singing like this, and I will keep enjoying it.'

'Yes, Mriganayani, when man begins to cherish something deeply, he gains strength by himself. If at all, it is only music that gives me happiness.'

'Then does that mean that my company doesn't make you happy?' Mriganayani asked in disappointment.

'It is not that, Mriganayani. Music is like worship for me, whereas you are the power behind it.'

Mriganayani's big eyes flashed with delight to hear the king's words. While they were talking, a chambermaid entered and said, 'Maharaj, our court singer Ramadasji wishes to meet you.'

The king ordered, that Ramdas be sent in at once. Ramdas bowed before the king and the queen and after greeting them with folded hands, sat down. The king asked, 'Ramdas, what do you see in the sky?'

'Dark clouds and rain, Maharaj?' Ramdas replied.

'In that case, take this *tanpura* and sing something for those clouds.'

At the king's orders, Ramdas commenced on the intoxicating tune of the *raga Malhar*. He sang with such deep concentration that he became completely oblivious to himself. Mriganayani and the king also listened similarly absorbed. When Ramdas stopped singing, the king said, 'Wonderful, Ramdas! You really sing beautifully. From today I shall call this rendering of *Malhar* the *Ramadasi Malhar*.'

# 4

It was harvest time. The wheat stalks swayed gently in the wind. The farmers reaped with their sharp sickles, while the swallows, blue jays, sparrows, wild-pigeons and flocks of parrots perched on trees at the edge of the field, twittering as they waited for their grains—as though claiming their share of the crop!

Exhausted with reaping, the farmers settled down to rest under the shade of the trees. It was their meal time. Young girls and women carrying *rotis* tied in cloth on their heads and pots of buttermilk came up the pathways, laughing and giggling. Under the trees they rested the pots of buttermilk and bundles of *rotis* on the ground, along with the water-jugs and they settled down to eat. After a hearty meal, they sat and gossiped.

Haria, the young village boy, could sing beautiful songs. At everyone's insistence, he started singing the *phaag*. The farmers kept rythm by beating on their metal plates with their palms. All the farmers and their women joined in the singing, and the whole atmosphere was jubilant.

Makrand was going towards his fields driving his bullock-cart along the *kuchcha* road. He too forgot everything and was lost in the joyous singing of the *phaag*. When it was over, the farmers picked up their sickles and resumed their cutting. Makrand also got up and was happy to see the harvesting of the crop in his fields. It had rained well that year, and there had been an abundant yield. The farmers' bags were bursting with wheat. Makrand thought to himself, that even after four years of marriage, he had not been able to make any ornaments for Parvati. This year he would definitely get a gold necklace and a few gold bangles for her. He would go to Gwalior for them with his money once the crop was sold. Lost in his thoughts, Makrand felt very happy. The farmers loaded their bullock-carts with the bundles of harvested crop. He climbed on to his bullock-cart and went homewards. Of course, on the way he stopped before the Mahadev temple at the outskirts of the village, to offer a bundle of wheat.

The strong, dusty *phagun* winds were blowing. Makrand Pandey alighted from his bullock-cart in front of his house. The farm hands began unloading the bundles of wheat-stalks from it. Instead of entering the house straightway, Makrand went to the garden at the back, where all kinds of flowers were blooming and the fragrance of roses filled the air. Seated, in a nearby bower, Parvati was admiring the beauty of the flowers. Makrand went up to her and gently placed his hand on her shoulder. Parvati was startled. '*Arey*, Parvati, you're talking to the flowers all by yourself !' Makrand exclaimed.

'They are saying something. How lovely and innocent are these roses!' she remarked.

'You love flowers a great deal, Parvati. I see that you're the only one to look after this garden. Do you have some links with these flowers from your previous birth?' asked Makrand.

'Maybe I do. When you're not at home I sit near these flowers and these roses are my friends. When I see them my heart is filled with joy, for their beauty brings nice thoughts to my mind,' said Parvati.

'Why should they not be beautiful? They are nature's produce after all, for they spread fragrance. Moreover, who do I have for company except you? To whom can I go and talk?'

It was clear to Makrand that Parvati loved roses and was fascinated by them. After a while both of them got up and went inside the house.

It was beginning to get dark. The village children were still playing. The Holi festival was round the corner and the children were jumping and dancing, playing the duff and the drum.

Parvati lighted the lamp as she entered the house. The house was flooded with light. The flame of the little lamp dispelled the darkness in the house, but that flame could not drive away the darkness of Parvati's mind. She had been sad all day, as was evident from her face.

Parvati served Makrand the meal in a metal plate and she sat on the floor before him, a melancholy look on her face. As Makrand ate he glanced at Parvati and said, 'Parvati, I've noticed that you've been sad for some time. What's worrying you, Parvati? Listen, I'm going to get some ornaments made for you this year, once I have sold the crop. I will take you to Gwalior and you can choose them.'

Parvati was more depressed after hearing that, but she said nothing. Makrand asked, 'Would you also like to have some new clothes?' Makrand went on about buying all kinds of things for her. Parvati remained seated and kept looking down at the floor, her face unhappy.

When Makrand insisted and wanted to know why she was sad, she raised her tearful eyes and said, 'Do you see this lamp?'

'I do,' said Makrand.

'What does the lamp give?' she asked Makrand.

'A lamp would give only light, what else?' Makrand replied and stared at Parvati.

Parvati said grimly, 'And what about the light of our house?'

'I see, now I've got your point, Parvati. That light is not in our hands. But I can't bear to see your tears. I love you with all my heart. Who do I have in this world but you? Parvati, I am a devotee of Lord Shankar. I will pray to him that he should grant me a son.'

Hearing this, Parvati's face lit up with joy. Happiness danced on her lips. After the meal, Makrand went to the village square to join the company of men. . . .

Barely four days were left for Holi. The whole village, both Hindus and Muslims, was busy singing the *phaag* songs and playing the duffs, cymbals, drums and timbrels.

Late at night, everyone went back home. Parvati too had gone to sleep but the lamp was still burning. Makrand called out her name and Parvati opened the door and then the couple retired to sleep.

Deep sleep is the only soothing balm for a troubled mind; the greatest sustaining force in life. Sleep, whose affectionate touch removes all fatigue. For now both of them were peacefully asleep. All sorts of pictures pass through one's mind in sleep. Parvati was having a dream. She saw herself as the wife of a very great king. Seated in a chariot she was going through a beautiful garden full of variagated flowers in bloom. An entourage of attendants was accompanying her. There were lovely trees with birds chirping in them, and a small river flowing close by. She went and sat in a boat, floating in the river. Her attendants were rowing the boat and in another boat a group of women were singing *raga bahar*. Their music permeated the atmosphere. Finishing their boating, all of them alighted and sat under a beautiful shady tree. The women entertained Parvati with different dances. When the dancing stopped, suddenly a fruit dropped from the tree into Parvati's lap. The happy women congratulated Parvati for the imminent birth of a prince. . . .

Suddenly, Parvati awoke and sat up utterly confused. It was not dawn as yet. She heard the jingle of the bells tied on the neck of the cow outside. She went up to the cow and kept the cut straw in its metal container. The cow went on chewing the fodder while Parvati stroked the animal. It was almost daybreak by that time. As the darkness diminished, a red light spread across the eastern sky. In the neighborhood, the farmers were milking their cows or buffaloes. Their wives were baking *rotis* on earthen *chulhas* and the sweet smell of the *rotis* had spread all round. The oxen were impatient to go out into the fields. The women, carrying earthen pots on their heads, made for the wells to draw water.

Makrand woke up yawning. He cleaned his teeth with a twig and after washing his mouth sat down. Parvati arrived with buttermilk in a jug. Makrand slowly drank the buttermilk and Parvati narrated her dream of the previous night to him.

Makrand said grimly, 'It's a nice dream, Parvati. But a dream is only a dream. I can understand how you are suffering. Now listen, if Lord Shankar is merciful, he would surely bless you with a child.'

With that Makrand got up. He bathed and then putting flowers and *bilwa* leaves in a small plate and with a jugful of water, he went to the temple at the far end of the village. He rang the temple bells for a long time and bowed to Lord Shankar sprinkling water, offering flowers and incense. Then he began praying and singing his glory. He had a good voice. Makrand folded his hands in prayer, prostrated himself and then said in a low voice, 'Oh, Shankar Baba, you are merciful. You are full of grace. You are *Bholenath*. You are a great giver. Grant a son to Parvati, *Bholenath*! I shall be grateful and distribute your *prasad*. I shall bathe you with consecrated water and I shall feed the people.'

After offering that prayer, Makrand returned home. From that day, he started visiting the temple everyday.

One day there was heavy rain accompanied with stormy winds and lightning. Behat village was flooded and the *kuchcha* roads were submerged under water.

Makrand felt melancholic, for his heart was full of conflicting emotions. He suddenly got up and came out of the house. In that heavy rain, he tied his dhoti higher, picked up the water jug and set out towards the temple, wading through the waterlogged road. Sometimes his bare feet struck stones and thorns pricked him. But Makrand with his firm resolve finally reached the temple. As he worshipped Lord Shankar he offered flowers and sang his praises. It appeared that the rain was singing *Megh-Malhar* as it poured ceaselessly on Makrand's head. And in the temple, Makrand sang the glory of Lord Shankar.

The rain poured heavily as Makrand waded through the muddy water, to return home. On the way, he noticed a gorgeous cobra under a tree. He stopped and folded his hands before it. He thought that Lord Shankar was pleased with him and had appeared before him in this form. Otherwise, he could not understand the mystery of the cobra in such wet weather. He stood there with his eyes closed, praying to the *Naga Devata*. When he opened his eyes, the cobra was not there. Makrand thought it was indeed a miracle. As he walked on, his foot struck a stone under the water and started bleeding. He reached home limping. Parvati was dumb-struck to see his bleeding foot. She said, 'You didn't listen to me. What would have happened had you not gone to the temple for just one day in this heavy rain? See how your foot is bleeding!'

'Don't worry, Parvati. The blood will stop on its own.'

'No, I'll tie a bandage right now.' And she bandaged Makrand's foot with a clean cloth and sat at his feet.

The days passed, the same sun and moon appeared each day. At times, Parvati wished that *Bholenath* would give her a son as lovely as the moon. . .

The marriage season had started. The marriage houses were decorated with festoons and plantain leaves. There was no electricity those days. The houses were illuminated with countless lamps and the *baraat* would arrive beating drums and playing cymbals. The women would receive the *baraat* with wedding songs.

At one end of the village lived the Muslim population. Jumman *Mian* an elderly man was a tall and sturdy Pathan, with long grey beard and moustaches. He was lovingly called Jumman *Chacha* by everyone in the village. He stood by everyone in times of trouble and was present at weddings and other occasions in every family. He was respected by the young and old. He constantly prayed to God and said his rosary.

Jumman *Chacha's* daughter Razia was an extremely charming girl. Her marriage had been arranged and the *baraat* was arriving that night from Gwalior. *Chacha* was very happy. Water was sprinkled in front of Jumman *Chacha's kuchcha* house. The village people gathered to help in the preparations for the wedding.

The *baraat* arrived at night accompanied by a lot of drum-beating and clanging of cymbals and *phuljharias* (sparklers). The whole village was lighted. The *maulvi* read the *nikah* and with that the marriage ceremony ended. The *baraat* departed in the morning. Razia, seated in the palanquin cried as she thought of her fields, her friends Radha, Kamala, Ragini, her games and frolic and Jumman *Chacha's* affection.

All the village women—both Hindus and Muslims—had gathered to bid dear Razia farewell. With choking voices they sang farewell songs. The whole scene was so pathetic for the girl was being separated from her parents. Jumman *Chacha*, Makrand and other people stood there with tearful eyes. The *baraat* departed. . .

Time went past. Makrand continued going to the temple everyday. Parvati lived on, in the expectation of having a son.

One day Jumman *Chacha* visited Makrand, as he sat outside the house on the charpoy, lost in thought. Makrand greeted him with a salaam and asked him to sit down. They talked at random. In the course of their conversation, Makrand said, '*Chacha*, it's five years since I married Parvati but she has not yet given birth to a child. It doesn't matter to me, but Parvati is a woman. Only she can know how much a woman longs to bear children.'

Jumman *Chacha* became very serious. He said, 'Don't worry, son. There is a very good fakir by the name of Muhammad Gaus who lives in Gwalior. Come with me to meet him one day. God willing, a son would be born in your house.'

It was time for the evening meal and Parvati brought food in two plates. Parvati had cooked *sarson ka saag* and *rotis* of maize flour. She had also put lumps of *gur*. The food was so delicious that both of them over-ate.

It was full moon, with the stars gleaming in the sky. The village fields, with mud-houses and *kuchcha* roads shone in the moonlight. The night was cooling and the moonlight was soothing.

When Jumman *Chacha* got up to go, Makrand held his hand and asked him more about fakir Gaus. He asked, '*Chacha*, who is this fakir Mohammad Gaus? What does he do? How is it that one's wishes are fulfilled by his blessings? Tell me something about him, *Chacha*.'

Jumman *Chacha* said in a serious tone, 'Makrand, my son, Mohammad Gaus is a Pathan Muslim. He was well-settled in life, but one day something got into him and he turned away from the world. He left his home and family and immersed himself in prayer and service of God. He forgot about everything and completely devoted himself to God. After becoming a fakir, Mohammad Gaus has been showering God's grace in the world. People in distress go to him weeping, but return laughing. Such fakirs do not take anything, they only continue to give. They have such a wealth of God's grace, that however much you take from it, the treasure never gets exhausted. When man's heart is dedicated to God, he forgets about wealth, caste and community, colour and appearance, hatred and deception. His heart shines like that moon in the sky. When a man, true to heart says something, it definitely comes true. Such is fakir Mohammad Gaus. He will surely fulfil your heart's desire. Would you come with me, son?'

'Yes, *Chacha*, why not?'

Then Jumman Chacha got up saying, *'Yah Khuda, Yah Khuda'*, and counting his beads went homewards.

After Jumman *Chacha* left, Makrand lifted the charpoy and kept it inside. Then he said, 'Parvati, tomorrow morning I shall go to Gwalior with Jumman *Chacha*. Please get up early and make *rotis* for me and Jumman *Chacha*, to eat on the way! And yes, Parvati, Jumman *Chacha* was praising your cooking a lot.'

Parvati asked with a smile, 'Why are you going to Gwalior? Is there something urgent?'

Makrand looked up and said seriously, 'Parvati, Jumman *Chacha* was telling me that the fakir's blessings works wonders and you get whatever you ask for.'

Parvati said, 'I don't have faith in what Jumman *Chacha* says. Are these fakirs God, that you would get anything you ask? This fakir saheb lives in Gwalior, where Maharaja Man Singh Tomar rules. How is it that Maharani Mriganayani hasn't given birth to a child so far? I don't believe you or Jumman *Chacha*.' With that Parvati fell silent.

Makrand tried to convince Parvati. 'But what's the harm in going to Gwalior in any case? We would also pay a visit to fakir Gaus Baba. Jumman *Chacha* is an elder of the village. I respect his wishes also. If, I'm blessed by Gaus Baba and if we do have a son, to bring light to our house, we shall go to have his *darshan*.'

Parvati was not convinced about Gaus Baba's powers. She said after a little thought, 'Very well, what do I understand about such fakirs and their like? Do go if you wish. I shall get up early and make *rotis* and I shall also keep some fodder to be given to the oxen on the way. Now, go to sleep. You've to leave for Gwalior early in the morning.'

# 5

It was a clear morning in spring and the sun had risen on the horizon. The *sarson*, which looked like a yellow sheet, had flowered behind the *kuchcha* houses in Behat village. The beautiful, small flowers with green leaves on the mango tree looked pretty, whereas red flowers adorned the bamboo shoots around the edge of the field. The peacocks spread their feathers and danced merrily while the cuckoos cooed melodiously on the branches.

As day dawned the farmers busied themselves feeding the cattle, while the children in torn clothes played barefoot in the mud.

Makrand got ready hurriedly. Soon Jumman *Chacha* arrived on his own bullock-cart and called out to Makrand, who promptly prepared to leave. He said to Parvati, 'I'm going and will return by the evening. If the grain merchant comes in the meantime, tell him to wait till I get back.' And the next moment he was out of the house greeting Jumman *Chacha*. Soon the cart began to move towards Gwalior, bumping along the *kuchcha* road full of stones.

Their hearts were full with joy on seeing the beautiful, wayside country. Wild flowers had bloomed at the edge of the road and the sugar-cane fields. People were bathing in the ponds. Young village women, smiles on their innocent faces, were returning after drawing water from the wells. The hard-working, sturdy farmers laughed spontaneously, like the sweet notes of the *veena*.

Jumman *Chacha* stopped the cart near a sugar-cane field. They pulled out some sugar-cane and took to the road again. On the way, Makrand asked very hesitatingly, 'May I ask you a question, *Chacha*?'

'Sure,' *Chacha* said very spontaneously.

'*Chacha*, is there any harm, if one seeks the blessings of Mahadev for the fulfilment of a wish and also the blessings of a fakir? Can one seek blessings of both?'

Jumman *Chacha* replied, with a sweet smile on his face, 'Son, there is no harm at all. Mahadev Baba is God. He is like *khuda* whom the fakir worships and comes close to, so his soul is pure. He does not get involved in worldly matters. There is great power in prayer, son. He does good to the world because of the power granted to him by God. A fakir only gives, he never takes anything.' Jumman *Chacha's* words allayed Makrand's inner fears.

The bullock-cart reached Gwalior. The fort standing on the rocky hills could be seen from afar. They entered the city, observing the people going to and fro, up and down, the guards doing their rounds and the traders selling their wares along the roadside. But, the roads, lined by thick trees were not too crowded and were quiet. Jumman *Chacha* stopped the bullock-cart near a big *maidaan*. They alighted from it and started walking. They didn't walk far when they saw a few *qavvals* singing. Smoke was rising from a fire. Quite a few men and women—both Hindu and Muslim—were listening to the *qavvali*. As they joined them, Makrand cast a quick look all around. A tall, sturdy man with a bare body emerged from a hut shortly. He had a flowing beard, long tresses of entangled hair and was wearing a green *lungi*. Makrand observed him closely. His lustrous face indicated that he was no ordinary fakir. Makrand asked, 'Is he the same fakir, Jumman *Chacha*.'

'Yes, son. He is fakir Muhammad Gaus. Did you look at him?'

'Yes, *Chacha*. His face is so bright.'

'You're right, Makrand. One's face turns bright by offering prayers. That is exactly why, what the fakir says comes true.'

In the meantime, fakir Muhammad Gaus arrived on the spot. People stopped singing and bowed to him. Some people even touched his feet and respectfully joined their hands.

Fakir Muhammad Gaus looked at the sky. He sat resting on his knees. People came up and started narrating their tales and the fakir, nodding his head, went on blessing them, for their wishes to be fulfilled.

Suddenly, people's attention was drawn to a shrieking boy near the bush. He had been bitten by a poisonous snake which had slid out of the bush. The boy had fallen unconscious, and was carried to the fakir. Looking at the boy, he called out loudly, 'Come here, you *Haria Naag*.' Immediately, the cobra came up to the fakir and stopped, coiling itself before him. 'Why did you bite this boy? If you do this to people visiting this place, you will have to go elsewhere. Go back now and never do it again.'

*Haria Naag* crawled back. Fakir Muhammad Gaus took a pinch of ash from the burning fire, recited something and then applied the ash on the boy's forehead. The boy sat up yawning. The effect of the poison was gone and all the people present raised cries of praise for the fakir.

Makrand was flabbergasted. He had never seen such a miracle before. He said to Jumman *Chacha*, 'What you said has turned out to be right, *Chacha*.'

'There is great power in the prayer of the fakir.'

While Jumman *Chacha* and Makrand were talking, a bullock-cart with three or four men stopped before them. They got off the bullock-cart and brought an unconscious young man raging with fever and laid him before the fakir. He looked at the youth, and rubbed a pinch of ash on his forehead. In a little while, the youth sat up. People were wonderstruck by this miracle. Fakir Muhammad Gaus was overwhelmed. Then he suddenly laughed and gazing at the sky cried aloud, '*Yah Khuda, Yah mere Maula*' and broke into a *qavvali*.

The undulating waves of musical notes went deep into people's hearts. People were fascinated by the lovely voice of Muhammad Gaus and his ecstatic rendering of *qavvali*. Makrand also joined in. When the singing was over, fakir Muhammad

Gaus looked at Jumman *Chacha* and Makrand. Then pointing at Makrand he said, 'Your name is Makrand Pandey. You have come for the fakir's blessing. You belong to Behat village. I bless you. Your wife will give birth to a son.' And he started laughing loudly. Makrand fell at his feet.

After a while Jumman *Chacha* and Makrand got up. Jumman *Chacha* drove the cart back to Behat village. He returned on the same *kuchcha* road full of tall trees and fields covered with *sarson* and reached Behat at sunset. The moon had risen and stray stars could be seen clearly in the sky. The lamps were already lit in the village huts. The sweet smell of *bajra* and maize *rotis* being baked on the earthen *chulhas* filled the air. Makrand thanked Jumman *Chacha* and returned home. He realised that Parvati would be anxious because it had got quite late. She opened the door.

Parvati asked, 'So, you're back after visiting Gwalior.'

'Yes, Parvati. Gaus Baba is really a miracle man. Right before my eyes he brought a dead boy back to life. Whatever he says, actually happens, Parvati.'

Parvati did not believe what Makrand said. She said, 'You're tired after the long journey. Come and have your meal for you must be hungry. I too haven't eaten anything so far.'

'You should have eaten. Why did you wait for me?'

'I'm an Indian wife. How could I eat without feeding my husband?'

# 6

Vrindavan was situated on the banks of the Yamuna about three *kos* away from Mathura. The black sand with silvery particles gleamed like a saree studded with diamonds. The atmosphere was enchanting, with herds of deer leaping and colourful peacocks dancing merrily. There were countless cuckoos and other birds flying about freely. Monkey leapt from tree to tree; the female monkeys carried their young ones.

The spring breeze had turned warm. Vrindavan with its dusty roads looked different from other places. Ascetics eating *prasad* off plantain leaves and cows wandering all over the town were a normal sight. The pealing of *arati* bells and devotional songs filled the air.

It was four in the morning. The *sadhus* of Vrindavan were already up and the air of Nidhivan was filled with the sweet fragrance of flowers, trees and creepers. The heat of the day had worn out, but darkness still pervaded.

Swami Haridas lived in a small hut in Nidhivan. His day began with the *darshan* of his *Bihariji*. Then, he went to the Yamuna for his bath. Keeping his loin cloth on the deserted *ghat* of the Yamuna, he stepped into the river to bathe and then retuned to Nidhivan by the *kuchcha* road. After worshipping *Banke Bihari*, he tuned his *tanpura* lying nearby and sang *bhajans* with complete devotion in praise of *Bihariji*.

Ecstasy overcame him. In that state of spiritual joy, he started singing the *pada* urging Radha to go to the forest to meet Krishna. He was so absorbed that he lost all consciousness of time. The sun was up and the sand in Nidhivan glittered. Monkeys in large numbers wandered about in search of food; some even ate the leaves of the trees. After the song was over, Swami Haridas stood up and took a few leisurely steps.

The devotees arrived and sat down to listen to him preaching. As Swamiji was about to start, a hefty man dressed in Punjabi clothes came and sat there. Swamiji asked him the reason for his visit to the ashram. He introduced himself, 'I belong to Lahore. My name is Vijnani. I am interested in *bhajans* and worship of God. I have come here with the great aspiration to see you.' And he fell at Swamiji's feet. Then he rose and said, 'Swamiji, I have heard that you are fond of two things—music and fragrance. I know no music, but I have brought a bottle of perfume for you.' With these words, he placed the bottle of perfume before Swamiji.

Swami Haridas was looking ahead intently. He emptied the bottle of perfume in the sand. This upset Vijnani. Seeing him so disturbed, Swamiji said to one of his disciples, 'Take him for the *darshan* of *Bihariji*.'

When Vijnani reached the temple, he was astounded to find that the scent of his perfume had filled the whole place. He came back to Swamiji. He became so fond of Vrindavan that he decided to settle down there.

One day it was very hot. The animals and birds were lying still among the bushes. In the evening, Swami Haridas along with his devotees came and sat under a tree. People were sweating profusely. Vijnani could not bear the terrible heat and said, 'Swamiji, I have never faced such heat in my life.'

On hearing this, Swamiji asked him to fetch the *tanpura* from the hut. Vijnani got up and brought it. Swamiji looked at the sky and began singing the *alap* of *raga Malhar*. He sang *Malhar* for a long time, his eyes fixed at the sky, first in slow tempo and then fast. He sang full throat and the sky became overcast. The clouds rumbled, the lightning flashed and soon after, it started raining heavily. Swamiji continued singing. The rain falling on the sands of Nidhivan, spread a sweet scent all around.

The animals and birds living in Nidhivan were different. When Swami Haridas started singing, all of them crowded around to listen to his nectar-sweet music. Even serpents of all kinds appeared. Swamiji continued singing and they listened, raising their hoods. When he finished, the serpents would disappear. It was said that the *ragas* and *raginis* had manifested themselves before Swamiji in the form of these serpents.

As usual, the music of Swami Haridas showered nectar on the lifeless creatures. Today, Swamiji had sung for a longer time. The sun had already set. He returned to his hut and sat praying silently.

From an early age, Swamiji had grown up with a sense of detachment. It is said, that his father Gangadhar and mother Ganga Devi were concerned about their son's mental attitude. Swamiji did not enjoy any kind of work. Deep down, he constantly thought of the enchanting form of Radha and Krishna. His father tried to engage him in some job. But Haridas would sit for hours together in the Radha-Krishna temple outside Haridaspur village, singing *bhajans* and returned home when the evening lamps were lit. That had become his normal routine. His parents often tried to argue with him, that he was old enough to work for a living. But he would simply listen to them, vacantly. Nothing, except Radha-Krishna attracted Haridas who was bent on following the path of worship. His parents started worrying about his marriage, but Haridas did not marry despite all their efforts. . . .

It was a dark night. The moon in the sky was hidden behind thick dark clouds. The *kuchcha* road of the village, the fields, mud-houses—everything was engulfed in that dense darkness. Lightning crackled now and again. The whole village was asleep. Haridas too.

He dreamt about Lord Krishna dancing *maharasa* on a full moon night on the bank of the Yamuna. Radha and Madhav, dressed beautifully and decorated with ornaments, were dancing enchantingly with the *gopis*. The jingle of the anklets, the musical notes of the flute, the playing of the *veena* and *mridanga* filled the entire bank of the Yamuna with music. The twenty-five year old Haridas was startled out of his sleep by that dream. He silently bowed to his parents, who were fast asleep and left the house to go to Vrindavan. Haridas walked on in the rainy night and reached Vrindavan where Krishna had performed his *leelas* and where the *gopis* had indulged in their love-play. The flower laden trees, the thick tulsi-forests and the gushing Yamuna was where Haridas sat admiring the beauty of the river. He thought to himself that it was the same bank where Krishna had once played his flute and where Radha and Madhav had done the *maharasa*. The Yamuna must have been a witness to everything they did, like listening to Madhav's footsteps and the taming of the great Kaliya serpent. Madhav must have decorated Radha's braid with all the flowers as they sat on these very *tamala* and *kadamba* trees.

Haridas was overwhelmed with emotion. He bent down and rubbed the sand of the Yamuna on his head. He prostrated himself before the sacred river. He paid his respects to the flowers and the trees of Vrindavan and then walked away.

He went towards a beautiful spot in the forest, where the green foliage of the trees and the beautiful flowers seemed to be bursting into laughter accompanied by the sweet chirping of the birds. Haridas was fascinated by the loveliness of the place and named it Nidhivan. Sitting there, under the shade of a tree, he had a sudden desire to sing. With deep concentration, he started singing the glory of the Lord. So completely was he lost in his devotion to the Lord that he became Swami Haridas. Nidhivan was where his devotion had blossomed. Here, his pursuit of music became a divine gift.

# 7

Clusters of blossoms had already appeared on the mango trees. The bulbuls perched on the branches, were pecking at them. Multi-coloured butterflies hovered over the *karaunda* bushes. Behat village looked splendid with yellow and pink flowers on the bamboo shoots. The women arrived at the wells with their pitchers.

After a while, they heard some tapping and found the eastern sky clouded with dust. They feared that a gang of robbers was approaching so they hurried home. But, in no time, a big army appeared waving Akbar's flag. The army did not stop near the wells, but some soldiers, cupping their palms, asked the women for water. The army was equipped with lances, bows and arrows, swords and canons. One of the women asked a soldier, 'Where are you all going?'

The soldier replied, 'We are going to conquer Mewar. Let us see if God helps us or not.'

'Why, what is the difficulty? Akbar Shah has such a large army and so much wealth. Why will you not be victorious?'

The soldier replied gravely, 'What you say is right. But. . .'

'But what?' The woman asked again.

'It's only that these Rajputs are very valiant and desperate fighters. They do not care about their lives. They sacrifice their lives to protect their honour. They give such a fight that the enemy flees in panic. But this time we will fight with all our might. And God will help us.'

'How long is the journey?'

'It will take fifteen days to reach Chittor. But these people hide in the Aravalli mountain ranges. They loot the rations and burn the standing crops in the fields. They adopt guerilla tactics in war. Let us see what happens in the battle this time.'

With that, the soldier rode his horse faster to join his companions.

Akbar's army marched ahead kicking up clouds of dust and raising the cries of *Allah-O-Akbar*. For a long time, the layers of dust hung over Behat village. The woman wondered to herself, why should people fight wars at all? What was the bloodshed for?

Then she told herself, 'We are poor people without any possessions. We don't crave for wealth and luxury nor do we want to conquer the earth. Our fields are our only wealth. The yield of our fields is what makes us happy. But those people who have everything, wealth and prosperity, feel that they do not have enough.'

She was an elderly woman. Her son tilled the land and she herself was the village midwife. Upon reaching home she put the pitchers in place and went to the kitchen to put the milk to boil. As she was about to take the milk vessel off from the *chulha*, Makrand rushed in saying, '*Bua* come quickly. Parvati is in pain. I hope she doesn't deliver the child right away.'

*Bua* closed the door of her hut and hurried after Makrand to his house.

Parvati was groaning with pain. *Bua* took one look at Parvati and immediately put the water to boil. She took some rags and closed Parvati's room from inside. Parvati shrieked aloud in pain and tossed about. After some time the wails of a new-born were heard. Makrand sat outside praying to God that Parvati would be alright. He walked up and down, eager and impatient. A little later, *Bua* came out smiling and said to Makrand, 'Makrand, it's a son! Now listen, I'll want a good reward. God has heard your prayer after such a long time.'

Makrand was happy beyond words. He said, 'I'll give you whatever you want. But first tell me, is the child all right?'

'*Arey*, absolutely fine. As beautiful as the sun and the moon. Very fair and he has such large eyes! He'll grow into a very handsome boy.' With that, *Bua* announced the birth of a son in Makrand's house to the whole village and then went home.

Makrand and Parvati were overjoyed at the birth of their son. After making so many vows, a happy day like this had come.

The village women crowded in Makrand's house. There was a great hustle-bustle. They sang *sohar* and the young women danced to the drumbeat.

Makrand had not yet seen the face of his son. Parvati took the new-born child in her lap. Makrand passed by her room and Parvati called out to him in a gentle voice and showed him their son's face. Affection surged in Makrand's heart at the sight of his son. The child was lovely. 'He has taken after you, Parvati,' Makrand said.

'All the women said he has taken after you,' Parvati replied with a smile. Makrand also smiled and came out of the room.

Outside people were busy feasting, on *laddoos, kachauries, puries* and pumpkin curry. They were also served curd with *bura* sugar in leaf cups. Lamps had been lit in the houses and the huts in the village.

Makrand was exhausted. He closed the door and sat near Parvati. She was looking intently at their son in her lap.

'Parvati, what are you staring at?'

'Nothing. But I was thinking, that his forehead shines unusually. Even when he cries, there is a rhythm in it.'

Makrand burst out laughing and remarked, 'You're wonderful, Parvati. You hear music in the crying of the child. So, you've become a mother. It is not you, but your affection that makes you hear that.'

They went on talking till late in the night. Makrand possessed a very sweet voice. He picked up the *tanpura* and started singing *bhajans.* And a little later, he fell asleep. He thought that he would train his son in music when he grew up. Even in deep sleep he kept muttering. . .

Makrand had a dream in the early hours of the morning. A bull was chasing him to kill him. He ran fast to save himself. Seeing a small river, he jumped into it. The enraged bull drove its horns into the sand on the river bank. Makrand somehow crossed the river and reached the opposite bank and thus saved his life.

The dream startled him and he woke up. He was breathing fast and he wondered why he had such a terrible dream. He had never dreamt anything like this before. Then, it suddenly occurred to him, that he had sought Mahadev's blessings to have a son. He had made a big mistake, for it was ten days since the son's birth but he had not yet gone to the temple. He decided to go there with his son early next morning.

The stars were still shining in the sky, as there was still time for dawn. The industrious farmers were singing *bhajans* while the women got busy with their household chores. The milkmen were milking the cows and buffaloes. Some women with their pitchers has started off for the well. Makrand got up. He had his bath and plucked *bilwa* leaves and flowers. He brought a jugful of milk from the milkman. Parvati had also got up by that time. She was trying to pacify the new-born child, who had been crying. Makrand came to her, and said, 'Parvati, after a little while we shall go to worship at the Shiva temple. Would you be able to walk or should I get the bullock-cart ready?' Parvati thought for a moment and said, 'I shall walk?'

Parvati bathed the child and dressed. And then, with the child she followed Makrand. On the way, farmers going on their bullock-carts towards their fields, offered to give Parvati a ride up to the temple, but she declined.

Walking slowly, they reached the temple. When they entered, they were surprised to see a serpent around the *Shiva linga*. At first they were scared. But then they plucked up courage and started the puja. They offered water, milk, *bilwa* leaves and flowers to the *Shiva linga* and *prasad* after lighting the incense. The serpent slithered away. Parvati and Makrand laid the child on the floor in front of the *Shiva linga*. The child started moving its legs and arms, while they prayed with their eyes closed.

As they sang the glory of the Lord, they suddenly heard the rumble of clouds. The sky became overcast and there were flashes of lightning as the rain lashed down. For a long time,

Makrand rang the bells of the temple and the air reverberated with their sweet peal. A flower, placed on top of the *Shiva linga* suddenly dropped on the child's head. Makrand and Parvati were overjoyed and they prostrated before Mahadev, for their son had been blessed by him.

After the rain stopped. Makrand and Parvati returned home, along the wet pathways. Parvati held the child close to her bosom all the way.

Parvati and Makrand were very happy with the child. One day Makrand decided to visit the field. He found that the *mehndi* hedges and the neem tree had flowered while the fruits had dropped off the berry-trees. As Makrand walked along, lost in his thoughts, he met Jumman *Chacha* on the way. After the usual greetings, Jumman *Chacha* said, 'Makrand, my dear, you may not seek the blessings of *pirs* and fakirs. But if you do, make it a point to visit them after your wish is granted. When are you planning to go to Gwalior to meet Gaus Baba?'

Makrand apologised, 'I had completely forgotten. It is good of you to remind me. We shall go to Gaus Baba tomorrow morning.'

'Yes, son. We shall go tomorrow. I shall get the bullock-cart ready in the night. You come with the child. He would also be blessed by Gaus Baba,' said Jumman *Chacha*.

The whole village came to know that Makrand was going to Gwalior to meet Gaus Baba. The people of Behat village were eager to go with him for they had already heard about Gaus Baba's miracles.

In the morning Makrand and Parvati got onto their bullock-cart. Jumman *Chacha* was in his own cart. Behind them the villagers, Brahmins, Vaishyas, Muslims all came in their own bullock-carts for the *darshan* of Gaus Baba.

Although, Parvati was accompanying Makrand to Gwalior, her mind was assailed by all kinds of doubts. She was afraid of incurring the wrath of Mahadev. She thought that if something untoward happened to the child, it would be a disaster. But, she could not refuse to go to Gwalior, because she was afraid of displeasing Gaus Baba. What would happen in such an eventuality?

The bullock-cart moved along the dusty roads. Parvati was overcome with boundless affection for the child. She thought that when the child grew up, he would be of help to his father. He would get married, and bring home a beautiful bride. The house would be filled with the laughter of their children. Their family of three would grow large.

Then she thought of the child's education. An uneducated man always remained uncouth and uncultured. She dreamt that she would send him to Gwalior for proper education. At the same time she felt sad at the thought of being deprived of his presence in the house if he went to Gwalior. How could she live without him? Parvati was so absorbed in such thoughts that she did not realise that they had already entered Gwalior city. She was shaken out of her dream when Jumman *Chacha* called out from his cart, 'Makrand, we have reached Gwalior.'

'Yes, *Chacha*,' Makrand said with a smile.

The bullock-cart had hardly gone a little farther when Maharaja Man Singh Tomar's army, fully equipped with all kinds of weapons, was seen leaving the city. The bullock-carts, stopped where they were. Jumman *Chacha* asked a man standing there, 'Where is this big army of the king marching to?'

The man replied that Behlol Lodhi's army had taken up strategic positions some fifteen *kos* away and the Maharaja's army was going out to confront the enemy. Soon, Maharaja Man Singh appeared dressed in armour riding an elephant. He had big mustaches reflecting his enraged mein. He carried all sorts of weapons—swords, lances and others. Soon the army passed on.

Jumman *Chacha* was no doubt old, but his blood boiled with anger. He said, 'Makrand, the kingdom of Gwalior is like our mother. We have played and grown up in its soil. To protect our motherland is our first duty. You people go to meet Gaus Baba. I will go to the battlefield with my sword. And now, what would happen to me in any case? Even if I die fighting for the motherland in my last hour, I will consider it my great fortune.'

Jumman *Chacha* was greatly excited. Makrand tried hard to convince him that his age was not one to fight on the battlefield.

'*Chacha*' he said, 'the beads of a rosary have greater strength than the blows of a sword. You should only seek God's blessings for the victory of Maharaja Man Singh Tomar on the battlefield.'

Finally, Jumman *Chacha* gave in to Makrand's pleading. Deep down, he cursed his old age. He said to himself, 'This wretched old age. Had I been young, I would have certainly gone into battle and nourished the grape-vines of my motherland with my blood.'

Such were Jumman *Chacha's* thoughts when the caravan of the bullock-carts turned toward the holy spot where Gaus Baba lived.

# 8

They went a little further and heard singing in the distance. Smoke rose into the sky. They stopped their bullock-carts. Gaus Baba was seated under a tamarind tree and was surrounded by devotees, singing devotional songs. With his dishevelled tresses, flowing beard and thick moustache, Gaus Baba looked very impressive.

Makrand and Jumman *Chacha* got off first, followed by Parvati carrying the new-born child. Other people from the village walked along with them towards Gaus Baba, who was listening to the singing with his eyes closed. In between, he raised his hands gracefully and moved his fingers in response to the singing.

After some time, the child in Parvati's lap started crying. Parvati tried very hard to pacify the child but he did not stop. Gaus Baba's concentration was disturbed. He opened his eyes and raised his hand as a gesture of blessing. The child quietened down. Makrand got up and fell at Gaus Baba's feet. Raising Makrand up, he asked, 'What has brought you here, son? What have you brought for the fakir and what would you take from him?'

Makrand replied, 'Baba, I have got a son by your grace. We have come from Behat to seek your blessings for the child. Others from our village have also come with us.'

On hearing Makrand's reply, Gaus Baba said, 'There is great power in our prayer to God. If someone thinks of him honestly and sincerely, he does not forget his devotees. God in his mercy, filled your wife's empty womb. Thank him, not me.'

All those from Behat joined their hands and thanked Gaus Baba. Parvati carried the child to Gaus Baba. He observed the child very closely, and then laid him on his lap. The new-born child moved his hands and feet as if he were playing. Gaus Baba played with him, snapping his fingers and the child occasionally smiled.

Gaus Baba felt very happy as he looked at the child. After a while he closed his eyes and muttered something. The people tried to catch his words but they could not understand anything. Parvati was impatient to have her child back. She even moved forward to take the child from Gaus Baba's lap. But Makrand held her hand and made her stay where she was. A little later, Gaus Baba opened his eyes and started saying slowly, 'Look here Makrand. This child shows great promise. He will shine in the world like the sun. His lustre will brighten the country for centuries to come.' And then he fell silent.

Makrand asked, 'Baba, what would he do to shine like the sun? We are mere farmers. Maybe he would become a big zamindar, when he grows up.'

Gaus Baba burst into loud laughter at Makrand's remark. He repeated what Makrand had said and continued laughing.

Parvati asked shyly with folded hands, 'Then Baba, what would he become?' Gaus Baba looked intently at Parvati and said, 'Child, time itself would show what is lying hidden in the womb of the future. Have patience.'

While this conversation was still going on, a man came running to Gaus Baba and stood before him with folded hands. Gaus Baba asked him 'Tell me, from where are you coming?'

'Vrindavan', the man replied.

Gaus Baba asked with a smile, 'Tell me, how is my friend Swami Haridas?'

'He's well, Gaus Baba. He wants to know when he would have the pleasure of seeing you. He is very eager to meet you. Since the danger of war is always looming over Gwalior, Swamiji has urged you to go to Vrindavan.'

'True indeed, Swami Haridas is really a devotee of God. And God has been kind to him. That is why, when he sings his voice has a nectar-like sweetness. It is possible to think of God by singing from the bottom of one's heart. Once, Swamiji and I were talking, the kings and *nawabs* had been causing bloodshed in order to expand their kingdoms. Swamiji had said something which I have never forgotten. He said, "Man hungers only to expand his kingdom and pile up more wealth. He always wants to be intoxicated with power, but he forgets God, who has sent him to the earth only to do noble deeds. Man can find peace not by shedding blood but by spreading love, like the flow of the Ganga. Everyone is a devotee of God. This sky, this earth, this light, this water, these oceans, rivers, mountains and these rains have all been gifted by God to us. However much you may try to take advantage of his grace and kindness, it never gets exhausted. But man does pass away after he has lived the span of life granted to him."'

Gaus Baba said to the man, 'Tell Swamiji that I will go to Vrindavan very soon and have the privilege of seeing him.' Then he looked at the sky. People around were astounded, that the child still lay in Gaus Baba's lap vigorously moving his hands and feet. . . .

Gaus Baba had eaten a *paan* that day and so his lips were a glowing red. Then, something got into Gaus Baba's head, he took out a little bit of the *paan* from his mouth and put it into the mouth of the child [Tansen] lying in his lap. The child's lips became the same red. When the Behat villagers saw this, they started whispering among themselves. They wondered about Gaus Baba's curious behaviour. 'Makrand, your son is no good for us now. He has become impure after having eaten that *paan* chewed by a *Mussalman*,' they said.

Anxiety and astonishment appeared on Makrand's forehead. A strange expression came over Parvati's face as well. Keeping the child in his lap for some time, Gaus Baba said, 'This child has a great future. He will shine like the sun in his life.'

With that blessing, Gaus Baba placed the child in Makrand's arms. People stared at Makrand's panic-stricken face. Makrand begged, 'Baba, now you keep the child. Our Brahmin community will not accept him. We will come to see him sometimes.'

Gaus Baba broke into a smile on hearing that. He said, 'This child was destined to come to me. You people can leave now.'

Gaus Baba picked up the child and took him to his own hut. Parvati wept bitterly. Makrand tried his best to console her. Still weeping hysterically, she got into the bullock-cart. The caravan's screeching wheels moved again to go back to Behat. The memory of the child brought incessant tears to Parvati's eyes. She kept on saying, 'Bring back my child. I am not bothered about what the community does to me.'

But she was helpless and beat her forehead at her misfortune.

# 9

The sky was red with the morning twilight. The cool morning breeze carried with it the fragrance of the mango blossoms. Muhammad Gaus had woken up. Next to him lay Makrand's son in deep sleep. Muhammad Gaus got up and gargled his mouth. Then he cleaned his teeth with a *neem* twig, as he walked up and down. After some time, he heard the child crying inside the hut. Hurriedly washing his mouth, he rushed to pick up the child and to pacify him, 'My Tanna, oh my Tanna.'

The child was hungry and cried incessantly. Gaus Baba put his thumb in the child's mouth. The child started sucking the thumb. Then he slowly dribbled cow's milk into the child's mouth. The child went off to sleep again.

The sun had risen high in the sky. Gaus Baba held the child to his breast and walked up and down in his hut. A little later, fifteen people arrived with a sick youth. They were panic-striken, for his condition was critical. The people fell at Gaus Baba's feet. He examined the youth and put some ash from the fire into his mouth. After a while, the young man vomited. A young snake came out of his stomach and crept away. People were surprised to see the snake. Gaus Baba said to the youth, 'You are drinking water from the pond. The water is dirty. While drinking it, you had also swallowed this little snake. From now on, drink water only from a well. And if you drink water from the pond, drink it after boiling and straining it. Now you may go.' All of them thanked Gaus Baba and left.

After they had gone, Gaus Baba sang aloud. He had a beautiful voice and the whole atmosphere was filled with his musical notes. The child woke up and started crying. Gaus Baba realised that not only was his voice not harsh but also had a hint of music in it when he cried. He walked about for some time carrying the child in his arms. His devotees came and went. . . .

It was about three o'clock in the afternoon. Man Singh Tomar had a sudden desire to call Gaus Baba to his *darbar*. But, on second thoughts, he felt that it would be more appropriate if he himself went to see the fakir at the *dargah*.

The royal elephant was decorated and the king set out with his entourage. His subjects cheered the king all along the way.

The king dismounted from the elephant and went up to Gaus Baba who was meditating under a tamarind tree. The king sat on the ground. When Gaus Baba came out of his meditation, the king bowed to him respectfully. They talked at random for some time. Then Gaus Baba got up and brought his *tanpura* from the hut. Man Singh Tomar took that *tanpura* from him and started singing the *alap* of a *dhrupad*. Its musical notes pervaded the whole atmosphere. For a long time the king sang the *dhrupad*. When he stopped, Gaus Baba praised his singing. The king accepted his praise, bowing his head in all humility.

A little later, Gaus Baba himself took over the *tanpura* and began singing. He was an excellent singer. When he finished singing, Man Singh Tomar showered him with praise. Gaus Baba said, 'My singing is nothing. There is a friend of mine in Vrindavan. He is a wonderful singer. Do listen to him when you get a chance.'

'Who is he?' the king asked.

'Swami Haridas. The way he sings—it is just wonderful. By listening to his singing even a dead man comes back to life.'

'Where does he live?'

'There is a place in Vrindavan called Nidhivan where that ascetic lives and prays to his God.'

'Very well. When I get a chance, I shall certainly go to Vrindavan to meet him.' After a while the king returned to his palace. Gaus Baba walked leisurely under the shade of the trees, carrying Tanna in his arms and continuously humming. . . .

Parvati almost went mad with the separation from her son. She would neither eat nor drink. Makrand was greatly distressed to see his wife's condition. He was constantly bitter about social conventions. The Brahmins in the village were not prepared to heed anything that Makrand said. Bound as it was by traditions, society was not ready to accept that Makrand's son could be readmitted into the Hindu fold after the *paan* eaten by a *Mussalman* had been put in his mouth.

But, among the villagers, were some youths possessed with new ideas. One day, the *panchayat* was called and all the people of the village including the Muslims were invited to attend it. Everyone, including the young men and the women of the village gathered at one place. Parvati also went there. She stared at everybody blankly, her eyes wide open.

The five members or the *Panches* sat apart and the proceedings started. The village head, Suraj Pandey said, 'It is a question of our beliefs and conventions. We cannot take the food eaten by a *Mussalman*. For centuries we have lived with these beliefs which we have inherited from birth. Now it is for the *Panches* to decide if we can bring Makrand's son back from Gaus Baba and admit him again into our Hindu society. . . .'

Hearing Suraj Pandey's words, people started whispering among themselves. Some adamant people said, that under no circumstances would they accept Makrand's son back. It was matter of conviction for them. Some people went to the extent of saying that if Makrand loved his son so much, then he and Parvati too, should give up their religion and become *Mussalmans*.

Hearing such a suggestion, Jumman *Chacha* was on his feet. He said, 'Members of the *panchayat* and people of Behat village, I want to make one request to you. Look at us. Even we *Mussalmans* have become *Hindustanis* after coming to Hindustan. And now Hindustan is our motherland. We love the earth of this land. We were born here and will find our final resting place only here. As far as religion is concerned, it has not been made for God. Religion, castes and communities have all been made by us. Tell me, if different moons and stars rise for the Hindus and the *Mussalmans*. Does the sun say, it would shine only on the *Mussalmans* and not on the Hindus? Do we have different skies for the Hindus and the *Mussalmans*? Is this earth, this air, separate for us? Then why these distinctions? That day when my daughter was married off and we had to part, why did the women of the village cry? What really matters is love among ourselves. Religion is meant to bring us together. Religion brings people closer, it does not throw them apart. Kindly give a serious thought to what I am saying and have some consideration for Parvati. Only a mother would understand the pain of being separated from her child. In my opinion, we all should go to Gwalior and bring back the child.'

People listened to Jumman *Chacha*, but they did not budge from their stand. The *panchayat* dispersed amidst great uproar. People went back to their homes. They saw Makrand and Parvati rising and cursing their fate with tears in their eyes and walking towards their house as though their world had been torn apart. For long Parvati's tears flowed.

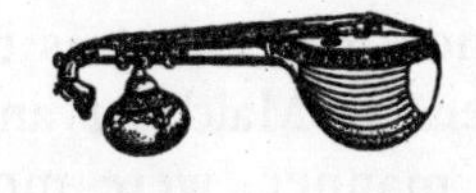

# 10

Built on the heights of Badalgarh, the Agra Fort sparkled. The torches in the fort were lit. Watermen had sprinkled rose water in the royal garden and incense was burning in the lamp-stands. The whole atmosphere was fragrant. Persian carpets had been spread everywhere. *Motia*, *kevra*, *campak,* jasmines, roses and so many other beautiful flowers were in bloom in the royal garden. When the rays of the light fell on the Persian lamp-stands, it seemed as though thousands of diamonds were glittering. Maid servants and other menial girls, conquettish in manner, were moving up and down, bedecked with all kinds of jewellery and wearing *kinkhab* and *vaskets.*

The moment the arrival of *Shahenshah-e-alam* Jalaluddin Akbar was announced, everyone became alert. Soon Akbar arrived with his courtiers. He looked visibly anxious and grave. Akbar went and sat on a throne studded with gems. The courtiers sat on the seats below.

After a pause Akbar said, 'Raja Man Singh and Phaiji, I am very upset over the news about Mewar. Have the Mughal swords become blunt that we have not yet been able to triumph over a handful of Rajputs? If I don't conquer Mewar, our dream of conquering Gujarat will remain a dream. It seems that I shall have to personally go onto the battlefield.'

For some time there was silence. Then Raja Man Singh said, '*Shahenshah-e-Hindustan* does not have to worry. It is our responsibility. Every line of anxiety on your forehead is our anxiety. I promise you, *Shahenshah*, my sword will not return to its sheath until we have conquered Mewar.'

Akbar was relieved by Man Singh's promise. He felt reassured by it. He was well aware, that a Rajput would keep his word even at the cost of his life.

Soon, the jingle of anklets was heard in the royal garden. Gulab *Bai* was dancing to the sound of the *tabla*. She was dancing the *mayuri* dance, displaying the movements of a peacock spreading out its feathers. The bells of her anklets were jingling and the *sarangi* was producing melodious notes. All the courtiers present were encouraging the dancer with their acclaims, '*Wah! Wah!* Wonderful!'

After a while Akbar ordered, 'Stop this dance!' Then he turned to Phaiji and asked, 'I had sent for a dancer called Rai Parveen from Orchha. Has she come?'

'Yes, *Shahenshah*,' Phaiji replied.

'Then present her! I wish to see Rai Parveen's dance. I have heard that her dance is as beautiful as she.'

'Indeed, *Shahenshah-e-Alam*! Rai Parveen will be presented to you this very moment.'

Rai Parveen of Orchha, was thinking about her past and was sad at heart as she sat in the nicely decorated room. She had been forcibly brought from Orchha to Agra.

One day Akbar's courtiers had reported to him that in a small kingdom called Orchha, near Jhansi, lived a nautch girl called Rai Parveen. There was no one to match her in the entire country. She had rose-soft lips, a saffron complexion, playful, gay eyes and a youthful body. Akbar was highly impressed by such extravagant praises of Rai Parveen. He was impatient to see her.

As the temple bells rang in Orchha, Rai Parveen was engrossed in singing *bhajans* in front of the idol. She had just stood up after finishing her *bhajans,* when her maid came to inform her, 'Four horsemen have come from Agra. They wish to see you.'

'Horsemen from Agra wish to meet me now? But why? Tell them that they should meet Maharaj. I don't attend to any affairs of the state.'

The maid was about to leave, but then she stopped to think

and turning to Rai Parveen said, 'They have come from *Shahenshah* Akbar. They have brought some important message. What is the harm in meeting them for a moment? Are you sure, there won't be any trouble if you don't meet?' And then the maid stood silent.

Rai Parveen thought for a while and said, 'Ask them to wait in the outer chamber. I shall come after changing my clothes.'

The maid left and in a while Rai Parveen came dressed in a blue saree. The Mughal messengers were amazed to see her stunning beauty. They had never seen such a beautiful woman before. Rai Parveen asked them the purpose of their visit to Orchha.

Their leader said, '*Shahenshah* Jalaluddin Akbar has invited you to dance and sing in his *darbar*. You will roll in wealth if he is pleased. You will have to come to Agra.' Saying that, he observed the consternation on Rai Parveen's face.

Rai Parveen was perturbed. She was a dancing girl, no doubt, but she had regarded the ruler of Orchha as her husband. She was afraid, that her loyalty would be at stake if she went to Agra, and she would have nowhere to turn. She said to the men, 'You all go and rest in the State guest-house. I shall give you my reply after some time.'

Akbar's messengers went to the guest-house and Rai Parveen went to her *guru* Keshav Das who had trained her to write poetry. She had been composing good poems herself. Keshav Das was working on his book *Ramachandrika*. He was startled by Rai Parveen's sudden visit. He asked, 'What has brought you here, Rai Parveen? You seem to be worried.'

'Yes, *Guruji*, I am really worried. I have come for your advice. *Shahenshah* Akbar has called me to Agra to dance and sing in his *darbar*. His messengers have come with the message. If I go to Agra, I don't know what will become of me. I may lose all my honour and reputation. If I compromise my loyalty to my husband, then I can do nothing except commit suicide.'

Keshav Das thought for a while and said, 'Rai Parveen, you

better go to Agra. If you do not go, Akbar would blow up Orchha in a fraction of a second. People would die for no fault of theirs. You should sacrifice your life to defend Orchha if need be.'

Keshav Das said nothing more and Rai Parveen went to her palace. She packed her clothes, hid a dagger inside her blouse and left for Agra with the messengers of the Mughal Emperor.

They passed Jhansi, then Gwalior and after that came to Dhaulpur. The dark blue waters of the Chambal could be seen glittering from a distance. The horses stopped by the river bank. The soldiers called a boatman, who carried them along with the horses to the opposite bank. Then they mounted the horses once again and trotted towards Agra.

Rai Parveen's heart was in turmoil. She loved Orchha and the mountain ranges of Bundelkhand came before her eyes. She felt that she had betrayed her Maharaja by leaving for Agra without informing him. She thought, what would he say when he came to know about it? He would call her a characterless woman and a traitor, for he would feel insulted. He would lose faith in all womankind.

As she thought about this, her hand touched the dagger inside her blouse and she gripped its hilt. She was about to pull out the dagger, but the next moment she said to herself, 'No, I won't give my life. If Akbar tries to touch me, I will thrust this dagger into his chest.'

Lost in such thoughts, she arrived at Agra. She was flabbergasted to see the Emperor's wealth. There was no comparison between Orchha and Agra! But, then she thought that her Orchha was far better. She was respected and honoured there. Orchha had everything to offer. Maharaj Vir Singh Judev loved her. The Mughal Emperor purchased love with his wealth. But she could not accept that. 'No, I won't be purchased. I shall give my life to protect my honour.'

Passing through the corridors of the Fort, the horse stopped in front of a beautiful entrance. Rai Parveen was asked to dismount and was taken inside the palace. Maids greeted her courteously. Seated in a beautiful room, Rai Parveen felt out of place. She was lost in her dreams.

Sunlight shone on the quartziferous chandeliers in the room, as though millions of diamonds were glittering there. Innumerable maids were waiting for her commands. It was lunch time. The maids arranged delicious dishes in silver platters. It was a royal lunch with all kinds of pilaos, curries, chutneys, pickles and jams. The room was filled with the fragrance of cardamom and saffron. The maids urged Rai Parveen to eat. Rai Parveen awakened from her dreams. She glanced at the food-laden platters and said. 'I am not hungry.' But the maids still pressed her to eat. Finally, she picked two black grapes from a bunch and popped them into her mouth. 'Please take away all the platters. I am not hungry,' she said and exited. Rai Parveen stretched herself against a big round cushion. She was tired after a long journey, but she kept thinking about her situation for some time and then fell asleep.

As she slept, she dreamt about her first meeting with the Orchha king. She saw herself dancing before him and enjoying the praise lavished on her. Then, suddenly a maid entered and disturbed her sleep. Rai Parveen woke up and gave a blank look. The maid said politely, 'It is time for the *Shahenshah*'s recreation. Please wear these new clothes I have brought for you. It is the *Shahenshah's* orders that you should dance in the royal garden only in these clothes. I shall bring you a chest of jewellery also.'

Rai Parveen looked contemptuously at those clothes, 'You are a prisoner, Rai Parveen,' she said to herself. 'Your art may be a curse or a blessing. Wear these clothes not for the sake of the *Shahenshah* but for your art.'

All kinds of thoughts crowded her mind. Then she suddenly got up. She washed her face and hands, combed her hair and put on the new clothes. She decked herself with flowers and jewellery. She wore a light pink *dupatta* over a long, blue skirt flowing down to her ankles. The palanquin bearers took her to the royal garden.

People had already gathered for the *mehfil*. The

*Shahenshah's* arrival was announced. Soon, Akbar reached the garden with his retinue. He sat on a throne studded with precious stones. One of the flunkeys announced, 'The great royal dancer of Orchha, Rai Parveen!' and with that, Rai Parveen appeared before the assembly in a dancing pose, jingling her anklets.

She performed the rain dance, with her vigorous foot-work depicting the stormy sea, the rumbling clouds and the flashing lightning and the stance of a dancing peacock. The assembly was stunned into silence. Everyone was transfixed where he was. Suddenly, somebody threw a dagger from behind a bush at Rai Parveen. The dagger hit her leg and blood streaked out. She stopped dancing. She pulled out a dagger which was hidden inside her blouse and threw it in the same direction from where she had been attacked. A woman's loud shriek was heard and the people ran in that direction. They found the dagger stuck in Gulab *Bai's* chest and her lifeless body in a pool of blood. Akbar did not bat an eyelid. Looking at Rai Parveen's dance and her accurate aim, he only remarked, 'She is a remarkable artist. She is as brave as she is beautiful, *Vallah!*'

The royal physician applied some medicine and bandaged Rai Parveen's leg. She smilingly looked around. Wherever she looked she heard the exclamation, 'Wonderful!' Her whole body swayed with youthful verve. The red blouse, tight on her thrusting bosom, the intoxication of her rose-like lips and the spring in her eyes and on her cheeks, alongwith the red glow of the twilight in the eastern sky made the atmosphere enchanting. Rai Parveen's brilliance was enhanced by her light pink *dupatta*.

The dance session was over. Everyone was up on their feet as Akbar stood up. Rai Praveen's beauty had deeply touched his heart. He took off a precious necklace and gave it to her. Then he said to Phaiji in a low voice, 'Rai Praveen will be with me tonight.'

Rai Praveen heard this. Her face became colourless. Everyone went home and Rai Praveen was sent to the harem.

At night thousands of torches lit up the Agra Fort. The

lamps burnt in Rai Praveen's room, alongwith her heart. She thought, 'What I had feared has really happened. My purity will be destroyed. I have been faithful to my husband and now I will be turned into a woman of low character. Sensuous hunger will devour me tonight.'

Sorrowfully, Rai Praveen went on sobbing with her head on the cushion. She was not conscious of the time. At eleven o'clock there was a knock at Rai Praveen's door which startled her. She thought *Shahenshah* Akbar had arrived to drink deep the scent of her fragrance. But when she opened the door she found Phaiji standing there. He said, 'The palanquin is waiting. You are very lucky. You will spend the night with *Shahenshah*.'

Rai Praveen bowed her head and said, *'Janab*, I am your prisoner. I shall be with *Shahenshah*, but. . . '

'But what?' Phaiji asked in amazement.

'Kindly take a letter from me to *Shahenshah*. I shall decide what to do according to the reply he sends.'

'Very well. Write it down.' Phaiji stood silently while Rai Praveen wrote a couplet on a piece of paper.

> Oh you sensible *Shahenshah*.
> Listen to Rai Praveen's pleas.

It meant: 'Listen to my plea, Oh *Shahenshah!* Only the crows, the low-caste, eat the left-overs. Would you, the great *Shahenshah*, have me who is a left-over?'

Akbar frowned grimly when he read the couplet. Phaiji thought Rai Praveen was doomed. But Akbar ordered, 'Let Rai Praveen be sent back to Orchha with due respect this very moment.'

That very night, a convoy marched towards Orchha, carrying Rai Praveen in a palanquin. Rai Praveen was happy, that her art had protected her honour that night. Her hatred for Akbar was replaced by admiration.

# 11

As a child when Tanna cried, Gaus Baba heard in his cries, the tunes of a *veena* or a *jala-tarang* or sometimes the tapping of a *mridanga*. He was convinced, that the child must have been a great singer in his previous life.

Now Tanna had grown into an eighteen year old youth. Gaus Baba had personally given him training in music. He had sent him to learn at Man Singh Tomar's music school. He also intended to send him to his friend Swami Haridas at Vrindavan so that he could have a systematic knowledge of music.

His name too, had changed from Tanna to Tansen. At the threshold of youth, he had a fair complexion, a thin black moustache, lotus eyes and a serious expression on his face. He was deeply absorbed in his music. He heard melodies in the chirping of the birds and tunes in the blowing wind. Whether it was the gurgling of the river or the rumbling of the clouds or the crackling of lightning, he heard music just about everywhere. His parents often came from Behat village to look him up. Since he had been living with Gaus Baba, his attitude was that of a fakir. He would dress like one and prayed to *Allah*. He had learnt by that time that Makrand and Parvati were his real parents, whereas Gaus Baba had only brought him up.

One morning, even before sunrise, Tansen said to Gaus Baba, 'I have a desire to see Behat village for myself. I need your permission.'

Gaus Baba said, 'Go by all means. But come back before night fall. You have to pass through jungles on the way, son.'

'Yes, Baba, I would be back before then', Tansen promised and left for Behat. There were dense jungles on the way with trees bearing wild flowers and fields and barns. There were wells and gravel paths strewn with stones. Tansen walked and walked, stopping occasionally and reached his house in Behat by the afternoon. His mother was overjoyed to see him after a long time. Makrand was equally happy and there was great excitement in the village. The entire village population, men and women, young and old, turned up at Makrand's house.

In the evening Tansen thought he would go to the Shiva temple. He walked barefoot in that direction. There were thorny bushes along the pathways. Lost as he was in thought, a thorn pricked Tansen's foot and it started bleeding. He tried to remove the thorn. It was very painful and he felt a burning sensation in his foot. He sat holding it for sometime. It was a quiet place. After a while, he heard the jingling of anklets. Tansen raised his head and looked behind him. A young woman came towards him carrying an empty water-pot. She came closer and looking at Tansen said, 'What has happened to you?'

'Nothing much. A thorn has pricked my foot. I did try to pull it out, but half of it is still inside. It's very painful,' Tansen said and then became silent.

'Keep your foot steady. I shall pull it out with my hair-pin. You must bear the pain.'

'Well,' said Tansen.

The young woman held Tansen's foot and pulled out the thorn in no time. The pain in his foot subsided but the pain in his heart intensified.

'What is your name?' he asked.

'Tani. . .'

'Where do you live?'

'In Behat. And what is your name?'

'My name is Tansen. I too belong to Behat, but I live in Gwalior with Gaus Baba.'

'What do you do? I've never seen you in the village before.'

'You wouldn't have seen me. Didn't I say I live in Gwalior with Gaus Baba?'

'But what work do you do?' Tani asked eagerly.

'Work? Oh, I live like a fakir and sing,' replied Tansen.

'You mean you also sing?'

'I do.'

'Then sing for me.'

'I'll do it. But I was going to the Shiva temple and a thorn pricked me on the way.'

'Don't worry. Now get along. . .'

Tani was extremely charming and youthful. Life's sweet dreams peeped through her eyes. She had a golden complexion, and her cheeks were tinged with red. Her voice was sweet and pleasant, as though mingled with nectar. Talking all the way, they reached the Shiva temple. It was deserted, with no one around. Tansen went inside the temple and continued ringing the bells for a long time. Tani remained seated in a corner of the temple with her empty water-pot. Tansen stood absorbed in himself. He began with an *alap* and then sang:

My Lord! You alone are Brahma,
You are Vishnu,
You alone are Mahesh.

Tansen's music filled the air. Tani had never heard anyone sing so beautifully before. She was lost in the music and listened with her eyes closed. When Tansen stopped singing, she was awakened as if from some somnolence. She said, 'You sing so beautifully! When will you be singing again? I would really like to come and listen.'

'Of course. But right now I must get back to Gwalior and be with Gaus Baba. I do not feel like going, but I must.'

'When will you come again?'

'I'm not sure.'

'I shall wait for you. I hope you won't forget me after going to Gwalior and not come to Behat at all.'

'Oh, no. Be sure, Tani, I will come. And tell me, do you also sing something?'

'Some folk songs—that's all.'

'Then let me hear you sing.'

Tani sang a folk-song, tapping her fingers on the water-pot. After listening to her song Tansen exclaimed, 'Wonderful! What a lovely voice! And now, Tani, let me take your leave. I don't know what would have happened to me if you had not pulled out the thorn from my foot.'

Tani smiled, 'You would have still been in pain.'

'Yes, Tani. But although the pain of the thorn is gone, there is greater pain in my heart.'

Tani bowed her head shyly. Tansen returned home from the temple and Tani went bouncing towards the well to fetch water, thinking of Tansen all the time. She turned homewards after filling her pot. By the time she reached home, she was wet with the water that had spilled from the pot on her head.

It was almost night, by the time Tansen started walking briskly towards Gwalior with a staff in his hand. He reached Gwalior at about ten. Gaus Baba was quietly saying his rosary outside the hut. Tansen went up to him and said, 'Baba, I've got very late. Forgive me.'

Gaus Baba said nothing. He only gestured him to go inside and to rest. Tansen went in and quietly lay down. Tani's image floated before his eyes. He was reminded of the silent language of her eyes, the touch of her delicate hands and tresses playing about on her rosy cheeks. Tani had nestled in Tansen's heart. He kept thinking about her till late in the night and how much she had become a part of his life!

On the other hand, Tani was a picture of melancholy ever since Tansen left for Gwalior. She desired to meet him everyday, talk to him, laugh with him. But how was that possible? He was so far away!

She was lost in Tansen's memory all the time. Time flowed at its own pace. It was as if the two banks of the river desired to become one, but the current of time prevented them from doing so.

When Gaus Baba woke up in the morning, he found Tansen still asleep. He wondered, why he was still sleeping, because usually he got up early. Then he thought, perhaps he was tired as he had walked all the way from Behat. However, Tansen woke up after a while and greeted Gaus Baba. Noticing an unusual expression on Tansen's face, Gaus Baba remarked 'Tanna, man cannot achieve what he desires in his life without working hard for it. If you wish to attain success in music, you will have to forget yourself. Forgetting everything, you should have the same devotion to music, as to God. Then alone, will you be able to achieve something, son. You must immerse yourself in music. You must pine for music. You must live for music and you may as well die for it. That kind of pining, that turmoil in the mind can raise man to great heights. You are going to Vrindavan tomorrow. My friend Swami Haridas lives there. I have sent him a message that you are my son and I am sending you to him for training. Go to him and delve into the depths of music.'

Tansen listened to Gaus Baba with his head bowed. He was thinking that if he went to Vrindavan, he would go far away from Tani. He felt restless at heart. His eyes longed to see Tani. It was Tansen's first experience of love and she dominated his thoughts and emotions. She had talked to him in his dream. And now he was expected to go to Vrindavan. He was not mentally prepared for it, but how could he disobey Gaus Baba's orders?

# 12

Tansen started from Gwalior on foot for Vrindavan. Tani was left behind in Behat. But she had installed herself deep in his heart. At first, he thought of going to Behat to meet her. But then he thought, that his path was different from the path of love. He had to become a great musician. Yet, the memories of her lovely face, her curly hair, the simple trusting look in her eyes whirled around in his mind. He said to himself, 'Let me go to Behat before going to Vrindavan.' But then he persuaded himself, 'How can I betray the word I gave to Gaus Baba? He would come to know everything and feel that I had betrayed him.' Lost in these thoughts, he continued walking in the direction of Vrindavan.

Tani was in Behat, which he had left far behind. Tansen's handsome and sensitive face gripped her mind and she constantly thought about his singing. Overcome with sadness, she felt a surge of intense love for him. Every evening, she went to the Shiva temple, lit a lamp, sang praises of Shiva and silently prayed that she would have Tansen as her husband. Quite often, tears welled up in her sad eyes and she reassured herself, 'Tani, have patience. He will come.'

At last one morning, Tansen reached the ashram of Swami Haridas at Vrindavan after passing through Dhaulpur, Agra and Mathura. It was still dark and the stars were shining in the sky. Tansen went to sleep on the sands outside the Nidhivan. As Swami Haridas went to bathe in the Yamuna river early in the morning it was dark, and his foot suddenly knocked against somebody lying in the sand. Uttering *'Hare Krishna'*, he immediately stopped. Tansen woke up at the touch of Swamiji's foot and sat up.

'Who are you? Why are you lying down here?' Swami Haridas asked affectionately.

'I was very exhausted and slept off right here on the sands. Can you guide me to Swami Haridas?'

Swami Haridas smiled to himself and said, 'Did fakir Gaus send you here from Gwalior?'

'Yes, please.'

'In that case come along with me to bathe in the Yamuna. I am Swami Haridas.'

The road was still dark and both of them went to bathe.

Swami Haridas asked Tansen, 'Do you worship God?'

Tansen said, 'Yes, I offer prayers to *Allah.* Gaus Baba has said that anyone who prays to *Allah* realizes him too!'

'Wonderful! What good thoughts Gaus Baba has given you!'

Talking thus, they reached the bank of the Yamuna. As soon as Tansen had bathed in the river his fatigue was gone. Then they both returned to Nidhivan. Tansen remained seated, while Swami Haridas worshipped Lord Krishna. After the *puja* was over, Swami Haridas rose to his feet and taking up the *tanpura*, began to sing *bhajans.* Tansen said to himself, 'Good God! He sings so beautifully! He simply draws you to himself by his singing! I shall ask him one day what gives him the power to sing so well?'

One day Swami Haridas was sitting quietly after singing *bhajans.* A well-built man, dressed in regal costume, came to meet him. He bowed to Swami Haridas respectfully and sat down. Swami Haridas asked him, 'Who are you and from where do you come?'

The man replied, 'Swamiji, my name is Hariram Vyas. I have come from Orchha to meet you. I am employed in the state administration. I got fed up looking after the affairs of the state and I have come to you to find peace of mind. Show me the way to completely dedicate myself to God.'

Swami Haridas explained to him the greatness of God, and said, 'When you yearn to attain something, you will definitely have it. Man can achieve anything by perseverance and a strong desire.'

After that Hariram settled down in Nidhivan. Madhukar Shah, the ruler of Orchha, was very upset because Hariram had gone away. So he set out for Vrindavan one day.

Madhukar Shah reached Vrindavan on his elephant. He had come to take Hariram back with him to Orchha. After meeting Swami Haridas, he asked Hariram to come back with him. Hariram was so upset to leave Vrindavan, that he started weeping and clinging to the trees, plants and creepers. He felt that his dear ones were being separated from him. Madhukar Shah stood in silence. He too was beginning to be fascinated by Vrindavan and keenly desired to stay back there. He conveyed his wish to Swami Haridas. But instead of acceding to it, Swami Haridas persuaded him, 'Madhukar Shah, you are the ruler of your kingdom. Your duty is to protect your subjects. I order you to return to Orchha. There is Vrindavan in every particle of the earth. Of course, you will have to perceive it with your inner eye.'

Abiding by Swami Haridas' order, Madhukar Shah prepared to return to Orchha while Hariram stayed on at Vrindavan.

The elephant suddenly went amuck as the king was about to mount it. People ran helter-skelter in panic. Swami Haridas ordered Tansen to sing. The angry elephant came near Tansen, to listen to his singing. There was some divine power in his music. Tansen, the disciple of Swami Haridas, had now reached the highest pinnacle of music. . .

It was evening. Tansen was walking around in Nidhivan. He was suddenly reminded of Tani and thought one day he would go to Behat to meet her. Full of her memories, he started singing in a melancholy voice:

Oh beloved, whether it be day or night
Your image is in my mind at all times. . .

Agony smarted in Tansen's voice. Swami Haridas came to him and said, 'Tansen, my son, now you have become an accomplished singer. You asked me the other day, how I managed to sing so well. Now listen. Every *raga* and *ragini* has a core which you must recognize. You must merge yourself in the *raga*, like in an ocean, know its essence and then sing. Music is the power of sound. But it will be revealed only when you study its tune with dogged perseverance.'

Tansen asked, 'Swamiji, from where did music originate?'

Swamiji replied with a smile, 'Music is born out of tears. There is a musical rhythm in the crying of a new-born child. There is music everywhere—in the waves of the sea, in the flowing current of the river, in the sound produced by animals and birds, in the blowing wind and in the rain. Music is nature's great gift to man. That gift has been already granted to you. Now your training is over. I am asking you to bid good-bye to Vrindavan and earn your living by music.'

Swami Haridas' words were like an implicit order. The next day Tansen left Nidhivan after respectfully taking leave of Swami Haridas. A bundle was all he had to carry. Nidhivan was engulfed with the fragrance of *shephali* flowers in full bloom, and also the scent of the *juhi*, *champak* and jasmine flowers. The breeze coming from the Yamuna carried with it the smell of the river. Tansen did not feel inclined to leave. But he had to, because Swami Haridas had ordered him to.

It was morning. As usual, the breeze was cool and the birds twittered in Nidhivan. A peacock was dancing gracefully, like a beautiful woman. Lovely colours flashed on its feathers. Tansen kept staring at the peacock. He thought that music and dance were the greatest gifts granted to man. Who, had taught the peacock how to dance? Who, had taught the *koel* to coo the *panchama sur*?

Tansen was engrossed in these thoughts as he waited for Swami Haridas to arrive. He emerged from the hut in a few moments after finishing his *puja*. Tansen walked up to him with a heavy heart and started weeping bitterly, his head at Swamiji's feet. He was going away from his guru today. Swami Haridas raised him up saying. 'Wipe your tears, my son. One day your tears would surely bring melody to your music and you would have the lustre of a gem. Forget your attachment to Vrindavan and me. Such attachments become a hindrance in man's journey towards progress. I have trained you systematically in music. With your music you must spread light all around, so everything becomes bright. Recognise the power of music. Think of my happiness and the happiness of Gaus, when you shine one day in the firmament of music.'

Swamiji looked affectionately at Tansen who repeatedly kept placing his head on Swamiji's feet. Then, Tansen said in a voice choked with emotion, 'Swamiji, the grace you have showered on me and all that you have given to me are the greatest treasures of my life. Be assured that I shall bring happiness to every one with the music you have taught me. Now I am taking your leave, Swamiji. I cannot say where I am going. *Allah* would certainly show me the way.'

'Yes, Tansen. Have faith in *Allah* and dedicate your music to him. Everything acquires fragrance when it is dedicated to God, my son.'

Swamiji went back to his hut and Tansen walked away from Nidhivan.

# 13

As Tansen left Nidhivan, he wondered, where to go. He walked on and on and kept thinking. At first, he thought he would go and present himself in some royal court. But after living in a free atmosphere, he did not feel so enthusiastic about this. Then he thought that now he had completed his training in music, he could go to Gwalior and meet Gaus Baba, and follow his advice.

Four years had passed since he had come to Vrindavan from Gwalior. Tani had been on his mind all along. He said to himself, 'I shall go to Behat and meet Tani. How would she be? She must have got married. Would it be proper to meet a married woman? What would her husband say if he found his wife talking to a stranger?' But then he thought, 'I am fakir after all. Anyone is free to meet a fakir. My heart is pure. I am far from desire. I shall certainly meet Tani.' Plagued by such conflicting thoughts, he set out for Gwalior.

On the way, he had to cross the Chambal and other small rivers in a boat. The Chambal was deep. The boatman had taken too many passengers so the boat started sinking in midstream. It began to sway from side to side and passengers started shrieking and crying. Tansen jumped into the river and pushed the boat to the bank. People fell at his feet, but he stood there calmly. After bidding them farewell he started on foot towards Gwalior. People pressed him to go by bullock-cart, but Tansen declined, 'I am a creature who has lived with nature. I am used to observe nature's various moods. The flowing river inspires me. I listen to the varied sounds of the chirping birds and I compose new *ragas* with them.'

He reached Gwalior at night and slept under a tree. When

he woke up next morning, the birds were chirping and the wheat and gram crop was swaying in the fields. The *neem* trees had flowered, with *palash* and berry shrubs all around. When Tansen reached Gaus Baba's hut, he found him groaning. His stomach had bloated and he was short of breath. He lay with his eyes closed. Seeing Gaus Baba in that state Tansen shouted, 'Baba, I have come to you. Get up.' And he cried 'Gaus Baba! Gaus Baba!'

After a while Gaus Baba came to consciousness. He opened his eyes and said feebly, 'Tanna, you have come back! I know you have had a thorough training from Haridas. Music alone is prayer. You can attain the merciful *Allah* with the help of your music. Enlighten yourself with music. You would be able to realize *Allah*. Never turn your mind away from music!'

Seeing Gaus Baba's critical state, Tansen rushed out and fetched the court-physician. He treated Gaus Baba who recovered in a few days.

After meeting Gaus Baba, Tansen was even more inclined to live like a fakir. He picked up his *tanpura* and sling bag. He himself had no idea where he was going. He walked on, engrossed in his own thoughts. He had left Gwalior city far behind him when he noticed a bullock-cart going towards the city. Tansen continued walking as before. As the bullock-cart moved closer, a young woman instructed the cart-driver to stop. But the cart-driver said, 'Why here? Gwalior is still two *kos* away.'

The young woman was insistent, but the cart-driver did not stop. She jumped off the moving cart, and fell on the gravelly road, face downwards and her forehead started bleeding. Tansen saw this and rushed to help the young woman. The young woman was none other than Tani! Tansen wiped off the blood with his shoulder cloth. After a while Tani said, 'I was going to Gwalior just to meet you. Four years have gone by but you never came to Behat to see me even once. . . Did it not occur to you that a woman's heart was pining for you, was lying in the dust? Was anything lacking in my worship?'

Tansen's heart trembled to hear this. He said in a calm

voice, 'Tani, I know that you are in love with me. I could not come to Behat for I was helpless. I was in Vrindavan for four years, learning music from Swami Haridas. I couldn't find time to come to you, but your memory always dominated my mind. Tani, how are your parents!'

Hearing his question, Tani's tears flowed copiously. She said, 'Tansen, my parents passed away in the malaria epidemic which raged in our village. I am left all alone in the world.'

'Where are you living?'

'In the Shiva temple. I constantly pray there to Lord Shiva for your safety.'

'And what about my parents?' Tansen enquired.

'They have left the village and gone on a pilgrimage somewhere. They left more than a year and a half ago, but they have not come back, yet,' Tani replied and went on sobbing.

Gently, Tansen said, 'Tani you go back to the village and wait for me. I shall definitely come to Behat to meet you.' Tears in his eyes gleamed like pearls in a shell, shining in the light of the sun. The tears of a pure heart have the lustre of diamonds.

The cart-driver drove back to Behat. Tani, turned around to look at Tansen and went back alone to a desolate world.

After meeting Tani, Tansen felt gloomy. She had all the while been in his mind. At first, he thought he would go to Behat and spend his life looking after his father's fields and marry Tani. But then he realized that any such action of his would bring untold unhappiness to Gaus Baba. And how would Swami Haridas react? He persuaded himself that he had to become a fakir only for the sake of music. He would live and die only for music.

Caught in this inner conflict, Tansen again started thinking about his parents. He wanted to visit the sacred places of pilgrimage and search out his parents. He set off for Prayag, carrying the *tanpura* with him. On the way, by mistake, he entered a dense jungle full of *dhak* and *kachnar* flowers, teak, wild, big peepal, *neem*, banyan, mango and *jamun* trees. It lay in Rewa. The ruler of Rewa, Ram Chandra Waghela, had been camping with his retinue in the jungle since the last two days to hunt a lion. The lion did not come out of the den, even after they created a din.

Tansen was very tired. He ate some wild fruits and drank water from a nearby pond. Then a sudden whim came over him and he produced the sound of a lion. In his childhood, he had learnt to produce the sounds of different animals. Hearing the roar of a lion, the king's soldiers rushed to the scene. They were stunned to find a young fakir roaring like a lion, and the lion was going straight towards the fakir. When it was only at a short distance, Tansen started playing the *tanpura* and singing. The lion sat down, listening intently to the intoxicating notes. After a while it got up and disappeared into the jungle.

The soldiers informed the king about this. The king came up to Tansen and said, 'Call the lion again. I would like to hunt it.'

Tansen replied, 'No. Don't kill wild animals. They too have life in them. And they too have their brood. I cannot call the lion for you to hunt.'

The king was very angry at these words. He ordered his soldiers, 'Arrest Tansen and put him in prison. He has disobeyed my orders!' Tansen was taken a prisoner and put into a dungeon in Rewa. The prison was adjacent to the royal palace.

Being a fakir, Tansen did not in the least feel uncomfortable in the prison. He prayed to *Allah* all day along. But one day, early in the morning, he remembered Tani. He thought to himself, 'How does it happen after all? The more I try to forget Tani, the more she dominates my mind and heart. Is this what is called love? Indeed, love is something which you cannot stop thinking about. But I'm a fakir. What have I got to do with love and all that.'

Tansen was thus lost in thoughts about Tani as he sat in the Shiva temple. With his eyes closed, he imagined himself singing *bhajans* in the Shiva temple and Tani listening to him.

By royal order, no one in Rewa could sing or play any musical instrument before eight in the morning, because till then the king Ram Chandra himself, worshipped Shiva. That morning too, he was in the temple inside the palace, meditating with his eyes closed. He had offered heaps of flowers to the *Shiva linga*. Suddenly, he heard the words of prayer addressed to Shiva and his meditation was disturbed. He got up midway through his worship and looked in the direction where he had heard the singing. He was about to clap his hands to call the attendants, but then he noticed that all the flowers he had offered, were falling in the very direction of that voice. The king was stunned at the sight and started listening to the *bhajan* with great concentration. When the singer stopped singing, he summoned the servants and ordered them to check who it was and to present that person before him. The servants went in every direction and discovered that it was the imprisoned fakir. Tansen was escorted by the soldiers to the *darbar* carrying his *tanpura*.

It was afternoon and the king was busy giving judgements about the cases brought up by his subjects. The courtiers had taken their places. One of them said, 'Maharaj, this is the same fakir who was singing, defying the royal order. You have summoned him. Looking at his crime, he should be severely punished.'

Tansen stood before the king with the *tanpura* in his hand. His beard and mustache were overgrown. The king asked, 'Tell me, singer, what is your name? And where do you live?'

'I belong to Behat village in the kingdom of Gwalior. But I am a fakir and a fakir has no home.'

'What brought you here?' asked the king.

'My parents have gone on a pilgrimage. I was going to Prayag to look for them but I lost my way and now I am a prisoner in your kingdom.'

'Where did you learn music?'

'My teacher is Swami Haridas of Vrindavan.'

'Do you know that in my kingdom nobody can sing or play any musical instrument till eight in the morning because that is the time I conduct my worship?'

'No, I did not know it. But Maharaj, a person can pray to his *Allah* any time. A fakir thinks of *Allah* all the time.'

The courtiers raised their eyebrows when they heard

Tansen's audacious reply to the king. They thought that the king would mete out harsh punishment to Tansen. But King Ram Chandra Waghela said with a smile, 'Can you sing something for me?'

'I can,' Tansen replied.

'Then start playing the *tanpura*.'

It was summer and the sun was raining fire. Everybody was suffering. Tansen started playing on his *tanpura* and after the *alap* began singing the *raga Sarang*. Everybody in the *darbar* was flabbergasted, listening to Tansen's singing. In a little while there was a cool breeze and the whole atmosphere cooled. Tansen seemed to have acquired some divine power. Everyone in the *darbar* remained seated, unaware of everything else, still and motionless, like a painted picture.

When Tansen stopped singing, the king took off his precious necklace and handed it over to him saying, 'Tansen, I am very pleased by your singing. You are not singing, but drawing out life. From today you are appointed the main singer of the royal court of Rewa.'

Tansen bowed to the king. Then he returned the necklace to him and said, 'Maharaj, of what use are such things to a fakir?'

'No, Tansen. You are no longer a fakir, now you belong to my court,' and then the king ordered his chief minister to make proper arrangements for Tansen to stay.

The *darbar* rose for the day. Fakir Tansen was appointed the court singer of the kingdom of Rewa.

By the king's order, Tansen was accommodated in a beautiful palace, which provided all the royal comforts and luxuries. Full-sized mirrors, lovely Persian carpets, beautiful paintings, chandeliers, shields, swords and other weapons hung on the walls. There were also tiger-skins, with tiger heads. There were retinues of male and female attendants. Outside was the lush green grass and all kinds of flowers in bloom in the flower-beds. Tansen was flabbergasted to see the opulence and grandeur of the palace.

Tansen who had lived in the midst of nature in Nidhivan

was disturbed by that royal grandeur. There was nothing like Nidhivan there. Lovely lamps had been lighted in the bed-chamber. The chandeliers glittered like diamonds in the light of those lamps. A lovely carpet had been spread on the floor. The bed had plush, silken mattresses. The whole chamber was fragrant with the scent of jasmines kept in a bowl.

Tansen sat on the carpet and wondered at the life of kings. They fought bloody wars in order to have those comforts. But all that was meaningless. In spite of possessing everything, they really possessed nothing. Their minds were uneasy. Their ambition to continuously expand their kingdoms and add to their prosperity drove them to shed blood. It was all so nice in Nidhivan! The earth was the bed and there was the cooling shade of the hut, the cool fragrance of the waters of the Yamuna, and the chirping of the birds. Whereas in the palace everything was artificial. Everything was far removed from nature. 'Would I be able to live in this palace?' Tansen wondered.

After a while, Tansen rose and started walking leisurely near the flower-beds. He kept gazing at the roses for a long time. Then a charming maid came up to him and said '*Huzoor*, dinner is ready.'

Unwillingly, Tansen returned to the palace with the maid. The dining-room was filled with the aroma of all kinds of food. Tansen looked at the food and thought to himself, 'So many things to eat!' So far, Tansen had subsisted only on *roti* and a vegetable curry to go with it. So, he ate only the *roti* and one vegetable curry and ordered the maid to take away rest of the dishes.

It was quite late in the night. Tansen felt like building a hut in the garden. But the royal conventions would permit no such thing. He did not realize when sleep overcame him.

# 14

Tansen had settled down in Rewa. He did his daily *riaz* in the palace. The king was highly pleased. In course of time, he began entrusting him with more and more responsibility. Instead of consulting the chief ministers and the commander-in-chief in the affairs of the state, he depended on Tansen's judgement! This created bad blood and rancour against Tansen.

One day, when the *darbar* was in session, the king ordered Tansen to sing something. Abiding by the king's command, Tansen started on a *dhrupad*. His singing was extraordinarily charming that day. The listeners were transfixed and became oblivious to their surroundings. As Tansen finished, the king honoured him. The state officials became very jealous, and began hatching plans to get rid of Tansen from the kingdom.

One beautiful morning, the king had a desire to go hunting. He ordered that the convoy should leave immediately leave for the Bandhavagarh forest. Tansen also was to come.

It was a dense forest. The king, accompanied by Tansen on a horse, was looking out for the lion. At one point, Tansen dismounted and followed the king on foot. He had hardly gone a little way when an arrow whizzed past Tansen and got stuck in the trunk of a tree. Tansen went up to the tree but could find no one. Then he thought that someone might have shot the arrow towards his prey. He sat there for some time. In the meantime, the king returned and both of them came back to their tent empty-handed.

The king was sad, that he had been unable to hunt. It was already evening. The breeze was cool and pleasant. The forest was filled with the fragrance of wild flowers. Occasionally, the *langoors* and wild birds disturbed the peace of that hour. The king was strolling outside his tent with Tansen. The general noticing this, whispered something in the chief minister's ear. After a while, the general came to the king and said, 'Maharaj, the forest looks very beautiful today. It's full moon and the whole forest is bright with the moonlight. In this pleasant hour, why not listen to some music of the great singer Tansen.'

The king agreed to the general's proposal and they all prepared to listen. Then, suddenly an arrow came with lightning speed and instead of striking Tansen, went deep into the neck of the chief minister seated next to him. People ran helter-skelter. The chief minister started bleeding profusely and died soon after.

After this incident, Tansen realised that some conspiracy to kill him was underway. He became alert. The king was also enraged. He sent his spies to investigate, but they could find no clue as to who had shot the arrow at Tansen and why it happened. . . .

On another evening, the king was feeling somewhat low. Tansen was also sad at the thought that he had set out in search of his parents but had forgotten about them after settling down in this palace. He wondered if they had returned to Behat. What would Tani's condition be? She was all alone—how would she be living? Uneasy in mind, he went and sat by the lakeside all by himself, dressed in ordinary clothes.

Some time later, two beautiful young women arrived near the lake. Seeing Tansen, they hesitated and stood still. Tansen asked them gently, 'Who are you and what has brought you to this desolate jungle?'

The young women smiled and stood silent for a moment. Then the elder woman said, 'We have come to meet you. Your music has entered our hearts. You are as handsome as your lovely music.'

'Are you admirers of beauty.'

'Of course! Women's hearts always lean towards beauty.'

'My music and I are also dedicated to beauty.' Tansen replied in a philosophical tone.

While the younger woman sat by the lakeside, the elder one continued talking to Tansen. He asked her, 'What is your name?'

'Roopmati.'

'Who is your father?'

'He was the chief minister of this kingdom. He has passed away. He died in an accident.'

'Oh!' said Tansen and then there was silence for a while.

Then Roopmati asked, 'What do you like most in the world?'

'My music.'

'What about me? Don't you like me?' Roopmati asked and bowed her head.

'You are nature's beautiful creation. You look lovely and I think you have a lovely mind too.'

'I have silently worshipped you as a singer. In my lonely moments, I have always experienced you sitting near me. How long have I been waiting to talk to you! Today I got an unexpected chance. What is your opinion about me?' Roopmati asked, lowering her eyes, waiting for Tansen's reply.

'A woman's heart is beautiful in every case.'

'Not in all cases,' Roopmati said firmly.

'You are right. But a woman possesses both power and devotion.'

Both of them went on talking without realizing that a long time had passed. It grew dark and they bid each other goodbye and went their own ways.

Roopmati's younger sister, Taramati, was a poet and a painter. She was emotional and very beautiful. She had heard Tansen singing on one occasion when she had gone to the Shiva temple where he was praying in song. His voice had sunk deep into Taramati's heart. Beads of perspiration formed on Tansen's forehead as he sang. Taramati felt an impulse to wipe off his perspiration with her own hands but she refrained, to avoid public slander. When Tansen was about to leave after his worship in the temple, she wanted to go up to him and praise his singing. But she did not get an opportunity to do so.

That evening, the two sisters had gone to the lakeside and by a strange coincidence, found Tansen sitting there. Something came over Taramati the moment she saw him. She was serious outwardly, but happy at heart. As for Roopmati, she gave her heart to Tansen at the first sight and kept staring at him spellbound. She had heard praises of Tansen's singing and was eager to talk to him. Now she had found her chance. Roopmati was drawn towards Tansen like a magnet.

Taramati felt hurt when she saw her elder sister talking to Tansen. She walked away from them and sat near the lakeside. In fact, she eagerly wished to reveal her heart to Tansen. From that day, Taramati, was in agony, though she was hale and hearty. Locking herself in her room, she would be lost in Tansen's thoughts for hours on end. She would compose songs of separation and sometimes, would paint Tansen's portrait.

One night Roopmati found the door of her sister's room open. As she entered the room she found Taramati asleep. Roopmati found a portrait of Tansen painted by her sister near her head. Under the portrait she found sheets of paper on which were written innumerable songs addressed to Tansen. Roopmati was stunned. She wondered if Taramati was in love with Tansen. Lost in her thoughts, Roopmati returned sadly to her room. Seated on her bed, she thought to herself, 'Can two moths hover around one flame? Does Taramati really love Tansen? Will she be able to have Tansen for herself?'

Caught up in such thoughts, she told herself, 'No, I'm in love with Tansen. I have claim over him. If Taramati does not keep herself out, I will. . .'

Roopmati could not sleep till long past midnight. When she finally did, she dreamt: 'Tansen and Taramati are seated in a lovely garden, laughing and talking. Taramati is reciting her poems for Tansen. After listening to her, Tansen is embracing her. Roopmati goes there and pulling out a dagger from under her jacket thrusts it into Taramati's chest. Taramati is badly wounded and dies with a painful scream. Tansen pulls out the dagger from Taramati's chest and commits suicide with the same dagger. . .'

Roopmati was so scared by that dream that she suddenly got up and wrote a letter to Tansen. She had hardly written a couple of words when she suddenly glanced at the back of the palace. Roopmati saw that two soldiers were riding towards the palace at breakneck speed. Who were those horsemen? From where had they come? She wondered why they had arrived at the dead of night. Soon they were out of sight.

All kinds of thoughts invaded Roopmati's mind. She got up, picked up her sword, led a horse out from the stable and started off in the direction where the horsemen had gone. Roopmati first went towards the royal palace but the riders were not there. Then she went towards Tansen's palace. Both the riders had dismounted from their horses and were standing there. With sword in hand, Roopmati went up to the riders and was shocked to see that they were none other than Taramati and her maid Mudri, disguised as soldiers. In utter amazement Roopmati asked, 'Tara, what has brought you to Tansen's palace at this hour of the night? Why have you come in disguise like this?'

Taramati replied firmly, 'I have come to meet Tansen.'

'But why secretly and so late in the night?' Roopmati asked sternly.

'My heart prompted that Tansen was calling me.'

'Now, come back. We should not visit somebody's house like this. We are the daughters of the late Chief Minister. We have our honour to think of. I think you have the heart of a poet and an artist. I know that you want to listen to his music. But this is not the way. Come home, my dear sister.' Roopmati's voice was sad.

Tara pondered for a while and then the three women rode back to their mansion.

Roopmati was convinced after that incident that Taramati was in love with Tansen. A storm raged in Roopmati's heart. Two sisters in love with the same man! No, that was impossible. She said to herself, 'I am in love with Tansen. It is impossible that Taramati should have him.' She decided that if need be, she would get Taramati killed. Roopmati started hatching a plan.

One day she met Mudri in the palace. She was alone. Roopmati said to her, 'Mudri, you don't have any good jewellery to wear. You are our maid but live like a pauper. Come to my chamber at night, before going home. I want to give you something in secret.' Saying that, Roopmati waited for Mudri's reply.

Mudri replied with delight, 'Yes, *Bai Sahiba*, I shall definitely come,' and she went to Taramati's chamber.

Taramati was sad, because she was not getting a chance to meet Tansen. But she did not mention it to Mudri. She lay the whole day, pondering over something or the other.

At night before going home, Mudri went to Roopmati's chamber. Roopmati was actually waiting for her. She gave Mudri a meal and then gave her a lovely necklace and said, 'Mudri, you have been formerly in my service. I will make you immensely rich if you do just one thing for me.'

'Murder Taramati.'

'No, no. I can't do it,' Mudri said in a terrified voice.

'You are mad to disregard such an offer. You are depriving yourself of so much wealth!'

'Well, what am I supposed to do?'

'You will have to poison Tara.'

'Very well. I shall come tomorrow,' said Mudri and went home, dreaming of having inexhaustible wealth.

Mudri thought about her bright future all through the night. The night has been rightly said to be the most appropriate hour for planning conspiracies. Night is like a chessboard where all types of pawns are moved. Some get out of the way. Some are thrown out. So many secrets lie hidden in the darkness! Planning a conspiracy is also a game of the dark.

Thoughts about a conspiracy occupied the mind of Roopmati and Mudri. Roopmati wondered how she would have Taramati poisoned. Mudri wondered that if Taramati died, she would be the suspect. But if she herself died, at least her children would live happily with her wealth.

In the morning, Mudri came to Roopmati's chamber instead of going to Taramati. Roopmati gave her a bottle which contained poison and told her that the poison should be mixed with the milk and given to Taramati. Mudri went to Taramati's chamber, hiding that little bottle of poison inside her blouse.

Taramati was up already. She said to Mudri, 'You are very late today.'

'Yes, *Bai Sahiba*, I was delayed today. Please forgive me.'

'All right. Now go and get me some hot milk.'

Mudri went to the kitchen and returned to Taramati with a bowlful of milk. She was trembling with fear. Her hand, shook so violently that the bowl of milk dropped from her hand, as she tried to give it to Taramati. Taramati said, 'Go and get the dog to lick away the milk.'

The frightened Mudri went out and brought the dog. The dog licked the milk and died instantly. Taramati was stunned to see the dog choke and die. She roared like a lioness, 'Who mixed poison in the milk?'

Mudri stood there trembling, with her head lowered.

'Out with the truth. Otherwise, I'll chop off your head this very minute,' Taramati thundered again.

Mudri was terror-stricken. Tara brought down the open sword hung on the wall and threatened again. 'Tell me, otherwise I'll kill you.'

Mudri was so scared that she mumbled, 'Roopmati. . .'

'I see! Now I know. She is conspiring to kill me, is it? I shall see her!'

Taramati immediately dismissed Mudri from service. With tears in her eyes, Mudri returned to her house.

After that, conspiracies continued to be secretly hatched, by both sides, the dark shadows of time, without any hint. . .

One day the sky was suddenly overcast. The dark clouds and cool breeze reminded Roopmati of Tansen and she had an irresistible desire to be with him. She set out for Tansen's house, without informing anyone.

It was afternoon and Tansen had just returned after singing in the *darbar*. He was astounded to see Roopmati standing at the entrance of the palace. 'Roopmati, you! Why are you standing there? Please come in.' Roopmati went inside with Tansen.

Roopmati was greatly impressed by Tansen's beautifully furnished chamber. All the musical instruments were nicely arranged. Roopmati looked at everything with admiration. Then fixing her eyes on Tansen's face she suddenly asked, 'Can two moths fly around one flame, Tansen?'

Tansen replied with an amused smile, 'The flame is always one, there can be any number of moths.'

'What is the function of the flame?'

'To burn itself and to burn others.'

'What happens if one moth doesn't let another moth come anywhere near?' Roopmati asked.

'That is up to the moth. But what prompts you to ask such odd questions?'

'For no particular reason,' Roopmati replied. And after a pause she asked, 'Do you believe in love, Tansen?'

'Love is a pure sentiment. It is a spark which can set one's heart on fire.'

'And if someone is burning in that fire?' Roopmati asked.

'Well, it depends on how intensely the flame is burning. Roopmati, behind love lies the feeling of sacrifice.'

'And if someone, cannot give up one's beloved?'

'That is called an obsessive love.'

Roopmati stood up. Clinging to Tansen, she said in a soft voice, 'You are my flame and I am your moth. Oh, the comfort I find in your name!'

Tansen and Roopmati stood locked in embrace for some time. Then suddenly someone threw a poison-tipped dagger at Roopmati. It went so deep into Roopmati's back that it tore out her heart. Soaked in blood, Roopmati collapsed at Tansen's feet. She writhed in agony and finally lay motionless.

Tansen stood horrified, wondering how it had happened. Who had thrown that dagger at Roopmati? He looked around everywhere in the chamber. Finally, he found Taramati standing behind a curtain with a fierce look in her eyes. Looking at Tansen she said, 'Tansen, I'm a woman. I fell in love with you at the very first sight. I want to have sole claim on you. You were mine. You are mine even now. Even after knowing how much I loved you, Roopmati did not withdraw. I know I will die on the gallows. Let me have one final look at Roopmati. After all, she was my elder sister.'

Promptly, she went up to Roopmati's dead body. She pulled out the dagger from her body and after touching Tansen's feet, thrust it into her own chest and collapsed right on the spot, her eyes turned towards Tansen. Two hearts in love, stopped beating forever. The two sisters passed into eternal sleep.

Tansen stood aghast, looking at the dead bodies of the sisters in disbelief. That singer, who was devoted to the pursuit of the melody shuddered with horror at the sight of their streaming blood.

Tansen felt miserable and uneasy at heart. At times, he thought that following the path of love was like walking on the edge of the sword. However, those two were real sisters, born of the same mother. Surely, they could have settled the matter between themselves? But the next moment it occurred to him that the person in love aspires to have exclusive claim on the object of love. Taramati had never opened her mind and expressed her love for him. Roopmati had entered his life first.

Alas, what an end to that love! It was indeed blind love! Then he said to himself, 'Tansen, pursuit of music is your aim in life. You have to live and die for music. Keep away from such worldly love!'

# 15

After that incident in Rewa, Tansen was very disturbed at heart. He found living in the palace irksome. It could not be otherwise because he was a lover of beauty and his life was devoted to its pursuit. Tansen would lose himself in the beauty of flowers and the sonorous sound of springs. He found nature's music in the gurgling of the river. He was ever perturbed at the sight of swords, blood, tears and wailing. . .

Tansen sat in his palace, lost in melancholy thoughts. Then, he donned the royal robes and set out with a heavy step for the *darbar*. The *darbar* was already in session and he sat silently took his seat. After the proceedings of the *darbar* ended, king Ramchandra Waghela noticed him. He asked, 'Tansen, what's the matter? Are you not well?'

'Oh, it's nothing, Maharaj. I'm absolutely fine.' Then he added, 'Maharaj, I've come to seek your permission to go to Gwalior. If you would please grant me permission. . .'

'But why do you want to go to Gwalior?' the king asked emphatically.

Tansen replied, 'Maharaj, I want to go to Gwalior to meet my guru Gaus Baba. Later I also wish to go to Vrindavan to meet Swami Haridas.'

Ramchandra Waghela was not quite pleased. He said, 'Well, go if you really wish. But come back soon. You know very well that I do feel uneasy without you.'

'Yes, Maharaj, I promise to come back to Rewa at the earliest, after meeting Gaus Baba and Swami Haridas.'

'Very well, Tansen. You may go. But before going, sing to me a *ragini* that would constantly ring in my ears.'

'I shall abide by your order, Maharaj,' said Tansen and began to play on the *tanpura*.

It was the monsoon season. Today, for the first time Tansen sang the *raga Mian Ki Malhar* which he had composed. The sky was already overcast. As Tansen sang this *raga* the clouds up in the sky started rumbling.

When he finished singing, Tansen got up and bowed to the king, who stood up from his throne and embraced him and offered him a bagful of money. With tears in his eyes, the king bid Tansen farewell.

Tansen sat in his palanquin and came to his palace. On one hand, he was deeply pained to leave the king and on the other hand he was happy that he was going to Gwalior and Vrindavan. He would be meeting Swami Haridas after a long time and after ages he would be talking with Gaus Baba. He was also overjoyed at the thought of meeting Tani, since he planned to visit Behat. Soon thoughts about Behat village with its berry-laden shrubs and lush green fields rushed over him. He wondered whether the thatched huts, fields and threshing floors would have changed. Would the dusty lanes where he had played as a child be *pucca* roads? He told himself, 'I will go and sing Lord Shiva's praises in the temple.'

He also started thinking about Tani, 'How beautiful she was! And what a wonderful mind she had! Most probably she was long since married and with her loving husband, she would have completely forgotten her past. Was it possible that she would remember me after so many years? And why should she remember? She must be having her own children. I will know everything once I go there.'

Tansen packed his bags and prepared to leave. The servant placed them on the back of the horse and Tansen set out on his journey to Gwalior.

On the way, Tansen was fascinated by the animals wandering freely in the thick forests of Rewa and by the sweet chirping of the birds. He thought to himself, 'Look at these animals and birds. They are so happy! They have no possessions—no houses, no wealth, no clothes and they are not worried about food. Are they happy only because they possess nothing? Human beings are unhappy because they crave for possessions. I shall go back to living like a fakir. All this wealth, these royal pleasures are meaningless. They are a bondage. They lead to craving, and sully the mind.'

Finally, the horse reached Prayag, the junction of the two sacred rivers—the Ganga and the Yamuna. Boats and canoes swayed gently on its rippling surface. Tansen decided to spend the night at Prayag and proceed in the morning after bathing in the Ganga.

He went to the river bank and after tying up the horse, washed his face and hands. It was evening and he felt like offering a prayer to the river Ganga. He did not have his *tanpura* with him. Sitting at a beautiful spot on the bank of the river, Tansen sang the *alap*. Soon his sweet voice, singing in praise of the Ganga filled the air. Whoever heard that singing, came rushing up to Tansen and was lost in that intoxicating music. He rested for the night on the bank of the Ganga and set out in the morning for Gwalior via Vithur. After almost three days, he reached Gwalior.

It was a lovely Gwalior morning. All around the trees were in blossom. Wild trees dotted the slopes of the fort. The sun had risen in the sky, and the daily hustle-bustle had begun. Bullock-carts loaded with grains were proceeding towards the market. Vegetables of all kinds were being sold on the roadside.

Tansen surveyed the scene and finally reached Gaus Baba's hut, full of emotion. He tied the horse on one side and dismounted. Then taking down the luggage, he went inside Gaus Baba's hut and fell at his feet.

Gaus Baba had aged a lot. His eyesight had dimmed. 'Who is it?' he asked on hearing Tansen's footsteps.

'I am Tanna, Baba, your Tanna!'

'So, you've come, my Tanna!' Gaus Baba said choking. 'How long, have I been waiting for you! How are you? I am sure you are married by now. Tell me all about yourself, son.'

Tansen replied, 'Baba, I am now a court-singer in the kingdom of Rewa. I am doing very well. No, I haven't married yet.'

'Oh, Tanna, that is very good. I am very happy that you are now a court-singer. But you must get married, my son. Man cannot bear the burden of life alone.' And then he added, 'Now that you are here, you will stay with me for some days, won't you?'

'Of course, Baba. I shall spend some time with you.'

'Very well,' said Gaus Baba. 'Go and have your bath and then eat something. Meantime, I will pray to my *Maula*.'

Tansen sat outside the hut and Gaus Baba began his prayer. When he came outside, Tansen said to him, 'Baba, I am seeking your permission to return to the life of a fakir. I find all that royal pomp and honour very irksome. I wish to fly freely, like a bird. I wish to soar high into the blue sky and astonish people.'

Gaus Baba listened attentively to Tansen. Then he said, 'No, my Tanna. The life of a fakir is full of hardship. It is one of endless sacrifice. You must become a householder. Man can live like a fakir even as a householder. You must marry and have a family. Your progeny would carry forward your musical tradition.'

Tansen was silent after listening to Gaus Baba. Just before him was Rani Mriganayani's palace. Outside the palace was a beautiful well from which women were drawing water. Maharaja Man Singh Tomar was already dead and Rani Mriganayani was living the life of widow, spending her time in worship and prayers. Her maid would bring sweet water from the well outside, to be used for cooking and Mriganayani also drank the same water.

A large group of women were drawing water from the well. Tansen went and sat there quietly, waiting for the women to leave, so that he could have his bath. When all the women had left, Tansen noticed an enchanting young woman looking into the well with a pot tied to a rope. For a long time she peered into the well and then, she let go her empty pot into the water. For nearly half an hour she went on pulling up that pot, and letting it go back again. Intermittently, she would look inside. The woman was not moving from the well. He got up and slowly went nearer. For a long time he kept on watching her as she let go the pot into the well and listened to all kinds of sounds. It aroused Tansen's curiosity. He wondered at the young woman's strange action.

Finally, Tansen went up to her and asked, 'What is this game you are playing? You let down your pot into the well and bring it up. You have been doing it for quite some time. Why are you doing it? It makes me curious.'

The young woman blushed. She said, 'I am not playing any game. By letting down the pot which is sometimes full and sometimes empty into the well, I am listening to the musical notes of the sounds. I hear the ***pancham swara*** in the dashing of the pot when it touches the water. I come here to listen to the music of those sounds which are sometimes soft and sometimes frightful,' the young woman gently replied.

'What do you do after listening to those musical sounds?' Tansen asked.

'I remember and imitate those sounds when I sing.'

'My God! How wonderful? May I have the pleasure of knowing your name?'

'Of course! My name is Hussaini-Brahmani.'

Tansen was astounded. He said, 'Hussaini-Brahmani—I don't quite follow.'

The young woman replied, 'Actually, our ancestors were Brahmins. They were converted to Islam later on, for political reasons. People call me Hussaini-Brahmani.'

'Where do you live?' Tansen asked.

'In the palace of Rani Mriganayani. I am in her service.'

'Well. Then what songs do you sing?'

'I don't sing. I do ***sadhana*** in music,' Hussaini said with tremendous pride. Then she asked, 'May I know who you are?'

'I am Tansen. I also sing.'

'Then sing for me.'

'Here? At this hour?'

'Yes, of course. Let me listen a bit. Please sing.'

Tansen fell for Hussaini's physical charm and her love for music. They moved away from the well and sat in the shade of a tree. It was the rainy season and dense clouds floated in the sky. Tansen began the *raga Mian Ki Malhar*, at first at a slow pace and then in faster tempo. Hussaini kept time with Tansen's singing by tapping on the empty pot in front of her. When Tansen stopped singing, she exclaimed with joy, 'How wonderful! How wonderful!'

Tansen turned to her and said, 'Now it is your turn to sing, Hussaini.'

'Well, tomorrow—right here at the same time. It is very late today. The Maharani must be waiting for me.' And then, looking straight into Tansen's eyes, she added, 'Let me have your permission to leave.'

'Very well, *khuda hafiz.* I shall wait for you tomorrow.'

Hussaini left, ecstatically in love. As for Tansen, he could think of nothing else but her. That is the way artists' hearts are drawn to each other.

Tansen returned to Gaus Baba's hut with turbulent thoughts in his mind. What was the right thing to do, to love God or to love a human being? His mind suddenly turned to Tani: 'How would she be? What would she be doing? She too, loves me from the depths of her heart. She would be terribly hurt if I go ahead with Hussaini. Would she be able to bear such a shock? I would be considered a traitor. No, I cannot fall in love with Hussaini.'

Gaus Baba asked affectionately, 'Tanna, my son, you seem to be terribly worried about something. What is the matter?'

'Nothing, Baba. I am learning from the book of life.'

Gaus Baba smiled and remarked, 'My son, life is like a song with its tunes of joy and sorrow. Listen to those tunes, grasp their meaning, but let your heart not break. It is only time, that drives human beings to take decisions. Man is merely a pawn on the chessboard of time.'

'You are right, Baba. I think I should go to Behat tomorrow. I seek your permission.'

'Sure, go by all means,' Gaus Baba promptly agreed, though he would have loved Tansen's company a little longer.

Night was beginning to cast its shadows and the stars were twinkling in the wide expanse of the sky. The birds had already returned to their cosy nests. Tansen lay on the charpoy under a tree. He kept awake far into the night. Sleep evaded him. Past events flashed before his eyes in quick succession. The images of Tani, Taramati, Roopmati and Hussaini flicked past. But before he realised it sleep overcame him. He slept soundly and woke up only in the morning when he heard the cock crow. He then started his *riaz*.

At about eight, Tansen rose and went to the well. Women were returning with their pots filled with water. In a little while, Hussaini appeared in a light green *dupatta*, carrying a pot and a rope. Tansen hid himself and observed Hussaini as she looked around expectantly for Tansen. Then she let go off the pot tied with the rope into the well and listened to her favourite sounds for a long time. Tansen quietly rose to his feet and standing behind Hussaini said, 'Here I am, Hussaini.'

Hussaini pretended to be annoyed. 'Off with you! How long I have been looking out for you!'

'Oh, Hussaini, forget the waiting. You are so beautiful! And more so in your light green *dupatta*. You will have to sing for me today.'

Hussaini was ready. She said, 'All right. Let us sit there.'

They both sat under the same tree.

In a little while, Hussaini started singing *dhrupad* in the classical style. Tansen was astonished to hear her music. 'Beautiful! Wonderful!' he exclaimed. And he felt love for Hussaini surging in his heart.

After that day, Tansen and Hussaini met daily near the well. Their meetings were no more a secret. The news of their love reached the ears of Gaus Baba and Rani Mriganayani. One day, Rani Mriganayani summoned Tansen to her palace to hear his music. Hussaini was also present. The Rani found his music so captivating that as Tansen was about to leave, she said to him, 'Tansen, I wish to give you a gift for singing so beautifully for me. It is so precious that you will be overjoyed. But you must preserve that gift carefully.'

'I am honoured. There will be no ground for any complaint.'

'All right,' Mriganayani said and then added, 'Hussaini, come here.'

Hussaini promptly stood up and went up to the queen. Placing her hand in Tansen's, Rani Mriganayani said, 'Tansen, I am giving you a precious jewel. Protect it well.'

Tansen stood dumbfounded. Then he said, 'I must consult Gaus Baba.'

'I have already discussed the matter with him.'

Tansen turned to Hussaini and said, 'Then come, Hussaini. Let us go back to our world of music. You will be my instrument and I, the voice, which sings to it.'

Tansen and Hussaini touched Rani Mriganayani's feet and then the two of them returned to Gaus Baba's hut. Gaus Baba was saying his rosary. Tansen and Hussaini fell at his feet. Gaus Baba was overwhelmed, and embraced them. Getting them married himself, he declared them husband and wife.

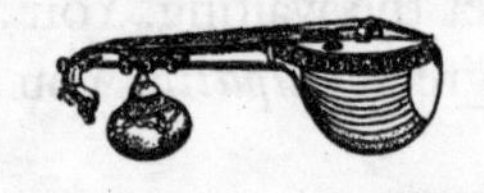

# 16

Hussaini's real name was Prem Kumari. She belonged to a Saraswat Brahmin family. When she and her family were converted to Islam, she was given the name Hussaini. But remembering her Brahmin origin, everyone referred to her as Hussaini-Brahmani.

Tansen's childhood name was Ram Ratan, but after his *nikah* Muhammad Gaus, gave him a new name—Muhammad Ata Ali. However, Tansen was not pleased with it. He preferred to be called only Tansen.

After the marriage, Tansen was possessed by Hussaini's enchanting beauty. He would sit before her the whole time. Her captivating eyes, so intoxicated Tansen that he simple reeled under their impact. He no longer practised music. He even stopped going out of the city; so totally were they absorbed in each other.

Then one morning, Tansen was suddenly reminded of his village. He wondered how his parents were. How their fields would be? The green stalks of wheat would have ripened and turned golden. The shrubs at the back of the house must be laden with fruits.

Then he thought about Tani—where would she be living? How would she be managing? Perhaps, she had raised lovely children. May be she was married in Antari village which was not far from Behat. He said to himself, that he would definitely go and meet her one day. If she complained, he would say that since she could not wait for him to get married, he too married Hussaini who was beautiful and learned in music. After all, one could not carry the burden of life alone. Moreover, how could he have disobeyed Gaus Baba's orders? Filled with such thoughts, Hussaini and he left for Behat on horseback; Hussaini sat in front and Tansen behind her. . . .

When Tansen and Hussaini reached the outskirts of Behat, they saw farmers working in their fields. They were ploughing the land and their wives were sowing the seeds. Young children, smeared with dust, were playing in the fields.

Tansen went straight to his house. He found the house locked. From want of care, the walls were covered with moss. The villagers came out of their houses when they learnt that Tansen had come. They told him that it was more than ten years since his parents had gone on a pilgrimage. May be they had settled somewhere else or. . . 'No, I shall rest only when I find them,' Tansen said with determination.

An old peasant handed over the key of the house to Tansen. He said, 'Here is the key of your house. My son, I have been selling the produce of your field every year. The money is with me. Please take it.'

Tansen replied, 'It is very kind of you. God has given me much wealth. You have been toiling on my land. Please keep that money for yourself. And yes, if my parents return, give them this house key. If they do not come back, then open a music school in the house.'

Then Tansen and Hussaini rode towards the Shiva temple. The aged priest was worshipping when they entered the temple. Tansen and Hussaini stood there with joined hands and prayed to Shiva in silence. When the priest finished his *puja*, Tansen said 'Baba how are you? Do you recognize me?'

The old man's eyesight had dimmed too much. He looked intently at Tansen and said, 'No, son, I can't recognise you. . . .'

'I am Tanna, Baba. Makrand Pandey's son. Don't you remember?'

'Oh, now I know. Where were you all this time? You have come after so long. Take this *prasad.*' And the priest gave them some *batashe.*

After eating the *prasad*, Tansen asked, 'Baba, there used to be a girl called Tani in the village. Where is she now? Do you know anything about her?'

'Yes, she used to live in the village. Everyday, she would to come here and worship Shiva. But, then she went away some time ago. We searched for her everywhere, but could not find her. Who knows where she would be now. No one in the village has any idea. Have you come to meet her, son?'

Tansen replied disappointed, 'Yes, Baba. Indeed, I came to Behat to meet Tani.' Then, he added after a pause, 'If she does come back, then please tell her that I have become the court-singer in the kingdom of Rewa. If possible, kindly arrange to send her there. I am leaving ten gold coins with you for her expenses during the journey. Give it to her in case she comes back. But if she doesn't come, then take it as my donation for this temple.'

Tansen and Hussaini came out of the temple and mounted the horse again and sped towards Gwalior. Tansen was impatient to be with Gaus Baba.

Deep at heart, Tansen was very sad and disappointed that he had not been able to meet his parents and Tani. He was deeply worried about her. In this wide world, she had none at all to call her own. She was absolutely without any means. Could not the village folk have stopped her from leaving? He had seen her crumbling hut. Who knows, where she had gone and how she would be living. And his parents—where were they?

It was already dark and Tansen and Hussaini were still on their way to Gwalior. Lost in his own thoughts, Tansen was racing his horse faster and faster. Suddenly, Hussaini felt very thirsty. She said to Tansen, 'I am very thirsty. My mouth is so dry! Please stop the horse near some well and get some water to drink.'

'Yes, yes,' Tansen replied as the horse still sped on. Then he noticed a well by the roadside. Tansen stopped the horse. He dismounted and then helped Hussaini to get off. He tied the horse to the trunk of a tree and then both of them proceeded towards the well.

There was a group of young travellers, busy having their meal of *roti* with pickle and chillies. On noticing Tansen, one of the young men stopped eating and walked upto him. He said, 'You are from the Behat village, aren't you?'

'That's right. I am from Behat. I am going to Gwalior.'

The young man said with a smile, 'They say you have become a famous singer!'

Tansen gave him a surprised look, 'Who ever said that I have become a famous singer?'

The young man said, 'A girl called Tani who lived in the Shiva temple in Behat. The priest of that temple also said so.'

Tansen was startled to hear Tani's name. He asked, 'Do you know Tani, young man?'

'Of course I know her. I should know the temple in my own village!'

'Then tell me,' Tansen said eagerly, 'Where did she go after leaving the village?'

'I don't know about that. But the villagers say that one day she sang *bhajans* in the temple for a long time. Then she tied her clothes and a garland in a bundle and left the village at night when it was dark.'

Images of the past crowded Tansen's mind. He said to himself, 'Oh it must be the same garland which I had offered to Mahadev one day. The flowers would have long withered away, but their fragrance must have lingered—the fragrance of my memory in Tani's mind!'

Once more dreams about Tani stirred in Tansen's mind. But they were dreams that belonged to the past. In the present, Hussaini, who was like sweet music in his life, was beside him. He was completely under the spell of her stunning beauty. Pushing back those memories, Tansen gave himself up to the pleasant moments with Hussaini. . . .

Now, the tenor of Tansen's life had completely changed. No music emanated from his lips—not a single note. He was obsessed with Hussaini. And all he did was to drink in her beauty.

Deep at heart, Hussaini was quite perturbed about it. She was beginning to have the nagging fear, that Tansen might get alienated from music. One day, when she found Tansen in a happy mood, she said to him in an extremely soft voice, 'I wonder what has happened to you. Imagine for a long time, you haven't even sung an *alap*. Just see the layer of dust on your *tanpura*. You know that your personality is best expressed only through music. If you keep away from music, you will also keep away from yourself.'

Tansen listened to Hussaini's remark with head bowed. He realized that Hussaini was talking sense. He wondered how he had neglected his music all this time. How foolish of him! He said, 'You're right, Hussaini, very right. Music is my life. It is my heartbeat. My whole being is contained in music. I can give up my body, but I can't give up music. Let us go to Vrindavan to my guru Swami Haridas. I have still to learn a great deal from him. Would you accompany me?'

Hussaini was overjoyed to see Tansen emerging from his inertia. She said, 'Surely I would go with you. Music is my life and breath. I too, will train under your guru.' Hussaini's face glowed with extreme happiness as she said this. They first went to Gaus Baba. After seeking his blessings, they went to Rani Mriganayani's palace and took her permission. While leaving, Hussaini clung to Rani Mriganayani and wept ceaselessly.

Mriganayani's eyes also moistened. Those were the tears sanctified by love and affection. Tansen and Hussaini mounted the horse and set out for Nidhivan of Swami Haridas at Vrindavan.

Passing through many places, the horse finally arrived at Vrindavan via Mathura. They went to Nidhivan and Hussaini was fascinated by the beauty of Nidhivan; the small, crooked trees and creepers laden with flowers, the unrestrained joyous cries of the birds. There were troops of monkeys all around eating gram. Hussaini was carrying a bag of sweets in her hand, a monkey came and swooped down on it. All the monkeys scrambled over those sweets; she greatly enjoyed that sight.

As they walked on in Nidhivan, they found a peacock, spreading out its feathers, dancing in ecstasy like a glittering fan of the rainbow's colours. Melodious notes were heard from the hut of Swami Haridas.

Tansen heard the music with utter concentration and was immersed in its flood of melody.

As Swami Haridas finished singing, Tansen and Hussaini fell at his feet. When he saw Hussaini, he promptly asked, 'Tansen, who is this woman who has accompanied you?'

Tansen replied very humbly, 'Swamiji, she is my wife. She too is a singer and wishes to learn music from you. I hope, you would have no objection to giving musical training to a woman?'

Swami Haridas said gravely, 'It does not matter. I make no distinction between man and woman. Men or women—they are all God's children. They all inhabit this earth. They eat the food which this bountiful earth provides.

They breathe the same air and drink the same water. They are born on this earth and on this earth they end their worldly existence. You both can live in that hut. I shall make both of you accomplished singers. I shall, Tansen, be sure of that.'

Tansen and Hussaini touched the feet of Swami Haridas and then they went to the hut which Swami Haridas had given them.

For quite some time they both lived in Nidhivan. Swami Haridas was engaged in some important religious performance, which did not give him any time to teach Tansen music. In the meantime, Hussaini started getting bored in Nidhivan. One day she said to Tansen, 'Now listen, we have been here for a very long time. I was so eager to learn music here, but your guru has not taught you anything at all. How long would you stay on here, waiting? If you ask me, it would be better to go back now.'

Tansen gave Hussaini a grave look. He did understand Hussaini's feelings but how could he leave his guru without his consent? He said, 'Look, Hussaini, I have come here on my own, but I shall leave only when my guru permits.'

Saying that, Tansen got up and went to Swami Haridas who quickly grasped what Tansen had in mind. That day, he explained to Tansen in detail the various mysteries in the realm of music.

But Hussaini felt really bored. One day, she was sitting under a tree in a melancholy mood. Suddenly, when she looked up, she was startled to find Swami Haridas standing before her. She stood up and went and sat near a bower. When Hussaini looked back, she found Swami Haridas standing there. She got up from that place and went and sat at the edge of the pond. As she gazed into the pond, she saw Swami Haridas its water. Hussaini rushed to the spot where Swami Haridas generally sat. She was astounded to find that Swami Haridas giving Tansen a practical demonstration of the rendering of a *raga*. Overwhelmed, by that miracle, Hussaini fell at Swami Haridas' feet. Respectfully, she joined her hands and said, 'Please forgive me, Swamiji. I had taken you amiss. Would you be good enough to teach me music as well?'

Swami Haridas gave her a benign look. He said to her very affectionately, 'Why not? I shall certainly teach you. Pick up the *tanpura* and start learning the essence of music right from now.'

Hussaini lost no time. She started playing the *tanpura* and right from that moment, began her formal training in music. He gave both Tansen and Hussaini a thorough training in singing *dhrupad*. . .

It was about four o'clock in the morning. After bathing in the Yamuna, Swami Haridas was worshipping *Banke Bihari* in his hut. Tansen stood outside in the meantime. Swami Haridas with his eyes closed, was absorbed in the *darshan* of Radha-Krishna. He imagined them dancing under a lovely *kadamba* tree on the bank of the Yamuna. While dancing, one of Radha's anklets snapped and she stopped dancing. Swami Haridas broke his sacred thread and stringing the anklet with it, tied it on Radha's foot.

Tansen was astonished to see that even in the state of meditation, Swami Haridas had broken his sacred thread. When Swami Haridas came out of the hut after his worship and found Tansen standing there, he said, 'Tansen, go to the temple and return after having a *darshan* of the deity.' Tansen promptly obeyed the order and set off for the temple. He was astounded to find the sacred thread tied to Radha's foot!. . .

Thus, Tansen and Hussaini received training in music from Swami Haridas. When the training was over, Swami Haridas said one day, 'Well, Tansen, it is now time for both of you to leave. Your training is over. Whenever you sing, first think of *Bihari* and remember that *Bihari* is listening to your music. If you sing with such feeling, you will be able to express yourself the best.'

Tansen and Hussaini fell at Swami Haridas' feet and then went to their hut. They packed their things and set out for the kingdom of Rewa.

# 17

As Tansen and Hussaini proceeded towards Rewa, Tansen was upset to leave behind the bowers of Vrindavan with blossoming flowers, forests and gardens, the beautiful banks of the Yamuna river and the charming birds and animals. At first Hussaini had not felt at home in Vrindavan, but later she too had come to love the place.

Their horse was racing towards Rewa. After some time, they reached a lovely forest, and dismounted to rest a while. A little later, Hussaini turned to Tansen and asked, 'Swami Haridas is a great sage. But I really don't understand how an ascetic like him is keenly interested in music.'

Tansen smiled at Hussaini's innocent question. Then he replied, 'Hussaini, the pursuit of music is also a way of realizing God. Music has a power which brings a human being closer to him. All great sages and fakirs always carry the *ektara*. They sing for God, and following that path, also realize God.'

Hussaini fixed her lovely eyes on Tansen's face and asked with childlike simplicity. 'You also sing wonderfully. Do you mean that you too, will realize God?'

A grim expression came over Tansen's face. He said sadly, 'Hussaini today you have touched a deep wound inside me. I have spent most of my life with Gaus Baba who is a fakir. His influence pervades every pore of my body. I too am a fakir at heart. I abhor all this royal pomp, wealth and show of ostentation. But I married you because Gaus Baba insisted. I wish to be free of all attachments and fly in the boundless blue sky like a free bird.'

Hussaini also became a little serious. She said persuasively, 'Now, you better rid yourself of such thoughts. We have bound our lives together and we shall share our happiness and sorrow.'

They sat in silence for some time. Finally, Hussaini said, 'Well, we should resume our journey. We have spent a long time sitting here. We ought to reach Rewa in the morning?'

They mounted their horse, and sped on, leaving behind echoes of loud trotting. . .

Although Tansen thoughts were like a fakir's, his body had gradually got accustomed to the comforts of the royal court. The desire to resume that tenor of life grew stronger as they reached the outskirts of Rewa.

It was early in the morning when they arrived. After a while, they noticed clouds of dust rising in the sky. They looked around. To their astonishment they heard loud trotting.

They wondered, if a ruler of some neighbouring kingdom or Emperor Akbar had attacked Rewa. Perturbed and agitated, they walked around aimlessly. A little later, when they saw the elephants coming with the riders, fluttering the royal flags of Rewa, Tansen's mind was at rest. The army of Rewa was returning after conquering the kingdom of Kalinjar.

In the district of Banda, stood the lofty fort of Kalinjar, like a sturdy sentinel. Surrounded by water reservoirs and springs of sweet water, the scent of wild ***karaunda*** fruits pervaded the fort. Its turrets rose high into the sky. There were eight or nine gates leading upto it. The surrounding ranges protected the fort from enemy attacks.

The kingdom was ruled by Raja Kirti Singh. Shershah Suri had besieged the fort of Kalinjar. A fierce battle ensued and the fort fell into Shershah Suri's hands. Later, in the war of Kalinjar, Shershah Suri himself was slain. Raja Ram Chandra Waghela attacked Kalinjar and restored its freedom. His army was romping back home, full of happiness at its conquest and was now about to enter Rewa.

Welcome arches had been erected at the gates of the palace. Women were singing auspicious songs. Ram Chandra Waghela was welcomed at the palace entrance, by the queen's ***arati***. She took the sword from the king's hand and touched it to her forehead. The soldiers slowly marched to their camps.

Tansen and Hussaini, with joy in their hearts, went to the king's palace. The king was in the queen's chamber. He was informed about Tansen's return. The moment the king heard this, he rushed out to embrace Tansen. He said, 'Tansen, I am not as happy about my victory over Kalinjar as I am about your return. Go and rest in your palace.' Then noticing Hussaini who was standing silently behind Tansen, the king said, 'Is this your wife?'

Bowing respectfully, Tansen said, 'Yes, Maharaj. Her name is Hussaini.' The king smiled happily and remarked, 'So, you have got married, is it? And you did not even inform me!'

Tansen bowed his head and said, 'I plead guilty, Maharaj. But it happened so suddenly that. . .'

'All right, all right! Anyway, I am happy you got married. Now go and rest. We are celebrating our victory over Kalinjar this evening. You will have to sing in the *darbar*', said the king and went back to the queen's chamber.

Tansen took Hussaini to his palace. The palace was in the same condition as he had left it. It was the same place where Taramati and Roopmati had given up their lives for his sake. The two sisters were madly in love with Tansen. As he came nearer, Tansen's heart filled with gloom. Hussaini went inside while Tansen stood there, lost in thought: 'Is the fire of love really so fierce that everything gets scorched in its intensity? I had never given those sisters any impression that I cherished any love for them. Then why did they give their lives for me? Really, the whole world seems meaningless. There is nothing, but misery in this world', thought Tansen. 'I do hope Tani too has not ended her life, pining for me. There is no trace of her anywhere after so much search. I hope she is not dead!' Tansen said to himself.

Suddenly, Tansen was shaken out of his thoughts when Hussaini called out to him, 'It is already so late in the day. Don't you want to bathe? Then, you are also expected to sing in the *darbar* this evening.'

Tansen went in and bathed. He had hardly finished his prayers when the messenger came in to announce that he was expected in the *darbar* immediately. Tansen donned the royal robes, tied his turban, and along with Hussaini, started for the *darbar* in the palanquin.

The assembly-hall of Rewa was gaily decorated. There were chandeliers of crystal glass with numerous dancing flames. The place had been sprinkled with *kevra* water. And the intoxicating fragrance of sandalwood and roses filled the air. There were canopies of orange-coloured cloth and entrances had been erected with trunks of banana trees. Expensive carpets had been spread. The commoners of Rewa had gathered outside the assembly-hall.

The senior administrative officials occupied their decorated seats. Soon the arrival of the king was announced. The people stood up to greet the king and flowers were showered on him. The king entered the *darbar* in a very happy state of mind and sat on the gem-studded throne. He wore a saffron-coloured silk turban, with a plume on the top. He was laden with all kinds of precious jewels. With a smile he signalled that it was time to start the celebrations.

The *mehfil* warmed up slowly. The dancing-girls danced with zest and brought joy to everyone present there. After they had finished, the king suddenly asked, 'Where is the master of music?' People immediately understood that the king was asking about Tansen.

Tansen was invited to present himself. He greeted the king by bowing his head. And the next moment the notes of the *tanpura,* the *sarangi,* the *flute,* and the *mridanga* reverberated in the air. Tansen sang an eulogy to the king praising his valour and the heroism of the soldiers.

The king was overjoyed. He took off a precious necklace and presented it to Tansen who stood before him in all humility. The celebrations came to an end. Everyone present in the *darbar* returned home. . . .

A spy of Rewa reached Bandhavgarh from Agra. He had visited Akbar's *darbar* disguised as a Mughal and wanted to pass on a secret of the Mughal *darbar* to Raja Ram Chandra Waghela. On his arrival, he saw that the palace was aglow with innumerable lamps. The spy informed the king that he wanted to see him very urgently, because he had brought very important information.

The king called the spy to the queen's chamber. The moment the spy entered, the king asked, 'What is the matter?'

The spy, who was still panting, said in a gentle voice, 'Maharaj, you are very well aware of the expansionist policy of Emperor Akbar. He wants to have the whole of India under his control. Yesterday, so many musicians sang in his *darbar*, but the Emperor was not satisfied with any of them. He said, "Is there no singer in Hindustan whose singing would really please me? If only, these court musicians are going to sing, I would not like to listen to any of them." The whole *darbar* was stunned to hear such an announcement from the Emperor. The courtiers simply stared at each other. After a while an aged Mughal general said, "Jahanpanah, there is indeed such a singer but he is not here. He is in the *darbar* of Raja Ram Chandra Waghela of Bandhavagarh." Akbar then promptly ordered that the singer be summoned to Agra at once and if Ram Chandra Waghela refused to send him, the kingdom of Rewa would be blown up like straw by the cannons of the Mughal army. The moment I heard Akbar utter such words I came rushing from Agra to give you advance information. Now it is up to you to decide whether you would like to send Tansen to Agra or fight a battle with the Mughal Emperor.'

Raja Ram Chandra Wahgela sat thinking. He loved Tansen more than he loved himself. The very thought of sending Tansen to Agra sent a cold shiver through him. Beads of perspiration appeared on his forehead. Then regaining his composure he said, 'Juzar Singh, you better go back to Agra. I will need sometime to think it over. Yes, you better keep a watch over the developments in Agra and keep me informed constantly.'

At the king's orders, Juzar Singh went back to Agra that very night.

The king then went to his chamber and kept pacing up and down. His face alternately showed expressions of anger and heroism. He drew the sword hanging on the wall and kissed the unsheathed sword. Then, he clapped his hands and called the attendants and ordered them, to inform the prime minister and the chief general of his army to come to the palace at once. The servants humbly took the orders and left.

Raja Ram Chandra would by turn touch the point of his lance, then hold the shield and the sword and then stand like a warrior on a battlefield. The prime minister and the general arrived. The king informed them about Akbar's wish and said, 'I shall shed blood. Even if it means our ruin, I will not entrust Tansen to Akbar under any pressure.'

The prime minister and the general kept quiet for a moment. Then the prime minister said, 'Maharaj, we know too well that you love Tansen more than your own life. But Maharaj, it is good statesmanship and political expediency to arrive at an honorable settlement with the enemy if he happens to be stronger than us. That is the best course of action in the interest of our kingdom. Akbar possesses wealth and military strength beyond measure. Fighting such a powerful enemy would mean certain defeat for us. In our view, it would be best to send Tansen to Akbar's *darbar*. That is the dictate of the times. . .'

Ram Chandra Waghela's face wore an expression of anger and determination to fight. At last, he said, 'You both may go and rest. I need a little time to think.'

The king could not sleep the whole night. All sorts of thoughts stormed his mind. The night was very long. The calls of the sentries broke the silence of the night. Occasionally, some unknown bird produced strange sounds.

Then, somehow he fell sound asleep. He dreamt that a fierce battle was raging between his army and Akbar's. Cannon balls flew from both sides. Soldiers riding horses and elephants were engaged in fighting. He himself, on horseback, was fighting Akbar. A blow of Akbar's sword struck his arm and he lay in a pool of blood. Akbar's army won the battle. He was taken prisoner and the Mughal soldiers arrested Tansen and marched with him to Agra.

The dream left the king panic-stricken. He got up from the bed and looked out of the window. The day had just dawned.

Tansen was singing *Bhairavi* in his palace. His voice was so pleasant to hear in the early morning! He stood spellbound listening to Tansen. And as he listened, tears glistened on his thick eyelashes, the tears of love he felt for Tansen.

Slowly, the day advanced, as the sun rose high in the sky. The kites transversed the depths of the blue sky, by spreading out their wings. The cows already milked, were licking their calves. The market place of Rewa was astir with life. It was time for the *darbar*. The king dressed up in his royal robes and reached the *darbar*. The courtiers greeted him by bowing respectfully. The king, his face writ with sorrow, sat on the throne. He sat quietly for a while. Then he looked up and called out in heavy voice, 'Tansen!'

Tansen bowed and responded, 'I am right here, Maharaj.'

The king said sadly, 'Tansen, it seems to me that very soon you will be separated from me. But Tansen, wherever you may be, don't ever forget me. You know how much I. . .' and the king's voice choked.

The *darbar* was stunned. Suddenly, a guard came in and bowing respectfully before the king said, 'Maharaj, the Mughal army commandant, Jalal Khan Kurchi, has arrived with the Emperor's *farman* and wishes to present himself in the *darbar*. May he be brought in, with your permission?'

'Yes, he has my permission. Let him come.'

Jalal Khan Kurchi appeared in the *darbar*, in military regalia. He offered salutations to the king and handing over the imperial *farman*, announced, 'Either send Tansen alongwith me or be prepared for a battle.'

Hearing the words of Jalal Khan Kurchi, the *kshatriya* blood of the king boiled. His hand went to the hilt of his sword, hanging at his waist. His eyes turned red with uncontrollable rage. The sandalpaste mark on his forehead shrank and then expanded, as though there was an earthquake. His twisted mustache looked as if the cobra had uncoiled itself and struck with its venomous fangs.

The minister at once understood what was passing through the king's mind. To give him some time, he turned to Kurchi and said, 'You may go to the royal guest-house and rest a little while.'

Immediately, the king thundered, 'Yes, indeed! Go and rest. You have challenged the *kshatriya* blood. We, who choose to die, also know how to free ourselves from the attachments of life. We are born to fight on the battlefield and have grown up listening to the painful cries of dying soldiers, as though they were lullabies. We have filled the empty, cranial bowl of *chandi* with blood. Kurchi, don't challenge me to wage a battle. We would prefer the comforting sleep of death, accompanied by death's soothing music. Now, you may go and rest. You may roam around and if you wish, even go hunting in the jungles of our Bandhavgarh.'

Kurchi opted to go hunting in the Bandhavgarh jungles, and left with his soldiers.

Meantime, Raja Ram Chandra Waghela filled with disturbing thoughts, weighed the pros and cons of the whole situation and finally decided in favour of sending Tansen, in the interest of his kingdom.

Kurchi did go hunting, but all kinds of doubts plagued his mind. In the meantime, the king issued an order that Tansen would be given an honourable farewell, when he departed from Bandhavgarh for Agra, in the morning. The announcement was made all over the city. Preparations were in full swing. The king, overcome with emotion, was seated on the throne. He said to Tansen, choking, 'Tansen, you are going away from me. Before you leave, sing a *ragini* that would ring in my ears all my life.'

Following the king's orders, the *tabla*, the *sarangi* and the *tanpura* were brought in. Tansen became very emotional and he sang *Mian ki Malhar*. Tansen had specially composed that *raga* by mixing the tunes of the *Malhar* and the *Kanada ragas* which were popular.

Everyone present in the darbar was moved to tears. Tansen himself was weeping. It was a heart-rending sight. Tansen was taking leave from the king. It was like an only son being separated from his father.

Finally, the *darbar* rose. Tansen went to his palace with a heavy heart and started weeping. Hussaini tried to comfort him as best as she could but the thought of being separated from the king was hard to bear.

At last everything was ready for Tansen's departure. Their belongings were loaded in the carts of the royal convoy. The whole city had turned up to bid Tansen farewell. He was made to sit in a beautiful palanquin. Hussaini was carried in a separate palanquin. The palanquin-bearers carried both of them towards the jungle where Kurchi was waiting for them. On arriving in the jungle, Tansen got off the palanquin and was astounded to discover that the king himself was one of the palanquin bearers! Tansen fell at his feet and exclaimed, 'Maharaj, what is this? You bearing the palanquin!'

The king replied, 'Tansen, it is our custom to carry the dead on the shoulder up to the cremation ground. From today, you are dead for me. That is why I carried your palanquin on my shoulder.'

Tears of love streamed from Tansen's eyes. He joined his hands together and said, 'Maharaj, I may be living anywhere, but my heart would be always with you!'

With a heavy heart, Raja Ram Chandra Waghela returned to Bandhavgarh and Jalal Khan Kurchi proceeded along the road to Agra with Tansen and Hussaini. On the way they passed the same jungle, the same mountain ranges, the same rivers and springs and the same nature smiling in its beauty—but Tansen's heart was so heavy that he did not even notice them.

# 18

Jalal Khan Kurchi and his soldiers reached Agra with Tansen and Hussaini after a two day journey. The morning sun scattered its golden light all around. As the convoy reached the city, they saw before them the Red Fort of Agra on the heights of Badalgarh. Pairs of pigeons were cooing on the turrets of the Fort. All over the Fort, heavy cannons were set up and sentries were standing on guard at the strategic points. Their bared swords flashed in the sunlight.

The convoy entered the Fort. The water-men were sprinkling water everywhere from their leather bags. Further down, the interiors of the Fort were being cleaned with rose and *kevra* water. The air was fragrant with burning incense. The maids dressed in exotic clothes and heavy jewellery, were hidden here and there, keenly observing the reception given to Tansen. Suddenly, a cannon exploded. Every hour the cannon was fired in honour of Tansen's arrival.

A beautiful palace had been allotted to him. Expensive velvet curtains with brocade work in gold and silver thread hung at the doors and the windows. A lovely marble bed had been installed, over which were spread beautiful mattresses. A rare type of wine was waiting for him.

Tansen noticed the flagons filled with wine. He promptly clapped his hands to call a maid. When the maid arrived, Tansen instructed her to take them away. The maid looked sarcastically at Tansen. She found it incredible that anybody in his position could turn away from something in which all men revelled! Noticing the impatient expression in Tansen's eyes, she promptly picked up those flagons and left.

The maid went to her companions who all ridiculed Tansen for showing such contempt for wine. 'An uncouth villager has come to Agra to become famous! Living in the royal palace and having such contempt for wine!' one of the maid cut in.

'He will soon be turned out. Just wait and see!' another maid piped in.

The third maid said, 'If he refuses to take wine when *Shahenshah-e-Alam* offers it to him, his head will be chopped off!'

The maids had found a topic to gossip about and made fun of Tansen. . . .

Tansen stretched out on the bed. He was very tired and soon went off to sleep. Hussaini, who was pregnant, was also fatigued. She, too, went to her chamber and went to sleep.

Tansen woke up in about an hour's time. But he stayed in bed. He remembered Raja Ram Chandra Waghela, Bandhavgarh and its scenic beauty. He kept thinking about the king, who had lent his shoulder to carry Tansen's palanquin. He said to himself, 'One day I shall sneak out secretly and meet my beloved king.' But suddenly doubts assailed his mind. He said to himself, 'Akbar is a very powerful king. If I go secretly and meet the king, Akbar would blow up the kingdom of Rewa with his cannons. I better live here, whether I feel happy or not. I shall certainly not create any trouble for the king.'

Possessed by such thoughts, Tansen went to Hussaini's chamber. Seeing that she was fast asleep, he sat near one of the windows, admiring the scene outside. He could see the crowded portion of the Fort, where the Emperor watched lion-fights.

A little later, Emperor Akbar arrived. The lion-fight took place, but since it was quite far, Tansen could not get a clear view. He stood at the window for a while, then came and sat on the bed.

He was suddenly reminded of Behat village. He thought to himself, 'Behat is not very far from here. I shall go there one of these days and try to get information about Tani. Who knows whether she is dead or alive? If she is alive, I shall bring her here and try to make her happy in the best way I can. After all, it was Tani who offered me love for the first time in my life. I have married Hussaini but it was Tani that I have loved.'

Then he started thinking about his parents who had gone away from the village for good. He wondered where they would be and how he could possibly trace them. . .

When Tansen finished his dinner and looked out, he found the whole palace illuminated with lamps lit on sconces. The lamps in the hanging chandeliers were spreading an unusual brightness all around and Tansen was lost in his own world.

Suddenly, a maid entered and informed Tansen that Rahim Khan Khana had arrived to meet him. Tansen had already heard about Rahim Khan Khana in Rewa. He was a friend of Raja Ram Chand Waghela. Tansen instructed the maid to bring him in.

Rahim Khan Khana, all dressed in royal robes, entered and Tansen greeted him with due respect and offered him a seat. In the course of their conversation, Rahim Khan Khana began his *shairi*. Tansen also recited some *padas* he had composed.

Then Rahim Khan Khana acquainted Tansen with the functioning of the Emperor's *darbar*. After a random conversation he got up and took Tansen's leave. 'I shall see you in the *darbar* tomorrow and listen to your music,' he said and left for his palace in his palanquin. . .

Akbar's *darbar* was full of poets, painters and musicians. There were many court-singers too. When they heard that the Emperor had summoned the singer Tansen from Rewa, they got jealous and upset. Baba Ramdas, Subhan Khan, Main Chand, Vichitra Khan, Muhammad Khandhadi, Sarod Khan were amongst the chief singers. Apart from them, there were many others as well. All of them were worried about losing their employment in Akbar's *darbar*—on account of Tansen. Hence, they started conspiring against him. They removed the strings from the *sarangi* and pulled out some strings from the *tanpura*. Deliberately, errors were made in playing the *tabla* and *mridanga*. They talked about their plans in undertones and waited curiously to hear how Tansen would be able to sing in that confusion. They wondered if the Emperor would be pleased with Tansen's singing or would he punish him and drive him out of the *darbar*.

The following day, Tansen got ready at about eleven o'clock in the morning to present himself in the *darbar*—unaware of the mischief planned by his adversaries. He had put on the turban presented to him by Raja Ram Chandra Waghela, and was all set to sing in the *darbar* in the presence of the Emperor.

In a little while, a palanquin was brought for Tansen. He got into the palanquin which took him to the Emperor's *darbar*. He was dumbfounded by the grand decoration of the Agra Fort. Passing through its many gardens and corridors, the palanquin was finally brought down in front of the *darbar*.

Tansen got off the palanquin and walked up to the *darbar*. Emperor Akbar had not yet arrived. All the courtiers had taken their seats in accordance to their status in the hierarchy. The eight jewels of Akbar's *darbar*—Birbal, Raja Man Singh, Raja Todarmal, Hakim Haman, Mullah Dopyada, Malikurshara Fhaizi and Abdur Rahim Khan Khana adorned the honoured seats in their royal dress.

Soon, Akbar's arrival was announced in the *darbar*. All the courtiers stood up respectfully. The Emperor, in full youth, came up and occupied his gem-studded throne. The maids began swaying the fly-whisks. Akbar's personality was impressive. He had big moustaches. On his turban glittered precious emeralds, diamonds and topaz. His sword hung at the waist, and he wore a silken robe with golden brocade and diamond studded shoes on his feet. His face was lustrous. It was a grand mix of wealth, power and opulence.

There was complete silence in the *darbar*. Then, Akbar addressed Mulikurshara Fhaizi: '*Mian* Fhaizi, what do you suggest? Should we first listen to our court-singers or should we straightaway start with Tansen?

Malikurshara Fhaizi replied, 'If *Huzoor* desires, we could first listen to Tansen. We have been hearing our own musicians singing all this time. Let us now listen to a new voice.'

Fhaizi glanced at Tansen who looked very handsome. His face wore a serious expression. He rose and bowing low, offered his salutations to the Emperor and then took his seat on the expensive Persian carpet where a lovely looking *tanpura* and a diamond-studded *pakhawaj* had been kept ready. But according to the planned conspiracy, the musician who was to play the *pakhawaj* was missing!

Tansen was puzzled. He looked around in confusion. Hussaini, who had followed right behind quickly grasped the situation. She came to Tansen's rescue. Coming forward, she bowed in salutation before Akbar and took charge of the *pakhawaj*. Tansen tuned the *tanpura* and started the *alap* of *Mian ki Sarang*. The *alap* itself was so beautiful and moving that everyone in the *darbar* alongwith the art-loving Emperor Akbar, were deeply immersed in its melody. After the *alap* Tansen sang the *dhrupad* so wonderfully that Akbar was full of admiration and the whole *darbar*, hailed him with cries of *Wah! Wah!* Akbar was so happy that he promptly gifted Tansen two crore gold coins. At the same time, he also announced that from that day, Tansen would be the main court-singer of his *darbar*. Soon after that announcement the *darbar* dispersed. . . .

Tansen and Hussaini were returning to the palace together in the same palanquin. Hussaini complemented Tansen in a gentle voice, 'You were wonderful!'

Tansen said with an affectionate smile, 'Why are you praising me, Hussaini? It is Fakir Muhammad Gaus, Swami Haridas and Raja Ram Chandra Waghela who really deserve the praise. We are just the dust of their feet, Hussaini. I have just presented today whatever they passed on to me.'

Hussaini agreed with Tansen, 'You are absolutely right, Tansen. This is all the result of their grace and favour. . .'

Passing through the lovely roads of Agra, the palanquin finally arrived at Tansen's palace. Hussaini immediately went to her chamber. Because of her pregnancy, she was feeling more exhausted than usual.

Tansen went to the garden and just admired the roses silently and tenderly. He found these flowers exceptionally beautiful. It seemed as though they gleamed with delight at Tansen's happy dream of the future. Tansen felt an impulse to pluck a flower and present it to Hussaini. Happy at heart, he then walked back to the palace.

# 19

Kafia, Jalal Khan Kurchi's daughter had been learning to play the *rudra veena* from Sheikh Dawan. He was a smart young man, with a fair complexion and a short, Mughal style beard, curly hair, big penetrating eyes and a tall figure. That day he had come to give her lessons, wearing a wine-coloured silken tunic. He secretly loved Kafia, but so far had not given her any indication of his love.

As usual, they settled down and soon Sheikh Dawan began playing the *rudra veena*. Kafia imitated him on her *veena*. In the process, he held her index finger and placed it on the correct string of the *veena*. For Kafia, it was the first experience of a man's touch and she shrank from within. Sheikh Dawan also felt a shiver in his body.

At the end of the training session, Kafia freely praised the *dhrupad* Tansen had sung in the *darbar*. Sheikh Dawan silently listened to her. He trembled at the thought that Kafia had probably started loving Tansen. He decided that Tansen should be removed from his way.

He sat with Kafia for a little longer, smiling sweetly at her and then left. His mind was in a whirl that day and he found it difficult to walk easily. At last, he pulled himself up and walked briskly towards the mansion of Jalan Khan Turani who was a senior army officer. . .

After Sheikh Dawan left, Kafia's friend Zeenat came to meet her after a long time. Her father had been a highly placed officer in the Mughal empire but had died in a battle, leaving behind his wife, daughter Zeenat and her two younger brothers. Emperor Akbar, out of compassion, had engaged Zeenat at a big salary, to supervise the servants in Tansen's palace.

Zeenat was a charming girl. Her cheeks once had a rosy tinge, but her father's death had cast a shadow of sorrow and gloom over her face.

Kafia was happy to see Zeenat. She greeted her friend warmly. Then they settled down for a game of dice and played for some time. During the course of the game, Kafia asked, 'Tell me, Zeenat, is it true that you have become a big ***haakim*** of the Emperor?'

'Oh, no, the Emperor has been kind enough to give me a small job, so that we can have something to live on.'

'What is the work you are supposed to be doing?' Kafia asked out of curiosity.

'Nothing much', replied Zeenat. 'You know, that musician Tansen who has come from the kingdom of Rewa? Well, I supervise the work of the maids in his palace.'

Kafia was delighted to hear that. She asked, 'Tell me, Zeenat, what time does Tansen do his *riaz*?

'Very early in the morning. But Kafia, I have heard people talking in the palace that the Emperor has issued an order that Tansen should sing for him in the afternoon, when he has his lunch and at night when he retires to bed.'

Kafia exclaimed, '*Yah Allah*! Would Tansen not get tired if he has to sing all that long? Zeenat, isn't he really handsome?'

Zeenat replied with a smile, 'Of course he is very handsome. It seems like you've fallen in love with him! But Kafia, remember that he is a married man. And his wife is due to become a mother very soon.'

Kafia said in a serious tone, 'Zeenat, I haven't fallen in love with Tansen but with his singing. He sings so wonderfully, doesn't he? And he himself is as handsome as his beautiful music. And by *Allah's* grace, he is good-natured too!'

Zeenat was astonished. She asked, 'How do you know that? Have you already met him or what?'

Kafia replied, 'Yes, I've met him.'

'Where did you meet him?' Now it was Zeenat's turn to be curious.

'I met him in the palace garden near the beds of roses.'

'Oh, I see!' Zeenat said with a mischievous smile. 'The matter has gone that far, has it?'

'Oh, it's nothing much. I hardly had any conversation with him. It was a brief meeting, that's all!' Then after a pause she said again, 'Zeenat, would you do me a small favour?'

'What,' asked Zeenat opening her eyes wide.

'Arrange a private meeting with him.'

'I shall try,' said Zeenat and shrugging her shoulders, she left for her home. . .

Jalal Khan Turani was not in, when Sheikh Dawan arrived at his mansion. Sheikh Dawan walked up and down in front, waiting for Turani. In the meantime, another court musician Subhan Khan passed that way. He was going to the market to buy some milk-cream. He was fond of taking opium with milk-cream. When he saw Sheikh Dawan, he stopped to talk to him. He said, 'Dawan *Mian*, it seems our days in Akbar's *darbar* are numbered. This new musician Tansen—by God, he really sings very well. He is very well-versed in the technicalities of music. When he sang in the *darbar* yesterday, it was really breathtaking.' Then he added, 'What are you doing here all by yourself, Dawan *Mian*? Come along, have a little opium. It will lift your spirits.'

Sheikh Dawan politely declined the invitation, 'Thanks a lot, *Mian*. But I do not take opium.' He stood silent for a while and then he said, '*Mian*, Tansen impressed everybody in the *darbar*, but didn't you notice that his rendering of the *ragas* was faulty?'

'You're right,' agreed *Mian* Subhan Khan. 'I too heard similar remarks.'

Sheikh Dawan grabbed the opportunity. He said, 'In that case, *Mian* Subhan Khan spread the rumour in the *darbar* that Tansen is an enemy of music and if he continues to sing, our music would be ruined. It would be the end of music.'

'You are absolutely right, young man! Tomorrow itself I shall spread this rumour in the *darbar*. I shall convey it to everyone. You've thought of a fantastic idea! You're indeed a man of imagination. If our *Shahenshah* is convinced about it, be sure Tansen is out and then we all would have a glorious time.'

Happy with himself, Subhan Khan turned to go to the market to buy milk-cream to enjoy with his opium, while the Sheikh stood waiting in front of Turani's mansion. A little later, the bearers lowered Turani's palanquin at the entrance. He stepped out of the palanquin and finding Sheikh Dawan standing near the entrance, immediately went up to him. After exchanging greetings, Turani put his hand around Sheikh Dawan's shoulder and led him inside.

They went in and sat in a well decorated room. After a while, a maid came in with wine and fruits and withdrew immediately.

When Turani asked him the purpose of his visit at that hour of the night, Sheikh Dawan started off about the wrong renderings of the *ragas* in order to build up some background.

Turani wielded a good amount of influence in the *darbar*. He was convinced that Tansen was indeed, singing the *ragas* in a faulty manner. Turani assured Sheikh Dawan that he would first mention the matter to Fhaizi. But Sheikh Dawan was not satisfied with that. He said, '*Huzoor*, the purpose won't be served with just that. Tansen must be driven out of the Mughal *darbar*. If this is not done he will deprive all musicians like us, of our livelihood.'

Turani was engaged with other problems but he assured Sheikh Dawan and sent him off. Sheikh Dawan, instead of going home, went to the mansion of Asad Khan, one of the generals of Akbar's army. The general was fond of music and Sheikh Dawan occasionally visited his mansion to play the *rudra veena* for him.

The general was out flat, in a drunken state. Sheikh Dawan said to his attendant, 'I must see *Janab* Asad Khan right now. It's an urgent matter. Inform him immediately that I've come to meet him.'

The attendant went inside and returned immediately to lead him to Asad Khan's room. When Sheikh Dawan entered, Asad Khan was waiting for him. After the preliminary exchange of greetings, Sheikh Dawan talked about his love for Kafia and how Tansen was becoming an obstacle in his way.

Asad Khan had been nurturing a secret animosity with Kafia's father Jalal Khan Kurchi. Akbar, instead of promoting Asad Khan, had trusted Kurchi more and elevated him. Asad Khan's heart burnt with jealousy against Kurchi. He had been secretly thinking of a conspiracy and was seeking opportunities to humiliate him. And now he found his long-awaited chance.

Sheikh Dawan convinced Asad Khan about the relationship between Tansen and Kafia. Asad Khan advised Sheikh Dawan to keep that matter a closely guarded secret. He said, 'Zeenat has been in service in Tansen's palace. Her father was my friend and he belonged to my regiment and fought with my soldiers.' Then he said after a pause, 'Do one thing. Somehow arrange for me to secretly meet Zeenat. All the rest will be looked after by Zeenat and me. But take care that the matter does not leak out. Otherwise, it would be hell for Zeenat and you.'

Sheikh Dawan assured Asad Khan, 'Very well. I shall take sufficient care to keep it a secret. I shall arrange a meeting between you and Zeenat one of these days.' Then Sheikh Dawan courteously took his leave and went home, feeling happy. He too started thinking of a number of plans against Tansen. . .

Zeenat and Kafia had been close friends right from childhood. They had played together and studied in the same place. Zeenat also was extremely fond of music. She had learnt music from her own father. She sang sweetly like a *koel*. But she sang only in her own house never outside so far.

Kafia went to Zeenat early one morning. Zeenat had just got up and was alone at home with her mother. She was not happy to find Kafia at her doorstep so early. But she did not openly express her resentment. Both of them sat down and started talking. Meanwhile, Zeenat's mother threw some grain for the hens. Her younger brother was standing on the terrace of the house and was shooing away the crows.

Kafia slowly came to the point. In a pleading voice she said,

'Zeenat you haven't yet arranged my meeting with Tansen. I want to see him immediately. I have to discuss something very urgent with him.'

'Really? Tell me, what's the matter.'

Kafia said, 'I've got information that some people in the *darbar* want to humiliate Tansen.'

'In what way?' Zeenat was curious.

'It is being rumoured all around that Tansen doesn't sing correctly and that he composes *ragas* and *raginis* at will and is thereby killing the very spirit of music. There are wild rumours that attempts are being made to drive him out of the *darbar*.'

To assuage Kafia's fear Zeenat said, 'Don't worry, Kafia. Tansen is a very great musician. Believe me, if somebody tries to spit on the moon, the spit falls back on his own face.'

'Nonetheless, please do arrange my meeting with him,' Kafia urged Zeenat.

'I really don't know how to do it. At the crack of dawn, he goes to the Emperor's harem and sings the morning *ragas*. Our *Shahenshah* wakes up only after hearing them. He remains with the *Shahenshah* the whole day, and returns very late in the night. Sometimes, he sleeps in the royal palace itself. Anyway, I shall still try.' Kafia thanked Zeenat and went back home.

All along the way Kafia kept thinking that there was some change in Zeenat's attitude. She seemed to have become quite cold towards her. Lately, she had not been talking to her with her usual liveliness. Could she not arrange her meeting with Tansen, if she really wanted? But actually she did not want her to meet Tansen. Then she thought that Zeenat was probably right that Tansen spent all his time in the service of *Shahenshah* Akbar. Kafia told herself, she would find some opportunity to meet Tansen.

Asad Khan and Sheikh Dawan on the other hand were quietly hatching all sorts of conspiracies. One dark night, the Agra city was bright with the light of torches burning all around. The royal palace was also illuminated. The *Shahenshah* had arranged a *mushaira* in the *Diwan-e-Khas* for which poets had come from far off. Lighted lamps were placed in front of the poets.

When a lamp was placed before Tansen, he recited his own composition in praise of the beautiful Dark Lord. At the end of his recitation, the *Diwan-e-Khas* reverberated with exclamations of praise. Finally, the lamp was placed before the poet Gang. *Shahenshah* Akbar, who had grown up amidst political authority, war and clanging of swords, was extremely happy to hear Gang's poetry which praised the *Shahenshah* to the skies.

After the *mushaira* ended, all the nobles and other courtiers went off in their vehicles, while Asad Khan and Sheikh Dawan walked briskly through the deserted roads to Zeenat's house. Listening to their hurried steps, the street dogs barked occasionally. They reached Zeenat's house walking with extreme care and caution. Inside, Zeenat was seated on her sick mother's bed, pressing her arms. The gong struck twelve outside the Fort, it was midnight already!

Asad Khan knocked at the door of Zeenat's house. Zeenat got up and taking the lantern opened the door. She was amazed to find Asad Khan and Sheikh Dawan standing there. She asked them what had brought them to her house at the dead of night. Taking a deep breath, Asad Khan mumbled, 'Zeenat, we have something very urgent to discuss with you. We are not forbidden to enter your house, are we?'

'Not at all. Do come in.' She lit the lamp in a small room and made Asad Khan and Sheikh Dawan sit there. She returned after keeping the lantern in her mother's room. After talking at random for a while, Asad Khan asked Zeenat about her position in Tansen's palace. Having got the required information, he came to the main point. He said, 'Tell me one thing, Zeenat. . .'

'What do you want to know? Please go ahead.'

'Tell me, is it proper to keep a lover separated from his beloved?'

'Not at all!' Zeenat promptly responded.

'Then, should the lover suffer in vain? What should one do if the beloved gives up one lover and starts loving someone else?'

'Clearly, she should be diverted from the intruding lover.'

'You are talking absolute sense. We expected such a reply from a sensible girl like you. Now, just look at Sheikh Dawan. He has lost his colour in just a couple of days. He is Kafia's earlier lover. But Kafia has given her heart to Tansen!'

Zeenat gazed quizzically at Asad Khan, wondering what she was expected to do about it. She asked, 'Well, well. What can I do in this matter?'

Asad Khan quickly said, 'You'll have to see that Tansen is. . .'

Zeenat was startled out of her wits. Sensing her hesitation, Asad Khan said, 'You will get anything you wish. Sheikh Dawan would weigh you against gold and jewels. I too, well give you a lot. Have this emerald necklace right now.' And he took off the necklace he was wearing round his neck.

Unaware of the court intrigues, Zeenat sat thinking for a while, whether she should undertake such a venture. Finally, she accepted the proposal. Asad Khan and Sheikh Dawan left Zeenat's house very happy at heart and went to their own homes.

After they left, Zeenat came back to her mother, who asked, 'Child, who had come to our house so late in the night?'

'Asad Khan and Sheikh Dawan.'

'Who are they?' asked Zeenat's mother, for those names did not sound familiar to her.

'Sheikh Dawan is the court singer and Asad Khan, his friend, is a general in the Emperor's army.'

'But what was so important that they had to come here at such an unearthly hour?'

'*Ammi*, you know very well, that there are some things in the affairs of the state that are very complicated. Men are driven to all sorts of things for the sake of their personal gain. They always crave for things which they can have and also for what they cannot have.'

'May be. What do I understand of state matters? Anyway, it's long past midnight. You're tired after a hard day's work.

Better go to sleep. You'll leave early in the morning for your work!'

'Yes, *Ammi*,' Zeenat said and got up. She put out the lantern, but could not sleep for a long time. Lying in her bed, she kept thinking about what Asad Khan had said. A storm was beginning to rage in her heart.

# 20

Akbar was lying on his silken mattress. He enjoyed Tansen's music for some time every morning while still in bed. After that, he went about his daily morning routine. At about eight o'clock Tansen left in the palanquin for his palace. The palanquin had holes on the sides, through which Tansen could see the road. As he proceeded towards his palace, Tansen saw a woman flitting past, into the bye-lanes. She appeared to be like Tani. Immediately, he asked the palanquin-bearers to stop and getting off the palanquin, he went in the direction where the woman had gone. But by then, she had disappeared into one of the narrow lanes. Tansen, was disappointed and returned to his palanquin.

Tansen had to present himself in the *darbar* soon afterwards. The Emperor was to make a special announcement in the *darbar* that day. When the *darbar* was full, the Emperor himself arrived. There was complete silence. All the courtiers and the commoners were waiting impatiently!

At last, Fhaizi got up and offered his salutations to Akbar and then addressed all those present, '*Shahenshah* Jalaluddin Akbar is about to make an important announcement!' Everyone in the *darbar* stood up.

The very next moment, Emperor Akbar declared, 'Honourable members, I am extremely happy to have the great musician Tansen in my *darbar*. Only once in centuries, can you expect to have a singer like him. I hereby announce that I am including Tansen among the "jewels" of my *darbar*.' The entire *Diwan-e-Aam* reverberated with cries of victory for Akbar and Tansen. Soon after, came the announcement that Tansen would sing in the *darbar* on that happy occasion.

The *tanpura* and other instruments were tuned and Tansen sang the *dhrupad* in a deep and serious voice.

*Charhau chiranjiva Shah Akbär Shahenshah*

When Tansen finished singing, the whole *darbar* broke into loud applause. But, some people in a corner started shouting, 'Tansen is the enemy of music.'

This was followed by another outburst of angry words, 'His singing is faulty. He has ruined our musical tradition.'

Then another cry was heard, 'He must be dismissed from the *darbar*. Otherwise, it would be the end of music.'

When Akbar heard those protesting voices, he frowned. He looked around angrily. Finally, when the uproar subsided, he announced in a resolute voice, 'From today, Tansen will be the chief court musician. All other singers will be under him and will have to follow his instructions.'

Stunned silence reigned in the *darbar* following this announcement. Sheikh Dawan and Asad Khan were miserable. They bit their lip and like beaten serpents were ready to strike at Tansen.

That day, the Emperor showered Tansen with money and accorded him royal honour. Tansen's heart burst with joy and happiness. As he reached home, Zeenat appeared before him and said, 'Congratulations, Master! *Begum Sahiba* has given birth to a girl!'

Tansen was very happy to hear that news. He said, '*Allah* be praised, Zeenat. And do you know what name I'll give her. I'll call her Saraswati!' And he hurried towards Hussaini's chamber.

Left to herself, Zeenat thought for a while, 'Asad Khan and Sheikh Dawan are under the wrong impression that Tansen too, is in love with Kafia?' Although she had an impulse to go and inform Tansen about the conspiracy that Asad Khan and Sheikh Dawan were planning, she decided against it. But after a while she thought again, 'Why not test Tansen?' And with the intention of discovering some secret, she approached him.

Tansen was sitting alone in his chamber on a *divan* passing his fingers over the *tanpura*. Zeenat went and sat on the ground near his feet. She sat there, twisting the end of her *dupatta* and said politely, '*Huzoor,* we are all very happy at your success today.'

'Thank you. It's very nice of you,' said Tansen and looked at her inquiringly because it seemed to him that she had something on her mind which she was hesitating to express. 'Do you wish to say something else, Zeenat?'

Zeenat looked at him and said, 'You know, *Huzoor*, that Kafia? . . .'

'Kafia!' Tansen knitted his eyebrows. 'Who is she?'

'The daughter of Sardar Jalal Khan Kurchi, *Huzoor*.'

'Well, what about her?'

'*Huzoor*, do you remember. . .'

'What?'

'You had once met her near the beds of roses in the palace garden.' Tansen tried to remember and said after a pause, 'Yes, I think I met her. But what of it?'

'*Huzoor,* Kafia wishes to have a meeting with you.'

'It's not possible now. But I shall tell you when I'm free. You can call her then.'

'Very well, *Huzoor*,' Zeenat said and quietly left.

As she left Tansen's chamber, she said to herself, 'Kafia is nowhere in Tansen's mind. Asad Khan and Sheikh Dawan are harbouring such a suspicion for no reason at all. I shall tell them when I meet them next.'

Convinced, they were under a very wrong impression, she firmly resolved not to get caught in their snare and got busy with her usual work in the palace. . . .

Abdur Rahim Khan Khana from the *darbar* was a great friend of Tansen. On the happy occasion of his appointment as chief court-singer, Tansen thought that he would visit Abdur Rahim Khan Khana to share his joy with him. He called for his palanquin.

Tansen received a shock as he entered Rahim Khan Khana's palace. Rahim Khan Khana was shouting at somebody at the top of his voice. Tansen wondered what could have happened to enrage his friend so much? He was under the impression that Rahim Khan Khana was a quiet man. He was in two minds, whether or not he should meet his friend at that particular moment. But finally, he decided that having come all the way, he might as well meet him. He instructed one of the attendants. 'Go and inform the master that I have come to meet him.' The attendant hesitated a bit, but ultimately went in with Tansen's message.

The moment Rahim Khan Khana learnt about Tansen's arrival, his anger vanished. He rushed out with a smile to greet Tansen and led him inside. Abdul, an attendant, was standing there, his head bowed. Rahim Khan Khana said to him, 'What do you say? When you went for your marriage, I had hammered it into your head that you should return within two days of the wedding, because I can't carry on without you. And you've come back today exactly after a fortnight. As punishment, I am ordering your dismissal!'

Tears streamed from Abdul's eyes. He folded his hands and said piteously '*Huzoor*, I was actually coming after two days, but my wife didn't let me leave. When I told her that you would be angry if I did not return in time, she wrote something on a piece of paper which she wanted me to show you.'

'Where's that paper?' Rahim Khan Khana asked sternly.

Abdul brought out a folded paper which he had tucked under his turban and handed it over to Rahim Khan Khana. It said:

You are going after showering love on Barbe
Let it not dry up, remember to continue the shower.

Rahim Khan Khana's face softened and a smile flickered on his lips. He asked Abdul, 'What's your wife' name?'

'She is called Barbe, *Huzoor*.'

'I see! I am very pleased by her couplet, Abdul. Wonderful! I forgive you and announce that from today, this style of poetry will be known by Barbe's name.'

Being a poet himself, Rahim Khan Khana was delighted to read those lines composed by Barbe. When Tansen read that composition, he was equally pleased. After Abdul left, the two friends settled down to chat. Rahim Khan Khana congratulated Tansen on his inclusion among the 'nine jewels' of Akbar's *darbar*. Tansen very graciously accepted the compliments but said, '*Janab*, the credit of this honour goes only to Swami Haridas. I want to seek the *Shahenshah's* permission to go and meet him at Vrindavan.'

Rahim Khan Khana readily endorsed Tansen's idea. He said, 'That would be wonderful. I too have to visit Mathura on an official mission. We can go together. I can go with you to Vrindavan after completing my job at Mathura. I would be delighted to have a *darshan* of Swami Haridas.'

Tansen was happy at the thought of undertaking a journey to Vrindavan with his dear friend. They talked for some time and then Tansen returned to his palace. . .

Emperor Akbar was seated on his throne, a grim expression on his face. The news from Mewar and Gujarat was causing anxiety. Akbar had sent an invitation to Maharana Uday Singh of Mewar to meet him in his *darbar*. But Uday Singh had not honoured the invitation. Akbar was upset by Uday Singh's audacity. The furrows on his forehead revealed the agitated state of his mind. Abul Fazl, Raja Man Singh and Fhaizi were telling the Emperor about the situation in Gujarat and Mewar. In Gujarat, Muzaffar Shah was refusing to pay the *chauth* levied by the Emperor. It seemed that the situation was getting out of hand. He was seriously thinking about the steps to be taken to deal with Mewar and Gujarat. Just then, Tansen and Rahim Khan Khana made their appearance in the *darbar*. They offered their respectful salutations and took their seats.

The moment Akbar noticed Tansen, his face relaxed and he asked, 'Well, Tansen? Are you fine?'

Tansen replied respectfully, 'By your grace I am very well, *Huzoor*.'

Akbar smiled, 'Have you composed any new *ragini*?'

'I am trying, your Honour! The moment I am ready with it, I shall present it to you.'

Akbar responded with a smile of satisfaction. Tansen thought that it was a good opportunity to ask a favour from him. He urged, '*Shahenshah-e-Alam*, I seek your permission to. . .'

'What permission, Tansen? Say it quickly. Don't keep me in suspense.'

'*Huzoor*, with your permission, I wish to go to Vrindavan to meet my guru Swami Haridas at whose feet I have learnt music.'

Akbar paused, 'Well, Tansen, do go to Vrindavan and meet your guru. But I shall expect you to be back soon.'

'I will be back as soon as possible, *Huzoor*.'

Rahim Khan Khana also seized the opportunity and said, '*Jahan-e-Alam*, I too have to go to Mathura on a political mission. If you permit me, I would also like to accompany Tansen.'

Akbar immediately agreed, 'Very well. Both of you may go together. But don't be away too long. Come back to Agra as soon as possible.'

Tansen and Rahim Khan Khana expressed their gratitude. Then they went home and packed a few necessities, mounted their Persian horses and left for Mathura. . . .

'Rahim Khan Khana and Tansen went to the bank of the Yamuna and after giving their horses water, visited various places in Vrindavan. As they dismounted, a crowd noticed them and identifying them as men from Akbar's *darbar*, followed them. On the way, they found the temple doors were open. Even from a distance they could have the *darshan* of Radha-Krishan. Rahim Khan Khana was so fascinated and joyful that he composed a couplet on the spot, praising the intoxicating beauty of Radha's lotus eyes and her unforgettable smile.

Tansen was already an admirer of Rahim Khan Khana's poetry. But after listening to his couplet that day, he became even more devoted to him.

A little later, Rahim Khan Khana told Tansen, 'As you know, *Shahenshah* Akbar has banned the killing of peacocks. I must find out from the officials in charge, if the orders are being properly carried out.'

And after taking Tansen's leave, he went on his mission. Tansen immediately set off for Nidhivan.

When Tansen arrived, Surdas, the blind saint-poet, had come from Parasauli and was singing his *padas* to the accompaniment of an *ektara*. He was singing with such devotion and from the depth of his heart that Tansen was overwhelmed. He silently bowed to Swami Haridas and sat on the sands, listening to Surdas' singing. He noticed tears flowing from Swami Haridas' eyes.

After Surdas finished, Tansen touched his feet and said, 'It was such a beautiful *pada*; I shall definitely sing this *pada* to *Shahenshah* Akbar.'

When Surdas learnt that it was Tansen who was admiring his singing, he said, 'Oh, Tansen, I have heard praises of your music.'

Tansen was touched by what Surdas said, 'It's all because of this great guru of mine, Swami Haridas!'

Surdas added, 'True. However, remember one thing son. When something is dedicated to God, it acquires a different kind of charm altogether. You continue to sing and dedicate your music to God. Then you'll see that your music will assume the fragrance of sandal.'

Tansen humbly joined his hands in gratitude. Then, he spent some time with Swami Haridas, acquainting him with what he had been doing. He gave him all the credit for the success that had come his way. Taking his leave, he returned to Agra with Rahim Khan Khana.

Facing the day-long hot winds, Tansen and Rahim Khan Khana at last arrived at Agra. Rahim Khan Khana could not help contrasting the serene atmosphere of Vrindavan with the hustle-bustle of the Agra city. He said, 'Tansen, living in Vrindavan was like being in heaven. Blessed are those fakirs and saints who live there in peace. We are slaves of our physical needs. We like comforts and enjoy power and wealth, but instead of happiness, we find only misery. I shall go back to Vrindavan some day.'

Tansen nodded his head smiling and they raced their horses homewards. As Tansen reached his palace, he noticed Sheikh Dawan and Asad Khan talking to Razia, one of the maids in his service. Tansen was startled at first, but then ignoring them, entered the palace. When he went in, he found Hussaini singing a lullaby to put Saraswati to sleep. Tansen sat beside her and joined her singing. Soon, Saraswati was fast asleep in the cradle. The night had already set in. After a hurried meal and a little chat, Tansen retired to his bed-chamber and was soon fast asleep. Hussaini sat on the edge of the bed gazing admiringly at Tansen, and wondered what he would be dreaming!

The next morning, Tansen had hardly woken up, when one of the Emperor's messengers arrived. He told Hussaini that the Emperor had invited some friends at *Diwan-e-Khas* to hear Tansen's music and he should come there in time. Hussaini went to Tansen who had just started stirring and informed him about the Emperor's message. He jumped up instantly and got ready in no time. He kissed little Saraswati and bidding Hussaini good-bye sat in the palanquin which took him to the *Diwan-e-Khas*.

The *Diwan-e-Khas* had been specially decorated and wore a festive look. The mild fragrance of *kevra* emanated from everywhere. The exotic colours of Persian carpets hit the eye. All the invitees had arrived from far off places, rulers and kings, were seated near the Emperor's throne. Soon, the *Diwan-e-Khas* reverberated with cries of victory to the Emperor. Every one stood up as Emperor Akbar entered, wearing a dazzling outfit and laden with jewels. They all bowed low to offer salutations, and then took their seats. Tansen sat in front of the Emperor on an ivory seat. The strings of the gem-studded *tanpura* rang out, followed by the palm-strokes on *mridanga* which sounded like the rumbling of the waves. Tansen began with an *alap* and then sang a *pada* by Surdas:

Jasoda cries again and again<br>
Is there someone in *Vraj* to stop Gopal from going?

As Tansen finished singing the *pada*, the *Diwan-e-Khas* was filled with thumping applause, '*Wah! Wah!* Wonderful!' But the clever Akbar asked Fhaizi, 'What is the meaning of the words, "again and again" in this *pada*?'

Fhaizi thought for a moment, and said 'Jasoda was weeping again and again and saying, "Is there someone in *Vraj* who would stop my Gopal from going?"'

Then Akbar asked Tansen to explain the meaning. Tansen said, 'Jasoda cries repeatedly. . .'

Then Akbar turned to Birbal, who said, 'Jasoda goes from door to door and says. . .'

Khan-e-Azam said, 'Here it means day after day. . .'

After listening to everyone Akbar asked Rahim Khan Khana, 'What do you have to say, *Mian*?'

Rahim Khan Khana replied, '*Shahenshah-e-Alam*, it is like this. Tansen has to repeat the same *pada*. Sheikh Fhaizi is a Persian poet and he can think of nothing except tears. Birbal is a Brahmin used to knocking at every door and hence according to him "again and again" means "from door to door". Whereas Khan-e-Azam is an astrologer and for him "again and again" can only means "day after day". But *Huzoor*, according to me, the words "again and again" mean that from every pore of her body Jasoda cried, "Is there someone in *Vraj* who would stop my Gopal from going?"'

Akbar was so pleased with Rahim Khan Khana's interpretation that he took out a precious pearl necklace and put it around his neck. Everyone applauded Rahim Khan Khana. Tansen too, rose from his seat and hugged him, and showered praises on him. . .

While Tansen was inundated with praise and words of admiration, unknown to him, Kafia, beautiful like a dream, sat sighing in her room. Her natural charm was further enhanced by the lovely jewellery she wore and the precious necklace dangling over her full bosom. Ever since she heard Tansen singing the other day, she had completely given her heart to him. She wished she could listen to Tansen's music for several hours and wanted to go on talking to him and to express her love. She wondered if there was any woman who would not fall in love with Tansen. He was so handsome and young. She had been learning to play *rudra veena* from Sheikh Dawan, but had never felt any love for him. The expression in Sheikh Dawan's eyes had often given her the idea that he was probably in love with her. But that did not arouse a response in her heart. Moreover, Sheikh Dawan had also never expressed his love in words.

Kafia was so possessed with her love for Tansen that she was very restless because she had not been able to meet him, except for that brief encounter near the flower-beds in his garden. Kafia's mother noticed that she was disturbed about something. One day, she asked her, 'Dear child, I see that you have not been your usual self for some time. Something is weighing on your mind. Tell me, my girl, what has happened?'

'What do you think could have happened, *Ammijaan*? It has been long since *Abba* left for Mewar. I become sad when I think about him, that's all!'

Kafia somehow convinced her mother that there was nothing particularly wrong with her, but she could not pacify herself. She thought, 'Why, am I so much in love with Tansen after all? Why should I love someone who can never become mine?' But the next moment she said to herself, 'Yet, what can I do? The more I try to forget Tansen, the deeper he goes into my heart. *Yah, Allah!* Tansen is so handsome! Will I ever be able to have him for myself? Perhaps not. But, if it comes to that, does the moth ever have the flame for itself? Yet, it burns itself away in the fire. Love is indeed such a fire raging in the heart. I shall burn away for Tansen. I shall become a flame and burn till the last moment.' And then Kafia began thinking of all the impossible situations which were most unlikely to ever materialize.

Kafia was aware how difficult it was to get anywhere near Tansen. Yet, she was possessed with a mad desire to meet him. She was looking for the slightest pretext that could take her to him, but no opportunity came her way. Finally, one day, when she just could not contain herself. She put on her best dress and jewellery and set out, telling her mother that she was going to meet a friend of hers. But as she stepped out of the house, she ran into Sheikh Dawan who had come to give her the ***rudra veena*** lesson. Much against her wishes, Kafia returned to the house and her desire to meet Tansen remained buried in her heart that day.

# 21

Sheikh Dawan had come after a long time to teach Kafia. His mind was preoccupied by so many conspiracies, but outwardly he appeared very calm. Kafia brought her *rudra veena* and continued her *riaz* for some time. But she soon discovered that today Sheikh Dawan had not come to help her in her *riaz* but to talk to her. Kafia then stopped practising.

She looked very charming in her onion-coloured dress over which she was wore a silken *dupatta* with golden embroidery. Colloryium enhanced the beauty of her eyes. Youth was bursting through her full blown body. She looked stunningly beautiful today. Sheikh Dawan admired her from a distance. Fixing his gaze on her for a while, he said, 'How are things with you, Kafia?'

'Fine,' Kafia gave a monosyllabic reply and bent her head.

After a pause Sheikh Dawan asked again, 'Tell me, Kafia, did you get another chance to listen to Tansen? Did you meet him?'

Kafia lifted her eyes to Sheikh Dawan and said gently, 'Yes, I saw him yesterday at *Diwan-e-Khas* from a distance and also heard him sing. Oh, his singing goes so deep in one's heart. It's really breathtaking!'

With a quizzical look in his eyes Sheikh Dawan asked, 'Well, did you meet him? Did you have a chance to talk to him?'

'Oh, no! I was very eager to seize a moment and talk to him. But I didn't get a chance at the *Diwan-e-Khas* yesterday. I know how difficult it is to get near him. He is now among the 'nine jewels' in the Emperor's *darbar* and is not easily accessible. But one day I'll surely go to his palace and meet him!'

'Yes?' Sheikh Dawan sounded amused. 'What will you say to him?'

'Anything that comes to my mind!'

That gave Sheikh Dawan a chance to come to the point. He asked point-blank, 'Tell me, Kafia, are you in love with Tansen?'

Colour rushed to Kafia's cheeks.

'You are free to think anything. Tansen is a great artist and who wouldn't love his art? Are you not impressed by Tansen's music?' Kafia asked looking at him enquiringly.

'It's not that, Kafia,' Sheikh Dawan tried to explain his stand. 'But he has harmed our music a great deal. He has ruined our traditional *ragas* and *raginis*. But surprisingly, people rave about his music!'

Kafia contradicted him, 'As for me, I would like to listen to his music all the time. And then, he is so handsome. *Allah* has granted him the gift of art and also a lovely frame!'

Now, Sheikh Dawan was convinced that Kafia was in love with Tansen. It was clear that he himself had no place in her heart. His male pride was deeply hurt. He hissed like an injured cobra, 'If two moths hover over one flame, what should the flame do?'

Kafia was a clever girl. She could see that there was anger in his eye. She pretended to smile and said, 'The flame can do nothing about it. It is for the moths to decide. The flame must burn.'

Apparently changing his tone, Sheikh Dawan said, 'Kafia, you know very well that I love you more than I love myself. Do you accept my love or don't you? I want your honest answer today.'

Kafia gave Sheikh Dawan a puzzled look. It had never occurred to her that her *Ustad* had been in love with her. She could not imagine this. Sheikh Dawan stared intently at her, awaiting her reply. Kafia did not reply immediately. When Sheikh Dawan persisted, she became grave and finally said, 'A woman's heart is always pure and clean. I had never imagined that you would ever talk to me like this. If I mention this to my *Abba*, he will have you skinned in public. Love is meant for those who, on their own merit, carve a niche in someone's heart. I respect you because you're my music teacher. I haven't ever been in love with you nor can I ever be.' Then, after a brief pause she said, 'Now you may leave and there is no need to come to our house ever again. Whatever I want to learn in future, I shall learn from Tansen!'

Sheikh Dawan felt hurt and humiliated and anger raged in his heart like a fire. He sprang to his feet and made a dash to Asad Khan's house.

Asad Khan was about to go out when Sheikh Dawan got there. Asad Khan greeted him. Sheikh Dawan began the conversation, 'Asad *Mian*, do something for me, otherwise I shall have to commit suicide right before your eyes.'

Asad Khan sensed his desperation and asked him to calm down, 'Oh, come on. Don't talk like that. Tell me what has happened to drive you to this extreme point?'

'What else? Today I asked Kafia point-blank if she loved me.'

'Well! What was her answer?'

'*Mian*, far from loving me, Kafia actually holds me in utter contempt. She has given her heart to Tansen. She insulted me and drove me out of her house!'

Having conveyed his anguish to Asad Khan, Sheikh Dawan sat staring at the ground in despair. But Asad Khan was a very clever man who knew how to play his game. He said, 'Razia. . . yes, whatever has happened to Razia? She is the only one who can help us in a moment like this. Let us go to her place immediately.' They both hurried off to her house. . .

Razia was a middle-aged, needy woman. Her husband was a drunkard and was averse to working. She had a son who was mad about flying kites all day long. There was no means of livelihood. Only Razia, earned a little money by working in Tansen's palace. When they reached her house she was getting ready to go there. She made Asad Khan and Sheikh Dawan sit on a broken charpoy. Then she got the hukkah ready and placing it before them, sat at their feet on the floor. After a while, she asked, 'You've honoured me by visiting my humble place. What can I do for you?'

Sheikh Dawan held a little money-bag before her and said, 'Razia, here are some gold *mohars* for your expenses.'

Razia was always in need of money, but did not grab it. She was an honest woman who accepted money only as a reward for some work. Never before had she been offered money in this manner. She was flabbergasted by Sheikh Dawan's unexpected gesture, and asked, 'Why are you giving me this money, *Huzoor?*'

Keep it, Razia,' Sheikh Dawan persisted. 'Of course, money is not God, but it isn't less than God either. Keep it. It will be useful to you.'

Seeing Razia's hesitation, Sheikh Dawan said, 'Listen Razia, we will make you wealthy. For that you must do one thing. Will you do it?'

Razia was all the more puzzled. 'What do you want me to do?' she asked.

'Tansen must be killed. . . .'

Razia looked at the two men wide-eyed. Were they in their senses? 'Kill Tansen—for what?' she said. 'No *Huzoor*, I can't do such a thing.'

Asad Khan insisted, 'What do you mean? You can certainly do it. We will make you fabulously rich. Come closer and listen to what I'm telling you to do.' Asad Khan whispered something in Razia's ear and then he said aloud, 'If you ever reveal this secret to any one, you and your son will be killed with this sword. Do you hear?'

Razia was so terrified that she almost trembled and said, 'Well, I shall do it.'

'Now, that's a sensible woman. May *Allah* be with you!' said Asad Khan and then they both left for their homes, imagining the success of their conspiracy. . . .

That day, Akbar's *darbar* bore an extraordinary glitter. All the 'nine jewels' were present. Akbar first glanced at Fhaizi and then he turned to Todarmal, 'Raja Todarmal, is there any critical political question to be discussed?'

Todarmal offered his salutations and said, 'There is no urgent matter to be discussed, *Shahenshah*. Of course, the news from

Mewar and Gujarat is not very good. But there is nothing much to worry about. The Mughal armies will humble their pride in no time. We will give them such hell that both will be swept away in the torrent of blood.'

Akbar's forehead wrinkled deeper. His face reddened and his moustaches quivered. There was silence in the *darbar* for a while. Then suddenly as Akbar's eyes turned to Tansen, his face softened. He asked, 'How are things with you, *Mian* Tansen?'

Tansen replied respectfully, 'All is well by your grace, *Huzoor.*'

Akbar smiled with gratification, and he looked relaxed. He said, 'I sincerely wish to invite your *Ustad*, Swami Haridas to my *darbar* and meet him.' Then turning to Abu'l Fazl he added, 'Call him to Agra.'

On hearing that Raja Birbal submitted, '*Shahenshah-e-Hindustan*, let me remind you very humbly that he is a fakir and has nothing to do with the world. Instead of calling Swami Haridas to Agra, it would be better that you go to Vrindavan yourself!'

'Why do you say that?' Akbar was surprised at Birbal's suggestion. 'I am inviting Swami Haridas to Agra with great honour.'

Birbal said, 'Forgive my impatience, but may I say something?'

'Of course, Raja Birbal, do say it,' Akbar said eagerly.

'*Huzoor*, do you remember once you forcibly called saint Chhit Swami to sing in the *darbar*?'

'Yes, I do remember it.'

'He was not at all willing to come to Agra and when he came he sang, "What do we saints have to do with Sikri?"'

Akbar was not offended by what Birbal said. He said, 'You're right, Raja Birbal. Those people are devoted to God. They're concerned only with God. I won't trouble Swami Haridas to come all the way. Instead, I will myself go to Vrindavan to see him.'

Loud applause greeted Akbar's decision. Everybody was impressed by the Emperor's humanity.

The sun had almost touched the western horizon when the

*darbar* got over. The twilight's redness filled the sky. Looking at the bright red glow, someone observed, 'When the sky turns so red, you can be sure there would be bloodshed!'

It was still semi-dark. Flocks of parrots were returning to their perches on the trees. The kites that soared high into the sky were slowly descending to the earth and the evening lamps were lit.

Tansen returned to his palace. The moment he entered his chamber, Zeenat brought him rose *sherbat* in a crystal tumbler. Soon after, Razia entered with a rolled up *paan* with silver *varag*, on a beautiful plate. Zeenat stood there and closely observed the curious expression on Razia's face. She seemed to be terror-stricken. Her hands were trembling and her face looked pale. For the first time Zeenat suspected Razia of having some evil design. As Tansen extended his hand to take the *paan* from the plate, Zeenat said aloud, '*Huzoor*, please don't eat that *paan*. I have a suspicion.'

Tansen withdrew his hand at once. Zeenat picked up the *paan* and went out. She dropped the *paan* before a dog which jumped at it and licked it. Immediately, the dog started wriggling and making queer sounds. It tossed about violently for sometime and then lay still. Zeenat immediately informed the officers concerned. The soldiers arrived to arrest Razia.

There was stunned silence in Tansen's palace. The news spread in the city like wildfire. Everyone wondered who could be hatching such a conspiracy in Tansen's palace. . .

A few days later, Tansen set out for Vrindavan along with Emperor Akbar. No one else accompanied them. Akbar was greatly excited at the prospect of meeting a great musician and a saint in person. But Tansen was in a dilemma, because Swami Haridas had completely stopped singing for quite some time. During the journey Tansen said hesitantly, '*Shahenshah-e-Hindustan*, I wish to submit something to you.'

'What is it?' Akbar was surprised.

'Actually, Swami Haridas does not sing any more. He stopped quite some time ago.'

'How is that possible? I will surely hear him sing. I cannot go back without listening to your guru.'

Tansen was puzzled. He knew there was no way Akbar could be made to change his mind. After a little thought he said, 'In that case, *Huzoor*, I have a suggestion.'

'What suggestion?'

'Pretend that you are a *sarangi* player. You should not be recognized as *Shahenshah-e-Hindustan*.'

Akbar wondered at Tansen's suggestion, but he was so eager to listen to Swami Haridas that he was ready to do anything. He said, 'Very well, I shall do as you say.' And Akbar put on the dress of a *sarangi* player and Tansen and he went to Nidhivan.

Akbar sat hiding in a bower while Tansen went to Swami Haridas, hut and found him seated in meditation. Tansen stood outside the hut waiting. Akbar was overawed by the beauty of the place. The rippling sound of the Yamuna river flowing nearby, the unrestrained flights of the birds and their sweet chirping, and above all, the serene atmosphere.

Overwhelmed, he started thinking, 'This place is so quiet! It brings one peace, whereas, there is unrest in my mind although as *Shahenshah-e-Hindustan*, I have everything. But all this glitter of jewels is meaningless. I conquer the world on the strength of my sword. In the bargain there is bloodshed, screams and death. That is the world of politics in which there is wealth and prosperity but behind which are the explosions of ammunition!' The serenity of Nidhivan had turned Akbar into a philosopher, who forgot for a moment that he was an Emperor who possessed the greatest power and at whose feet lay boundless wealth.

At last Swami Haridas arose from his meditation and noticed Tansen standing outside the hut. He came out and greeted Tansen, 'You have come, Tansen! Tell me, how are you? How has your music progressed?'

Tansen fell at the feet of Swami Haridas, who promptly raised him and embraced him. Tansen said, 'Swamiji, I am doing well, by your grace. I have come today to seek your blessings.' Then he paused for a moment and added 'I have a great desire to listen to your singing which is like nectar to me.'

Swami Haridas shook his head, 'No Tansen, I cannot fulfil your wish. You know I do not sing any more.'

Tansen was crestfallen. He went to Akbar who was waiting in the bower and apologized, '*Huzoor*, he won't sing! He cannot be forced to sing.'

But Akbar was adamant!, 'Say what you wish, but I won't go back unless I listen to his music!'

Tansen did not know what to do. He was caught between two adamant individuals. He felt disturbed and nervous. He thought for a long time and then an idea struck him. He went back to the hut of Swami Haridas. Sitting outside, he began singing a *raga* in a clumsy manner, deliberately going out of tune. Swami Haridas who was inside was greatly disturbed. He came out and reprimanded Tansen, 'Tanna, I have taught you this *raga* for so many years—and still you sing it so badly! All my labour is wasted! Give me that *tanpura*!'

Swami Haridas tuned the *tanpura* and began to sing and soon the melody of that music permeated the whole atmosphere. Everything stood still. The animals did not move and the birds did not chirp. And then, Akbar emerged from the bower where he had been secretly listening to the singing of Swami Haridas. He said, '*Allah* be praised! You sing so beautifully! It brings peace to one's soul!'

Swami Haridas was surprised, because he had not suspected the presence of anyone else in Nidhivan. He asked, 'Who are you?'

Akbar smiled, 'I am Jalaluddin Akbar, *Shahenshah-e-Hindustan*!'

Swami Haridas said, 'Oh, I see! Accept my greetings, *Samrat*'.

'I am really delighted to have listened to your music. As an expression of my gratitude I wish to present to you this dress and necklace. Kindly accept these gifts and oblige.' Saying that Akbar moved to take off the ornament from his neck.

Swami Haridas said, 'No, I won't take anything without bathing in the Yamuna. You too will have to bathe in the river.'

Akbar promptly agreed, 'Very well, Swamiji! I shall bathe in the Yamuna if you wish.'

The three of them went to the Yamuna *ghats* and bathed in the sacred waters of the river. After the bath, Akbar once again offered the necklace to Swami Haridas. But Swami Haridas forestalled him, 'Oh, *Samrat,* we are ascetics. What can we do with such necklaces? If you really wish to give something, get the stone steps of the Yamuna *ghats* repaired. They are worn out.'

Akbar glanced at the steps of the Yamuna *ghats* and was flabbergasted to find that those steps were not made of stone but of sapphires, inlaid with diamonds and other gems. Akbar fell at the feet of Swami Haridas and said, 'Kindly forgive me, Swamiji! I do not have such a huge stock of sapphires to repair these steps.'

Swami Haridas gave him a benign smile. The great Emperor had bowed before the power of the saint's penance. Akbar, feeling humble in the presence of Swami Haridas was thinking that the power of a saint was far superior to that of an Emperor. He said to himself, 'Everywhere people always extend their hands to beg for things, but here this ascetic declined to accept my gift and showed me thereby that what he possessed was something which the great Emperor of India did not have.' He bowed respectfully to Swami Haridas and said, 'Tansen, it is my great fortune that I could be in the presence of Swami Haridas. I am extremely happy. Let us now go back to Agra.'

They bowed to Swami Haridas again and respectfully bidding him farewell, mounted their horses. They pulled the reins and the horses started racing towards Agra.

As they returned to the world of pomp and glitter, Akbar asked Tansen, 'Tansen, tell me one thing. Why does your singing lack the fervour of Swami Haridas?'

Tansen replied with extreme humility, '*Shahenshah-e-Alam*, that is because Swamiji sings for his God and I sing for you!

*Huzoor*, when something is dedicated to God, it acquires a new character altogether. Saint Surdas had told me that.'

Akbar agreed with Tansen's explanation, 'You're right, Tansen. After all, *Allah* is *Allah* and man is man—no matter how much wealth he may own!'

Those words made Tansen happy and his heart went out to the great Emperor who had understood that fundamental truth about life!

At last, the panting horses reached Agra city and soon Akbar was back in his palace. Cannons were fired to greet him and their smoke rose to the sky. The citizens of Agra raised the cries of '*Allah-o-Akbar*!' which hung in the air for a long time.

# 22

Kafia's father Jalal Khan Kurchi had returned to Agra after his victory in battle against the Hada Rajputs of Bundi. Emperor Akbar, who was extremely happy with Kurchi's performance accorded him an honourable welcome.

To celebrate the occasion, Kurchi had invited the nobles and army officials for a feast. A gorgeous *shamiana* was erected and all kinds of delicious food was laid out for the guests. As the evening hour drew close, his mansion was flooded with the light of innumerable torches. One by one, the guests started arriving. They were welcomed by Kurchi and Kafia.

After some time, Asad Khan arrived, elegantly dressed. He was alone. His attention was drawn towards Kafia. She was wearing a green coloured *garara* and had applied collyrium in her eyes. Big, glittering earrings dangled from her ears, and a pendant swayed on her forehead as she turned her head to look around. Asad Khan gave her a knowing look and then surveyed the hall to see who all were attending the feast. He came up to Kafia who was standing alone and stood silently for a moment and then asked, 'How are you, Kafia?'

'Fine,' Kafia answered briefly.

'You look fine, indeed. Tell me, how is your *riaz* going?'

'How do you know that I am learning music?'

'Sheikh Dawan was telling me.'

'What? He told you that, did he?'

'Yes. He said he is teaching you how to play the *rudra veena*. It would be my pleasure to see your musical talent some day.'

'Oh, don't talk about it. I haven't learnt it properly yet.'

'What do you mean? Doesn't Sheikh Dawan teach you well?'

'It's not that. I myself forbade him from visiting our house.'

Asad Khan said with apparent disbelief, 'What are you saying? Why did you have to stop him from coming?'

'Nothing particular. I didn't wish to learn from him—that's all. If at all, I will resume my training only under *Mian* Tansen.'

'You are absolutely right. What could be better than training under Tansen? I can recommend you to Tansen if you wish.'

Kafia said somewhat brusquely, 'No, there's no need. I know him well. I shall talk to him myself!'

But Asad Khan would not give up easily. He said, 'Forget Tansen for the moment. Tell me, how do you like me? You see, I'm young and I'm in a high position. I love you from the bottom of my heart. If you're willing, I can send a proposal for our marriage to your father tomorrow!' And Asad Khan searched Kafia's face, trying to read her reaction.

Kafia said, 'I'm not interested in marriage at the moment.'

'But I'm interested,' Asad Khan said, taking a deep breath.

Kafia said with an enigmatic smile, 'Then go ahead! And don't forget to invite me for the feast!'

Asad Khan was upset that Kafia had taken him so lightly. He said, 'I'm not joking Kafia. Tell me frankly, how do you like me?'

'You appear to be a good person. You're handsome and are in a high position. What more?'

While they were having this conversation, Kafia's mother arrived. She said, 'Kafia, come along. *Mian* Tansen would be coming any minute. Be ready to receive him.'

Kafia bloomed like a flower at the very mention of Tansen and seeing her delight, Asad Khan got very frustrated. . .

Soon Tansen arrived. Hussaini could not accompany him as she had just delivered a baby. But Zeenat and a few other attendants did come with him. Kafia bowed to Tansen and greeted him and gave him a seat among the special invitees. She herself sat next to him and asked, 'How are you?'

'I'm fine,' Tansen replied simply.

'I swear by *Allah's* name, you don't just sing, but enter the hearts of people. It's a breathtaking experience.'

'I'm honoured!' Tansen again replied briefly and fell silent.

Kafia said, 'I want to meet you very much. With your permission, may I visit you at your palace some day?'

'Yes, why not?' said Tansen and glanced at Zeenat.

Zeenat realised what Tansen meant. She said to Kafia, 'I shall let you know when you can come.'

The feast went on till late in the night and finally the guests returned to their homes. . .

While other guests went by their palanquins or horses, Asad Khan preferred walking. All along the way, he kept thinking about Kafia: 'She definitely likes me. That's why she had said, "You're young, you're handsome and enjoy a high position. And you're a good man." It only means that Kafia loves me from the bottom of her heart. She is a woman and modesty is a woman's adornment. How could the poor girl openly acknowledge her love for me? Had she not loved me, she would have given some other reply.'

With such thoughts revolving in his mind, Asad Khan reached home. Soon after Sheikh Dawan arrived. At the very sight of him, Asad Khan said to himself, 'I shall also get rid of this obstacle in my path. His pockets are empty and he has the audacity to fall in love!'

Asad Khan did receive Sheikh Dawan, but his behaviour was somewhat lukewarm. Sheikh Dawan was quite put off and after a casual conversation, he got up saying, *Mian*, it's pretty late in the night.'

'So, it is,' Asad Khan agreed.

'I should be leaving, friend. I am sure you want to sleep after that sumptuous feast!'

'Indeed, my eyes are heavy with sleep, *Mian*!'

'*Khuda hafiz,*' Sheikh Dawan said and turned to the door, barely hearing Asad Khan's '*Khuda hafiz*'.

After Sheikh Dawan left, Asad Khan poured wine from the flagon kept near his bed and quickly gulped it down. And then, lying on the silken mattress, he kept thinking about Kafia and hardly realised when he drifted off to sleep. . .

Emperor Akbar was well-known for his love of art. He himself composed verses. He had genuine respect for the artist. Lately, he had been constantly hearing that Mirabai, the queen of Chittor, wrote lovely *bhajans* and also sang them beautifully. Akbar was often seized with a desire to listen to Mirabai singing her own *bhajans*. But this was very difficult, for there was no easy access to the palaces of the Rajputs. However, his desire grew stronger day by day. He resolved that one day he would somehow manage to listen to her.

At last, the Emperor sent his men on a secret mission to probe the possibility of his going to Chittor to listen to Mirabai. On their return, the men informed the Emperor that there was the Ranchhodji temple in the Chittor Fort where Mira alone worshipped and sang her *bhajans*. If the Emperor was prepared to go to Chittor in disguise, he would be able to listen to Mirabai's songs.

Emperor Akbar was highly impressed by that thoughtful suggestion. One day he said to Tansen, '*Mian* Tansen, I've a great desire to go to Chittor and hear Mirabai singing her *bhajans*. I've heard that while singing she is so overwhelmed with emotion that she starts dancing before the image of her *Girdhar Gopal*. Could anyone be really so devoted to the deity, Tansen?'

'Of course, one can be so devoted, *Huzoor*. Devotion to God is such that once you're touched by it, you remain immersed in it all your life.'

Emperor Akbar nodded his head in agreement.

However, he said, 'But *Mian* Tansen, it's said that Mirabai maintains no relationship with her Rana. They say that she regards only *Girdhar Gopal* as her husband. Could this be true?'

'It is indeed true, *Huzoor*. Devotional love is always like that. It unites one's soul with the Divine. It is like the mingling of water and sandal!'

'How beautifully put, Tansen! Then let us go to Chittor in disguise.'

'No, *Huzoor*. That's impossible. The Rajputs would lay down their lives but won't allow the shadow of other men to fall on their women. If we are caught in Chittor, it would mean certain death for us.'

Akbar's forehead wrinkled. He said in a resolute tone, 'Tansen, I shall see Mirabai even if I have to risk my life. Tomorrow morning both of us will leave for Chittor. No one should get the slightest inkling about it. Don't forget to conceal a sword and a dagger under your dress for self-protection.'

It was now impossible to disobey the Emperor's command. Tansen nodded his head in assent and went back to his palace. The next morning, they quietly left for Chittor in the guise of traders. They reached Chittor without any trouble via Kota, although the area of Bundi-Kota was under the rule of the Hada Rajputs. They tied their horses in a safe place at the base of the Fort. Then passing through several entrances, they finally reached the Ranchhodji temple and patiently waited outside. Akbar was holding a small bundle containing precious gems.

When they looked inside the temple, they were stunned by what they saw. Lamps were lighted in front of a beautiful idol of *Girdhar Gopal.* The scent of incense filled the air and fresh rose flowers lay in a heap before the idol. Mirabai was dressed in white, with a sandal mark on her forehead, and with small cymbals in her hands. She was absorbed in singing her *bhajans*, completely oblivious of her physical existence. The front portion of her saree had slid down her breasts and her black hair was dishevelled. Her anklets had broken and come off her feet. Mirabai, after her frenzied singing and dancing fell unconscious at the feet of *Giṛdhar Gopal.* She regained consciousness after some time. For a long time she shed tears of love.

After witnessing this unbelievable *leela* of divine love, Akbar felt humble before Mira. When she came out of the temple she saw Akbar and Tansen, disguised as traders. She was a little scared at first but the next moment she plucked up courage and asked, 'Who are you? How and with whose permission did you manage to come here?'

Tansen respectfully joined his hands before her and said,

'We are jewellers from Agra. We have come to sell our wares.'

Mirabai looked at them fixedly and said, 'Don't you know that if the Rana comes to know about your coming here, he will kill you instantly? Go away from here this very moment!' And with her plateful of *puja* offerings, she started going towards the palace.

But Akbar promptly took out a jewelled necklace from the bundle and said, 'Kindly put this necklace round the neck of your *Girdhar Gopal* on our behalf.'

Mira thought for a moment. She wondered if it would be right to touch the necklace belonging to another man. But then she thought that *Girdhar Gopal* belonged to everyone and she put it round his neck. Akbar and Tansen bowed to her and feeling gratified, led their horses towards Agra.

After Akbar's departure, Mira felt disturbed. How would she tell her Rana that an unknown man had presented that necklace for her *Girdhar Gopal* when she was alone in the temple? But finally she decided that she would tell him. What did she have to fear when her heart was pure?

At night the Rana came to her palace. Seeing that he was alone, she ventured to say, 'Ranaji, two jewellers came to the temple when I was singing the *bhajans* there. They have gifted a precious necklace to *Gopal*! I want to show it to you.'

The Rana was enraged. His eyebrows narrowed and his forehead wrinkled. The colour of his eyes changed. He thundered, 'Who allowed them to get to the temple?'

'I don't know!'

'You don't know? Are you not aware that our Rajput honour has suffered on account of their visit? Our queens are not exposed even to the sun and the moon. How did they reach the temple. Who were they? Tell me at once!'

But the Rana was too impatient to wait for an answer. He rose to his feet and cast an angry look all around. Finally, he summoned his trusted generals and consulted them. It was decided to call all the jewellers of Chittor and show the necklace to them. When the jewellers came, they were all dumbfounded to see the necklace. Then one of the jewellers said, 'Maharana, I had gone to Agra sometime ago and I sold this necklace to *Shahenshah* Akbar.'

Everyone was rendered speechless to hear that. They wondered what the Rana would do next. Like lightning, the Rana raised his sword and rushed to behead Mira. Mad with rage, the Rana shouted, 'Mira has ruined the reputation of the Rajputs. She sang before a *Yavan*. I shall wipe out that blot on our reputation by slaying Mira!' And he cast his blood-thirsty eyes all around.

Rana was about to strike Mira, but the general held him back. They persuaded him, 'Maharana, it is against the Rajput's tradition to slay a helpless woman.'

The Rana stopped where he was. Soon the sword was back in it's sheath. But the fire of revenge in Rana's heart had not subsided. He fretted and fumed, because personally he felt humiliated and moreover, the reputation of Rajputs had received a blow. . . .

The sun had risen in the east and life began to stir. Everyone was busy with their daily routine. Mira woke up and after bathing, started off barefoot towards the temple, humming a *bhajan*, holding the plate of *puja* offerings. She had absolutely no fear in her mind. What was there to fear when her heart was pure? Mira was absorbed in herself and immersed in devotion to her *Girdhar*.

She reached the temple and after lighting the lamp, burning the incense and offering flowers, she picked up her little cymbals and got absorbed in singing the *bhajans*. She became one with her Divine Lover. Her feet moved and the anklets jingled and she began to sing.

'I am in ecstasy, I am with my *Girdhar*.' She sang and danced, sang and danced, unaware of who she was and where she was! . . .

In the meantime, Rana was restless, with anger raging in his heart. He wondered, what he should do to take Mira's life. At last he got up and quickly poured strong poison in a cup.

Handing over that cup of poison to a maid he said, 'Go and give it to Raniji in the temple. Tell her that I want her to drink the contents of the cup immediately.'

With trembling steps the maid went to the temple. Mira was completely immersed in her devotion to *Girdhar*. The maid stood there, watching Mira sing and dance in ecstasy. Suddenly, Mira noticed her standing at the door and she stopped.

'What is it? What do you have in your hand?'

The maid mumbled, '*Maharaniji*, *Maharaja* has sent this cup for you and has ordered you to drink it at once!'

Mira smiled. She put the cup in front of the idol of *Girdhar* as an offering. Then she picked it up and looked into it. She saw the enchanting image of her *Girdhar Gopal* inside it. She turned and bowed to the idol and then with a smile gulped down the poison in the cup. As that poison went down Mira's throat, it turned into nectar. She felt ecstatic and started singing again in a deep voice.

'I have my *Girdhar Gopal*, none else.'

Indeed, Mira had been protected only by him. It was the supreme union of devotee with the Lord.

The Rana found it intriguing that Mira was still alive even after consuming that strong poison! How did that happen? What was the secret?

# 23

Razia had been put in jail. The soldiers were constantly torturing her to find out at whose bidding she had mixed poison in Tansen's *paan*. But even after being tortured endlessly, Razia did not give out the truth. At last the jail superintendent ordered the soldiers to brand Razia's body with heated iron bars and to throw her children to the hungry lions. On hearing that, her heart trembled. She implored with folded hands, 'I'll tell you, *Huzoor*! Have mercy on me!'

The superintendent roared at her, 'Tell me at once, who was it?'

Razia said in a trembling voice, '*Huzoor*, I mixed poison in Tansen's *paan* because Asad Khan and Sheikh Dawan told me to.'

'What did you say? Asad Khan and Sheikh Dawan? Did they give you some money to do such a heinous act?'

'Yes, *Huzoor*. There were some gold coins in a little bag.'

'Where is that money?'

'It's all gone. My husband was ill and that money was spent for his treatment.'

The superintendent said to the soldiers, 'Very well. Put her behind bars. And arrest Asad Khan and Sheikh Dawan immediately on charge of hatching this conspiracy.' The superintendent left immediately after issuing that order and got busy with other matters. And Razia in ragged clothes, went on crying, cursing herself for her complicity in the evil design of those two men. . .

Sheikh Dawan arrived at Asad Khan's house early one morning. When he barged in there, he found Asad Khan humming a romantic *ghazal*. In a little while, soldiers came there after putting up a notice at Sheikh Dawan's house.

Asad Khan was in panic at first to see the soldiers at his door. But, he was an army officer after all. He asked in an authoritative tone, 'Yes what brings you to my house?'

The soldiers *salaamed* him. Then one of them said, 'Razia has confessed her crime and said that you and Sheikh Dawan had a hand in the conspiracy to mix poison in Tansen's *paan*. We have orders for your arrest.'

Asad Khan was unfazed. He said, 'You have come to the wrong place. It must be some other Asad Khan. I am an army officer. We kill enemies, not friends. I say, you have come to the wrong house. First find out properly which Asad Khan conspired to kill Tansen!'

The soldiers were overawed by Asad Khan's overbearing authority and withdrew without arresting him. Asad Khan was very shrewd. He thought to himself that Sheikh Dawan was an artist and a very simple man at heart. He did not understand political intrigues. If the Sheikh got arrested, then there would hardly be any escape for him. Moreover, he had to be eliminated if Asad Khan wanted to have Kafia for himself.

Asad Khan returned to his room, with such thoughts in his mind. He said, 'Sheikh, Kafia has just sent a message that she is going to the lake with her friends for a picnic. There would be singing and dancing and lots of fun. She has sent an invitation for you as well. Let us go to the lake. What do you think?'

'What a question? If Kafia wants me to enter the jaws of death, I would be most willing to do so. I'm Sheikh Dawan, you know!'

'Very well. Then you better change your clothes. We shall have to go in disguise.'

'As you say!'

And immediately Sheikh Dawan dressed himself as an attendant. Asad Khan was in full military dress, with a sword hanging at his waist. Their horses soon started speeding towards the lake.

They reached the lakeside in no time. The place was deserted and Sheikh Dawan looked at Asad Khan, 'Kafia hasn't arrived yet.'

'She must be on the way!' Asad Khan said and then added, 'I say, just look up at the sky!'

Sheikh Dawan raised his head towards the sky. Asad Khan asked, 'What do you see there?'

'Nothing, only the clear blue sky. And some birds flying across the sky, that's all!'

'Raise your head still higher and see!' Asad Khan persisted.

Sheikh Dawan raised his head higher and in a single sweep Asad Khan severed his head from his body. The ground was soaked with Sheikh Dawan's blood. A weird smile distorted Asad Khan's cruel face.

He tied Sheikh Dawan's corpse to a heavy stone and dragged the body into the deep waters of the lake. Then Asad Khan mounted his horse and was soon in his house in Agra. The soldiers searched for Sheikh Dawan everywhere, but they could not trace him anywhere. And Asad Khan, despite Razia's revelation of his involvement in the conspiracy could not be arrested for want of evidence. . .

Razia was far from Asad Khan's mind. But if anyone was installed in the depths of Asad Khan's heart, it was only Kafia. When the evening shadows spread, Asad Khan arrived at Kafia's house. She was reading the Quran with her mother. Asad Khan sat on a cane seat. Kafia came up to him after some time and asked, 'You're looking very dejected today. What's the matter?'

'Oh, I can't even die!'

'But what has happened that you should start thinking of dying?' Kafia asked very innocently.

'As if you don't know! I'm madly in love with you. I only dream of you night and day. Kafia, I must have you or else, I will end my life.'

'I think something has gone wrong with you. I have never felt any love for you. If you care for your safety, leave this place at once!'

Asad Khan roared like an injured lion, 'I shall ruin you Kafia and then die. A day would come, Kafia, when you would throw your arms round my neck. My love for you is pure and I swear by my pure love that you will be able to live only by accepting me. I'm going for the time being. But, do ponder over your decision.' With those words, Asad Khan stormed out of Kafia's house.

Kafia was in a terrible rage after he left. Her Mughal blood surged up in her veins. 'I shall see to that rascal Asad Khan! Preposterous, that's what he is! I shall put him in his place, yes!'

Back at home, Asad Khan was seized with a raving desire to take revenge. He set his men to keep a watch around Kafia's house and take note of where she went.

In the meantime, Kafia's mother had heard every word of Asad Khan. She decided to report Asad Khan's obnoxious behaviour to her husband when he returned home in the evening. . .

Tansen was enjoying the full glory of Emperor Akbar's *darbar*. Akbar had come to love Tansen's music from the bottom of his heart. Other court singers were being relegated to the background and they received much less respect and attention. They were all worried about their livelihood and were planning all sorts of conspiracies against Tansen. But nothing seemed to work and they felt disheartened.

There was a singer called Brijnath in Akbar's *darbar*, who knew the art of exciting elephants by his singing. The elephants went berserk when they heard him sing, trampling people under their feet. One day, Emperor Akbar was going somewhere on a political mission. His elephant was kept ready with full embellishments. There were other elephants also.

Tansen was standing with others to bid farewell to the Emperor. Brijnath went round humming a tune in the ears of all the elephants. One of the elephants turned wild after listening to Brijnath's tune. Unfortunately, Tansen was standing right in front. The elephants raised its tusks and rushed towards Tansen. It was clear that Tansen's death was imminent. However, Swami Haridas had once taught him a *raga* to bring a mad elephant under control. Tansen at once began the *alap* and then followed up with the *raga*. In no time, the elephant lowered his trunk and knelt down near Tansen's feet.

Thus, even that plan of the court-singers to demean Tansen was unsuccessful.

It was evening. The whole city of Agra was lit up with bright lamps. Jalal Khan Kurchi returned home after supervising the military exercises. He removed his army uniform and after reading the Qụran, sat leaning against a cushion, feeling quite pleased with himself and started puffing at the hookah. Kafia was in her own room. Her mother went to Kurchi carrying a plate of snacks and told him about Asad Khan's impertinent behaviour. Blood rushed to Kurchi's eyes. He took the sword hanging on the wall and prepared to go and kill Asad Khan. But Kafia and her mother tried to stop him. His wife said, 'There are some matters that can be settled not by emotion but by reason.'

Kurchi sat down, his face still aflame with rage. But, he had resolved to avenge the insult of his daughter. Though he listened to the persuasions of his wife and daughter and kept quiet, he was furious. He was so agitated that now and then, his hand touched the hilt of the sword or his finger checked the sharpness of the blade of his lance, making the mother and daughter very nervous. . .

Tansen had now grown quite old. He was the father of four children—the daughter Saraswati, and the sons Tantarang, Vilas Khan and Suratsen. All of them had entered their youth. Tansen made them do their daily *riaz*. Saraswati was very good at singing the *Malhar raga*.

However, other court-singers still indulged in all kinds of evil designs to demean Tansen. One day, Tansen had not yet arrived at the *darbar*. Taking advantage of his absence, one of the court singers, Adam Khan addressed himself to Emperor Akbar, '*Huzoor*, the *Deepak raga* is among the best of our *ragas* and it is only Tansen who knows how to render it. If you listen to Tansen's rendering of that *raga* you would be enchanted.'

Akbar was very pleased to hear such praise being lavished on Tansen. Adam Khan had hardly taken his seat when Tansen arrived. Akbar insisted that Tansen should sing the *Deepak raga* that day. That order, struck terror in Tansen's heart. He felt that his death was now imminent.

If someone sang the *Deepak raga*, flames emanated from his whole body. Extinguished lamps were rekindled. Tansen thought for a moment and silently debated whether or not he would sing that *raga*. Finally, he decided to abide by the Emperor's wishes. He said, '*Huzoor*, I shall sing the *Deepak raga*. But I will only be able to do it on the banks of the Yamuna.'

Akbar agreed. Soon the announcement was made that there would be a *mehfil* on the banks of the Yamuna that evening. Promptly, the *shamianas* were put up. By the time the evening set in, the river bank was lit up with the light of thousands of torches. Some lamps filled with oil, were kept unlit in order to witness the miraculous effect of the *Deepak raga*. The venue of the *mehfil* was overcrowded.

Saraswati, Tansen's daughter, was standing at a little distance from the *shamianas*. Tansen had explained to her everything and warned her of any eventuality.

Tansen began the *alap*. As he continued the *alap*, people started feeling hot. When he started singing the *raga* with full gusto, people felt flames were rising from Tansen's body and were spreading heat all around. The extinguished lamps had started burning. The Emperor was feeling terribly hot. He came away from the *mehfil*. Others followed. There was a great commotion and the *mehfil* suddenly ended. Tansen, experienced a terrible heat in his body and ran towards the river. The moment Saraswati saw Tansen, she began singing the *Malhar raga*. In no time, the sky was overcast with clouds and the rain came pouring down. In that cooling rain, the fire rising from Tansen's body was extinguished. Tansen was saved. Akbar heaved a singh of relief. He regretted that he had pressed Tansen to sing the *Deepak raga*. Never again would he insist that Tansen should sing any particular *raga*—not the *Deepak raga*, in any case. He would respect his freedom as an artist. . . .

When Kafia heard about that incident, she profusely thanked

*Allah* for sparing Tansen's life. Zeenat had asked Kafia to come over that evening to meet Tansen. She looked forward to meeting him.

Tansen was quite fatigued but he thought it was a good idea to go to Rahim Khan Khana's house. They could chat and he would feel light at heart. For a while, they talked about political matters, but soon started talking about literature. Rahim Khan Khana recited some of his *dohas* to Tansen. Then in the course of their conversation, Tansen asked Rahim Khan Khana, '*Janab*, how is it that your son is still unmarried?'

Rahim Khan Khana lifted his shoulders and said, 'Well, let me know if you have a nice girl in mind.'

Tansen promptly mentioned Kurchi's daughter Kafia and narrated her beauty and good qualities. Rahim Khan Khana was impressed. He said, 'I shall send the proposal to Kurchi tomorrow itself.'

They had a pleasant conversation for some time and then Tansen took leave of Rahim Khan Khana and returned to his palace. By that time, Kafia had already arrived to meet Tansen and was seated with Zeenat, awaiting his return. The moment Tansen's palanquin was lowered on the ground, Zeenat and Kafia came down to receive him. But as Tansen stepped out of the palanquin, Kafia noticed an arrow coming with lightning speed towards Tansen. She screamed and had she not stopped that arrow with her palm, Tansen's life would have ended that day. Blood spurted from Kafia's palm and some blood spattered Tansen's clothes. .

It was quite late in the night and since Kafia had not yet come back, her father Kurchi set out to go to Tansen's palace to fetch her. As he came up to the palace, he heard some whispering in a bower. It was dark all around. Kurchi pulled out his sword and went walking stealthily in that direction. The moment he found Asad Khan hiding there, he attacked him. Their swords clashed and there was a bloody dual between them. Other people also rushed to the spot when they heard the clanging of the swords.

With a single blow of his sword, Kurchi ripped open Asad

Khan's stomach. Asad Khan was in a pool of blood and his eyes were fixed on Kafia as he gasped for breath. Kafia was saying to herself, 'What is this thing called love? It makes man so reckless that he blindly gives his life for it!'

Tansen too felt miserable at the sight of blood. He said to Zeenat, 'Zeenat, come inside. My mind is very sad today. Kurchi kindly take Kafia with you immediately, and inform the officer-in-charge that a murderer has been killed within the precincts of my palace.'

Kurchi returned to his palace with Kafia. Asad Khan's body remained right there. That dark night again witnessed a bloody conspiracy, but it was a conspiracy that met with another failure.

# 24

Asad Khan was dead. His body was taken from Tansen's garden and buried the next day. That incident had quite unnerved Tansen. He thought, 'After all, why are people constantly conspiring to kill me? What harm have I done to anyone? As a matter of fact, an artist always brings peace to everyone through his art. And he brings credit to his land. But here they are desperately indulging in all kinds of acts to take my life—sometimes they mix poison in my *paan* and sometimes they shoot an arrow at me! What should I do? Should I leave Agra and go away? What would happen if I and my family really become victims of such conspiracies? And if only I get killed, my wife and children would be left without any support.'

While Tansen was preoccupied by such gloomy thoughts, Hussaini came and sat by his side. She too, was upset. Finding Tansen in a sad mood she asked, 'Why are such things happening? That army general Asad Khan, who was killed yesterday—why did he want to kill you? After all, what harm have you done to him?'

'I don't know. To tell you the truth, I didn't even know him,' Tansen replied sadly. They went on talking for some time after which Husssaini went inside, and Tansen was left alone. He walked up and down in his chamber.

Sometime later, a palanquin was lowered in front of Tansen's palace. Lifting the curtain, a young woman stepped out. She was stunningly beautiful. She walked up to the entrance and said to the guard, 'I wish to meet *Mian* Tansen.'

'Your good name?' the guard asked.

'My name is Noor. I live in Agra. I want to meet *Mian* Tansen to discuss an important matter.'

The guard said to her very courteously, 'Kindly wait for a while, I'll go in and inform the master.'

The guard went in and informed Tansen. At first Tansen was in two minds. Should he or should he not meet a female visitor? Then he thought that he might as well meet her, since she had taken the trouble of coming all the way. He said to the guard, 'Very well. Bring her in and make her sit here. I will just go in to change my clothes and come back.'

The guard led Noor inside and made her comfortable. In a little while Tansen came and joined her. As he entered, Noor bowed and offered her salutations. Tansen asked her, 'What has brought you her, *Mohtarama*. Why did you have to take the trouble of coming all the way to meet me?'

Noor replied, '*Janab*, I am a special attendant to the *Shahzadi*. She is in a terrible panic ever since she heard about the conspiracies to take your life. She has sent me to inquire about your well-being. She has sent a message that she will be going boating on the Yamuna tomorrow evening and you must definitely meet her there. She will be waiting for you!'

Tansen pondered over this for a while and said, 'Listen, my life won't be safe if somebody comes to know that I had a secret meeting with the Princess. Please tell her that I will meet her in her palace.'

Noor said, 'No, *Janab*, you can't meet her in her palace. She will wait for you on the banks of the Yamuna tomorrow evening. And now I shall take your leave. I can't stay on here very long.'

Then, Noor got up and returned to Princess Zaibunnisa's palace. After Noor left, Tansen sat wondering why the Princess was keen to meet him secretly. What could be her purpose. It was possible that Noor was a party to some conspiracy. 'These court singers are bent upon taking my life. In what way have I harmed them that they should make repeated attempts on my life?'

Tansen felt very disturbed. He came out his chamber and started walking up and down in the garden.

Soon it was evening. Tansen's palace was lit with the torches.

Cotton wicks burning in huge lamps shed their light. Tansen returned to his chamber and was startled to find Kafia seated there waiting for him.

Kafia was very elegantly dressed today. Collyrium enhanced the beauty of her fish-like eyes. She smiled as Tansen entered and bowed to him respectfully. Then, both of them took their seats and started chatting.

Tansen was really struck by Kafia's charm. He stared at her admiringly. Kafia said, 'Your enemies tried to take your life in so many ways, but could not harm you in any way. Asad Khan got killed. And there is no trace of Sheikh Dawan. It is quite likely that he too has been killed or has fled and gone far away from Agra!' Kafia said all that, in one breath and then fell silent.

Tansen broke the silence and said, 'But Kafia, I had no animosity with Asad Khan?'

'True, you did not take him to be your enemy, but he thought. . .'

'What did he think, Kafia?'

'That I am . . .' Kafia stopped midway

'Say it clearly, Kafia. What did he think?'

'That I am in love with you!'

Tansen was speechless to hear that. Kafia said, 'Asad Khan was in love with me but he thought that I was loving you. That was why, he had decided to take your life!'

There was a brief moment of silence. Then Tansen asked, 'Kafia, is it true that you're in love with me?'

'Yes,' Kafia said shyly.

Colour rushed to her cheeks. And her eyes were full of desire—they were like overflowing cups. Tansen said, 'But you never openly expressed any such feeling!'

'You didn't give me any chance. I have been like a flame silently burning away. I've writhed like a fish without water. I've been thinking about you the whole time,' said Kafia and shyly looked down.

Tansen said after a little thought, 'Kafia, tell me honestly. Are you in love with me or with my music?'

Both! You're an artist and your music sunk deep into my heart at all stages of my life.' And after a brief silence she added, 'I know that as a woman, I should not openly express my silent love for you. But when too much water flows into a river, it breaks the banks. It is difficult to control what is uncontrollable.'

Tansen showed empathy with Kafia's feelings for him. He said, 'Kafia, I'm fortunate that such a charming girl like you should be in love with me. But everything should be kept within limits. You know very well that I am a married man and I have a family. Have you ever thought about that?'

'Love doesn't take all that into account. I'm a woman and I've a soft heart. And only you dominate my heart!' said Kafia and fixed her lovely eyes on Tansen.

Tansen said, 'I accept your love, Kafia. But it should remain a secret in our hearts.'

Kafia's face bloomed like a rose. She said, 'When would you send the marriage proposal to my *Abbajaan*?'

Tansen was taken aback. He said, 'Kafia, I told you I'm already married. And then, think of the age difference between us!'

Kafia heaved a sigh and said, 'Love has no consideration for age, community or religion.'

Now Tansen was in a dilemma. He said, 'Tell me one thing, Kafia.'

Kafia gave Tansen a questioning look. 'You see, everybody in this world loves the moon. But the moon remains far from all. Let it be so with us. We may continue to love each other. But you must be married to a young man.'

Kafia trembled at Tansen's suggestion. She said with tears in her eyes, 'I knew you would say this. I came like a wave to you and now I will pass through the most difficult stage of my life with a storm in my heart. Is it the inevitable fate of people in love that they should eternally shed tears? You're a man, yet you're afraid of what the world may think or say; whereas I, although a woman, wish to face the world. You're forgetting that a woman gives her heart only once in her life. She adorns her body everyday, but falls in love only once in her life. I shall burn like a flame till the end!'

Tansen was astounded that Kafia had talked so much at a stretch. He tried to pacify her, 'Kafia, life is nurtured not by emotions but by realities. You have to forego many things in life. Yes, you must burn. Burning is the sweet melody of life. But don't be disheartened. Since you love me, you must also abide by my advice. Love has the same intense feeling as music. Think that you are loving me. You will find my presence in every *raga* and *ragini*. You will feel me in your pursuit of music. Kafia, only those with unfulfilled love in their hearts are able to attain something unusual. Separation in love fills one's heart with a keen desire to do something big in life. Being together is the end of love, whereas separation is its triumph. We would be like two banks of a river. We would keep looking at each other but would not embrace. You will have to take my advice and get married. You will have to start your new life. You will have to attain all that you should attain. When you are happy, I would be happy too.'

Kafia turned round and said, 'My happiness has ended today right before you. By your command, I shall continue to live, but it would be a life of dejection!' With that Kafia started sobbing.

Seeing Kafia's tears, Tansen's tender heart grew restless. But he controlled himself and said, 'Kafia it is quite late. You should go home.' And they both stood up.

Tansen went to see her off up to her palanquin. As she was leaving, when Kafia looked at Tansen, tears glistened like diamonds and trickled down her fair cheeks. The bearers lifted the palanquin and went towards her house. She wept and sobbed all the way.

Kafia debated with herself if she had done the right thing in openly expressing her love to Tansen. There was a raging storm in her mind. She was returning, defeated in her love. She thought, she would never marry all her life. She would secretly cherish Tansen's memory. But the next moment she had different thoughts. She wanted to change her defeat into triumph. There was no game in life which one could not win. Kafia ordered the palanquin-bearers to change the course and go towards the Agra Fort. The palanquin-bearers followed the order.

The Agra Fort was lit up. At the gate, the guards were told that Jalal Khan Kurchi's daughter Kafia was going into the Fort for an important mission. The guards allowed the palanquin to be taken in. It went towards Princess Zaibunnisa's palace.

The Tartar women with bared swords were guarding the palace. One of those women asked, 'Who are you? What's your business here?'

Kafia lifted the curtain of the palanquin and introduced herself. The palanquin was taken upto the palace of the *Shahzadi*. Kafia stepped out of it and walked upto the *Shahzadi's* chamber.

The *Shahzadi* was seated alone in her chamber with her head covered and was reading the Quran. Kafia sat quietly on the carpet. The *Shahzadi* was extremely beautiful and almost the same age as Kafia and they were close friends.

When the *Shahzadi* spoke, her voice sounded like the notes of a *veena*. She was also very much interested in music and poetry. She occasionally hummed some tunes and also wrote some poetry. . .

When the *Shahzadi* finished reading the Quran, she turned to Kafia with a smile and asked, 'How are you, Kafia? Tell me, what brings you here at this hour? Are things all right with you? How is your *riaz* with the *rudra veena*?' The *Shahzadi* came and sat near Kafia. Both the girls sipped the *sherbat* which the maid had brought for them. Seeing that Kafia was dejected, the *Shahzadi* asked, 'Kafia, you are not in your best mood. What is the matter?'

'You are right. I am really sad.'

'But why?' the *Shahzadi* asked.

Tears streaked down Kafia's fair cheeks. She said, 'My dear friend, you're my dear friend. I've come to seek your help. Would you help me?'

'Yes, tell me. What do you want?'

Kafia said in a melancholy tone, I'm very genuinely in love with Tansen. But. . .'

'What do you mean?'

'I've come to you today, defeated in love. Look at my tears. Look at my eyes. Think of the storm raging in my heart. Tansen has no doubt accepted my love but has declined to marry me. Now it is up to you. Tell *Shahenshah-e-Alam* to arrange my marriage with Tansen,' Kafia urged the *Shahzadi.*

The *Shahzadi* was very sensible. After thinking a little she said, 'Kafia, I had no idea that you have been in love with Tansen. An artist like Tansen is born once in several centuries. But you must remember that he has grown quite old. Moreover, he has a family—a loving wife and equally loving children. Kafia, divided love has no meaning. A lotus can contain only one dewdrop. Other drops just get scattered. Love enjoys a sole claim on the lover. The sky does not get overcast with tiny clouds. Take my advice and even as you continue loving Tansen, go and get married to a young man. Of course, you'll have to show complete fidelity to your husband. As for my *Abba Huzoor*, although *Shahenshah-e-Hindustan*, he cannot force anyone in the matter of the heart. He will say nothing to Tansen in this matter. And if I dare to suggest anything to him, he would be furious with me.'

After hearing the *Shahzadi's* reply there was nothing more Kafia could say. She took leave of the *Shahzadi* and with a broken heart and with heavy steps returned to her palanquin and went home. . .

Kafia was feeling very miserable and so was Tansen, but he was helpless. He was not in a position to accept Kafia, who was whirling like a straw in a violent storm. She tossed about restlessly all through the night, but later fell asleep without realising it.

She woke up in the morning when she heard the cock crowing. The sky was slightly clouded. The morning sun was playing hide and seek with the clouds. Kafia was absorbed in watching that play of light and shade. Then she said to herself that she too, like the sun in the sky, would have to emerge through the dark clouds. Tansen had said, 'Adore music, Kafia. You would be able to find me only in music.'

Kafia at once got up from her bed. She went straight to her *rudra veena*. For a while she sat before it and then her fingers started sliding along the strings. And what she played on it that morning was in fact the music rising from the depths of her melancholy heart.

Listening to Kafia's *rudra veena*, her mother came up to her and remarked with a happy smile, 'Really, Kafia, you have become a great artist! You have put your soul into your music. You have never played so well before!'

Kafia looked at her mother sadly. The storm within had shattered her. But she said nothing to her mother. She merely let a faint smile flicker on her lips and finally got up to start the daily morning routine. . . .

It was the evening. The *Shahzadi* came with her maids to the bank of the Yamuna for boating. The roads through which palanquin passed were closed to the public. A boat, shaped like a swan, was anchored on the banks. This boat was to be rowed only by women. No male was to be seen anywhere around. The *Shahzadi* was waiting for Tansen near the river-bank. He arrived after some time. He was stopped by the guards at first, but was allowed to come when the *Shahzadi* gave the signal. Tansen offered salutations to the *Shahzadi* and stood bowing his head. She asked, 'How are you, great artist?'

'By your grace, I'm very fine.'

Looking concerned, the *Shahzadi* said, '*Mian* Tansen, I know that the court singers are after your blood. So far, their plans to take your life have been unsuccessful, but we cannot be sure what is hidden in the womb of time. In my view, you should protect yourself well. Let me know if you need any help from our side. I have called you here for that very purpose.'

Tansen heard the *Shahzadi* in silence. He said, 'I wish to leave Agra and go back to my guru Swami Haridas at Vrindavan.'

'No, that's impossible,' the *Shahzadi* reacted at once. 'If you go away, it would be the end of music in Agra. Our *mehfils* would lose all charm. They will lack lustre. *Abba Huzoor's* heart would be sad. You must stay on in Agra. The Mughal *darbar* appreciates artists. In our *darbar* artists are nurtured and they thrive. However, I'm giving you something which would always protect you.' And she gave Tansen a gem-studded dagger. Then she said, 'I wish to listen to your music all by myself. Will you give me that chance?'

'Why not? Any time you command!'

The *Shahzadi* smiled, 'In that case, join me on the boat!'

Tansen abided by her wishes and on the boat he sang *raga Darbari Kanada* for her. She took off a precious necklace from her neck and presenting it to Tansen said, 'This is my gift to you. Keep it with you. It would always remind you of me.' Tansen accepted the gift with a graceful bow.

It was already night when the boat touched the banks of the Yamuna. Tansen respectfully took leave of the *Shahzadi* who kept gazing at his receding figure for a long time.

# 25

Tani had lost her parents. Some distant relations who lived in a far off village, tried to take her with them. But Tani refused to leave her village. Tani was all alone. She spent most of her time in the field. In the evening, she went to the Shiva temple where she prayed and sang *bhajans*, and then trudged back alone to her home.

She lived in a *kuchcha* hut, which was almost in a state of collapse. Whether it was the heat of the sun or the fury of the rains, she felt the impact of everything in her hut. At night sometimes she would light the lamp, but quite often, she slept off in the dark. Peasant women from nearby huts provided her food, because she never liked to cook anything for herself. Sometimes she ate that food, and sometimes it remained untouched.

Seeing her mental condition, the villagers often discussed her future. They felt that her life could be redeemed if she were married to a nice boy. They made several attempts to fix her marriage, but Tani always said, 'I'm already married!' When the villagers pressed her to tell them to whom she had been married, she only said, 'I'm married—that's all!'

Tani was in the prime of youth. The supreme truth of life peeped through her large eyes. When she covered her bulging breasts with the front end of her saree, people realised how she had grown.

Some frivolous young men of the village were attracted by Tani's youthful appearance. One evening when Tani was going to the Shiva temple along the path, a youth waylaid her. At first Tani said to him calmly, 'Get away from my path.' But that youth did not oblige. As he rushed forward to catch hold of Tani, she struck his face with her fists so hard that his nose started bleeding. The young man stumbled on the ground and Tani proceeded to the Shiva temple.

That young man was full of vengeance. He went towards the temple. Tani was singing *bhajans* and the temple was deserted. It was already dark when Tani finished. The young man stealthily followed Tani. He soon caught up with her and held her tight at the waist. Tani kept on shouting, 'Leave me, let me go!' But when the young man did not release her, she whirled around with all her strength, so that the young man lost his grip on her. Tani caught hold of his legs and pushed him flat on the ground. Then she showered a few blows on his face and stomach and mounted his chest like the goddess *Chandi*. The young man pleaded for mercy and promised never to harass her again. Tani finally let him go for she had already beaten him black and blue. He got on to his feet with great difficulty and shaking the dust off his body, limped towards his house. By that time, Tani had already reached her hut.

It was a dark night. Tani lighted the lamp and its dim light spread in her little hut. For a long time, Tani sat staring at the flame of the lamp. She looked very grim today. She was suddenly reminded of her parents. For a long time, she passed her hand over the spot where her father used to lie down. Then she got up and started packing up the utensils one by one, passing her fingers over them. She touched all those utensils to her head and then replaced them on the ground.

Suddenly, she was reminded of Tansen. She got up. It was past midnight and the village was asleep. Occasionally, she heard the wandering dogs barking loudly in the stillness of the night. She came out. She first went to Tansen's house. She stood staring at the locked house. Then she took a little earth from its threshold and after touching it to her forehead, tied it in her saree. With weary steps, she returned to her hut, lost in gloomy thoughts. Then, she tied up her clothes and her mother's ornaments in a bundle. She came out and stood for a long time staring at her hut. Tears streamed down her cheeks.

The full moon shone gloriously in the sky, showering its

silvery light all around. Flowers on the neem trees spread their fragrance in the cool air of the night. When the moonlight fell on the leaves of the banyan trees, it looked as though thousands of lamps had been lit there. The peepul leaves were fluttering in the strong breeze. The fields were bright in the glittering moonlight. Tani walked on and on. She gazed at her village, its streets, its pathways, its earth, as though they were her childhood friends whom she was leaving behind to go alone to an unknown destination. Tani walked the dusty roads all through the night.

The night passed and gradually the twinkling stars became dim. The birds started chirping. The darkness of the night lifted and the eastern sky brightened with the red glow of the dawn. Tani continued to walk and finally reached Gwalior. She sat under a tree to rest. There was a well nearby where some women were drawing water. Tani walked up to the well and washed her face and hands. She drank some water and went to the market, where she sold an ornament at a jeweller's shop. She tied the money in a pouch and went to where she saw some bullock-carts standing. Tani sat in one of them, which was due to go to Kashi.

The bullock-cart continued moving all through the night. The bells tied round the necks of the oxen rang through the night's stillness. All around there was darkness except for the dim light of the lantern in the bullock-cart. Passing through several villages and forests the bullock-cart finally reached Kashi after a fortnight. It was good luck for the passengers that no untoward incident took place during the journey, because in those days, bandits usually attacked and looted travellers.

On reaching Kashi, in the early morning, the passengers started going to their respective homes. Tani also picked up her bundle and got off the bullock-cart. But where could she go? She had no acquaintance or relative there. As a child she had heard about a very beautiful temple of Vishwanath in Kashi. She thought she could go there. The Lord in that temple would indicate some place for her to stay.

Asking directions along the way, she finally reached the

temple. She was very hungry. Still, she first bathed and had *darshan* of Shiva. When she came out of the temple, she found an old woman feeding the poor. Tani also joined that crowd.

While Tani was eating, she attracted the attention of the old woman, who came up to Tani and asked, 'From where are you coming, my dear? You seem to be from a good family.'

Tani remained silent. The old woman stroked her head and asked again, 'Tell me, child, from where are you coming?'

This time Tani could not avoid replying. She said, 'I belong to Behat village near Gwalior. My parents are dead. I am all alone. I have come to seek the protection of Kashi Vishwanath.'

'Where are you staying?'

'Nowhere. I've just arrived today.'

The old woman's heart went out to Tani. She said, 'Now, get up from here. You'll stay with me. I've got a nice place for you. I am a singer. You too, can learn singing and live in comfort.'

Tani vehemently shook her head. 'No, I don't want to learn singing. Singing separates you from dear ones. I don't like music. I shall find some place to stay on my own.'

The old woman was a little disappointed. 'Well, as you wish, I was only speaking in your own interest,' she said and went her way.

Tani remained seated at the threshold of the temple for long. After some time she got up and proceeded towards the banks of the Ganga. Tani found place in a nearby *dharamshala*. After that she bathed in the Ganga everyday and worshipped and sang *bhajans* at the Vishwanath temple. Some time later, some women helped her to get a small room for which she was charged no rent. Thus, Tani lived comfortably in Kashi.

In those days, the Tulsi *Ramayana* was being recited on the Dashashvamegh ghat. Tani derived great comfort by listening to that recitation. But there were moments when Tansen's memory caused a turmoil in her mind. . .

One morning Tani was sitting on the banks of the Ganga applying sandalpaste marks on the foreheads of those who came to bathe in the river. They left their clothes with her when they went to bathe and when they returned, Tani would anoint their foreheads with a *tilak*. For this, they would give her some money.

Once a man and a woman came to the *ghat* where Tani sat. Tani asked, 'Brother, from where do you come?'

The man replied, 'We come from a far away place. There is a village called Behat in Gwalior district.'

Tani asked with curiosity, 'You're coming from Behat!'

'That's right.'

'I come from Behat too! The village must have changed a lot in all these years. What about the Shiva temple? Is it the same or has it changed?'

'Everything is as it has always been. Nothing has changed.'

Then Tani asked about the people she had known in Behat. 'What about Makrand Pandey and his wife? Have they come back to the village?'

'No, they haven't come back. They had gone to bathe in the Gangasagar. While returning, the boat capsized and both the husband and the wife got drowned.'

Tani sighed sadly and asked, 'Who is living in their house now?

'No one. They had a son—Tansen. But he never came back to live in the village. The house is locked since Makrand Pandey and his wife left for their pilgrimage. Parts of the house are damaged by the rain.'

'Where is Tansen living now?'

'Oh, dear woman, don't ask about Tansen. He has become a very big man. He is among the 'nine jewels' of Akbar's *darbar*. There is no other singer like him in the whole country. He lives in great comfort. Why should he be bothered about his little house in the village? He lives in a palace!'

'In a palace? Where is his palace?'

'In Agra, not far from Akbar's palace. It is not easy to meet him.'

'I see!' said Tani and looked down.

The man and the woman got so involved in Tani's questions

that they even forgot to ask her anything about herself. They bathed in the Ganga and went back.

A little later, there was a terrible dust-storm. The placid waters of the Ganga were whipped into stormy waves that came crashing on the bank. Canoes floating in the river were tossed about by the waves. While the Ganga was in fury, Tani's heart was in turmoil with the onslaught of past memories. Every rising wave of the Ganga was telling her as it were, 'Tani, just see how times change! Look at Tansen and look at yourself! Most probably he has even forgotten you. You are like a passing cloud which appears in the sky, casts its shadow on the earth and then disappears somewhere in the wide expanse, unknown to anyone. But you can't even return from where you are. It's now too late, Tani!' For a long time, Tani also tossed about like the stormy waves rising in the Ganga.

Tani had loved Tansen with all her heart. She had hoped that sometime, somehow, she would be able to meet him and make him her own. What lovely dreams Tani had about future! But today she was heartbroken to hear that Tansen was among the 'nine jewels' in Akbar's *darbar* and no one could easily meet him. She thought that she was so poor and he was living in a palace! How could there be love between the poor and the wealthy? But the next moment she thought, 'No, that's not possible. Tansen could not have forgotten me. He will definitely recognize me if he sees me!' And then she said to herself, 'Yet, how can I be so sure? With wealth and power, man forgets everything!'

Tani closed her eyes and remembered her first meeting with Tansen in the village. She came out of her reverie only when some people passed by her singing *bhajans* glorifying the sacred Ganga.

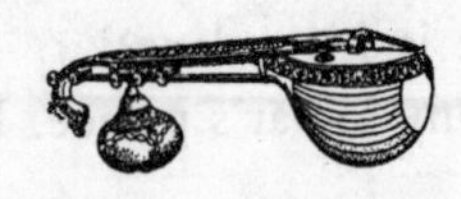

# 26

The Kalinjar Fort seemed to be rising up to the sky. The place was picturesque with its thickets of *neem*, acacia, mango and *jamun*. The scent of wild *karaunda* was pervasive. Kirti Singh, the ruler of Kalinjar, was courageous and brave. From the foot of the fort, which was at a height it was possible to launch successful attacks on the enemy with artillery and rifles.

The Kalinjar Fort was of great strategic importance. Shershah Suri had his eye on it and one day he attacked the Fort with his large army. A fierce battle ensued, the Fort fell into his hands. He had not only the soldiers of Kalinjar slaughtered but also the civilian population. He went back to Agra after conquering the Fort and appointed his son-in-law, Ali Khan, as its governor.

Raja Ram Chandra enticed Ali Khan by offering him a large sum to buy the Fort. Akbar appointed one of his generals, Majnu Khan as the *subedar* of Manikpur. Majnu Khan launched an attack on the Kalinjar Fort. When Raja Ram Chandra heard that the Mughals had conquered Ranthambore, he handed over the Kalinjar Fort to Majnu Khan in order to avoid bloodshed. But Akbar being a reasonable ruler, gifted him a large estate in Alkhabad.

Akbar's life was spent largely in fighting battles and establishing a big empire. Tansen had composed a number of verses glorifying Akbar's victories. The Emperor aspired to become the all-powerful ruler of the country. Rulers of many big kingdoms came to Agra to offer their salutations and offered him lavish gifts. However, Raja Ram Chandra of Bandhavgarh was a very self-respecting, as well as valiant and resolute ruler. Once the Emperor Akbar observed that all the rulers had come to his *darbar* to pay their respects to him, except for Raja Ram

Chandra of Bandhavgarh. He sent his emissary to Bandhavgarh with an order that Raja Ram Chandra should promptly present himself at the Mughal *darbar*.

The emissary went to Bandhavgarh without losing time and conveyed Emperor Akbar's orders. Raja Ram Chandra in response sent his son Virbhadra to Akbar's *darbar*. The Emperor was not satisfied. As he was in Shahabad, he ordered a regiment to attack Bandhavgarh and bring Raja Ram Chandra to his *darbar* as a prisoner. But Virbhadra influenced the members of the *darbar* who convinced Akbar that instead of launching an attack on Bandhavgarh, he should send some respectable and influential persons and persuade Raja Ram Chandra to come to the Mughal *darbar*.

Tansen played a significant role in this matter. Akbar accepted that proposal and he sent Raja Birbal and Jahin Khan to Rewa. They used their persuasive abilities to the utmost and as a result Raja Ram Chandra went to Agra to meet Akbar. Raja Ram Chandra's mind was dominated by the feeling that his forefathers had obliged Akbar when Humayun fled westwards, after being routed by Shershah in the battle of Kanauj. He had left his wife Hameeda Bano under the protection of Raja Virbhanu of Bandhavgarh. Raja Ram Chandra felt a sense of pride and even conceit and that was the reason why he was unwilling to go to Agra.

But Raja Birbal and Jahin Khan persuaded him. He was not at all happy to bow in submission before the Mughal Emperor. Tansen kept him company throughout his stay at Agra, entertaining him with his music. He was sad when Raja Ram Chandra went back to Bandhavgarh, leaving in his heart his sweet remembrances. . .

Tansen resumed his routine singing in the *darbar* and sustained himself by the grace of the Emperor. He had grown older and once again he started thinking of taking to a life of asceticism. But he was a householder and had a family to maintain with its responsibilities.

At times, when he was alone, memories of Behat village surged in his mind. He was reminded of many childhood incidents. The houses of the village, the fields, the Shiva temple, Tani—everything came to his mind. He wondered where Tani could have gone. Was she alive at all? If she were alive, where was she and how was she living? Would he be able to meet her any time? Suddenly, he remembered that it was time to go to the *darbar*. He got dressed and left.

Emperor Akbar was very happy that day. Rani Jodhabai had given birth to a son. He ordered Tansen to sing for the occasion. Tansen tuned up the *tanpura* and sang in celebration of that happy occasion.

Akbar swayed with joy as Tansen sang. He promptly took off a necklace from his neck and presented it to Tansen. Later Tansen had to sell the necklace to fulfil an important commitment. Other court-singers had always been jealous of Tansen for all the special attention he received from the Emperor. When they learnt that Tansen had sold the necklace gifted to him by the Emperor, they seized this opportunity, and reported it to Akbar, 'He has insulted you by selling that necklace which you so graciously gifted to him.'

Akbar's eyes turned red with rage. He immediately summoned Tansen and ordered him to produce that necklace. Tansen felt very miserable. He confessed that he had sold it and sought the Emperor's permission to produce it after a few days. Helpless, Tansen saw some ray of hope only in Raja Ram Chandra, and so he set out for Rewa. When Raja Ram Chandra heard about Tansen's plight, he gave him a pair of his gem-studded wooden sandals saying, 'The value of these sandals is much more than Akbar's necklace.'

Tansen returned very humbly to Akbar's *darbar*. He said, '*Huzoor,* kindly accept these gem-studded wooden sandals in lieu of the necklace you gifted me.' Looking at those wooden sandals, Akbar's pride was humbled.

He said, 'Tansen, you are a truly great artist. Apart from me, there are countless others who admire your music. Keep these sandals. I am sure some admirer of yours has given them to you.' Tansen bowed to the Emperor gratefully and returned to his palace.

·That was a period when Akbar faced revolts, all over his empire. He had boundless love both for music and also the sword. He loved Tansen's music in the *darbar* and also the resounding thud of cannons and clanging of the swords on the battlefield.

Muzaffar Shah, whom he had appointed the governor in Gujarat, was persistently refusing to pay the *chauth* levy. Akbar repeatedly summoned him to the *darbar* and tried to persuade him but he remained defiant. When Akbar sent his officers to Gujarat to recover the dues from Muzaffar Shah, they were insulted and driven out of the *darbar*. Those officers returned to Agra and reported the matter to the Emperor. Akbar was furious and he pulled out his sword and commanded, 'Prepare for battle. We shall march towards Gujarat at the crack of dawn!'

The next morning, Akbar's army marched off towards Gujarat. The Emperor, dressed in armour, himself rode the elephant. The 'nine jewels' accompanied him. The army consisted of three thousand infantry men, four hundred and fifty cannons and innumerable elephants and horses.

Raja Udai Singh of Chittor had refused to surrender to the Mughal might. But Akbar did not intend to provoke the Rajputs at that particular juncture. He marched straight towards his destination and besieged Gujarat.

Muzaffar Shah offered token resistance and was caught alive. He was taken prisoner and presented before Akbar who ordered, 'Take him alive to Agra. We shall punish him by throwing him into an empty cage of a lion.'

The royal order was immediately carried out. Muzaffar Shah was put in an iron cage like a helpless bird. He was served food in earthen bowls. Although, Muzaffar Shah was a rebel, he tried many tactics so that Akbar would free him. But, Akbar was very shrewd and this time he refused to take Muzaffar Shah at his word. Akbar's army began to march towards Agra.

While returning to Agra, Akbar camped for a while, on the banks of the Sabarmati river. In that brief period, Akbar's flunkeys brought information that there were two charming sisters who sang very beautifully. They could be presented before the Emperor if he so commanded. Akbar, who was by now tired of battles and blood, was keen to return to the world of music. He agreed and ordered that the girls be brought to him.

The Emperor was pacing his sprawling, gorgeous tent, wearing slippers, studded with glittering diamonds. His turban too, had the dazzle of diamonds, pearls, sapphires and topaz. A jewel-studded sword hung at his waist. The attendants informed him that the two sisters had already arrived. 'Bring them in at once,' ordered Akbar.

The next moment two charming girls, fearful like deer, stood before Akbar. He was so fascinated by their beauty that he muttered, 'What wonderful creations of nature!'

Soon, Tansen also arrived. The girls started singing. They sang so well that both Akbar and Tansen were highly impressed. The girls trembled at the thought of their fate and wondered if their chastity would be violated. Suddenly Akbar ordered, 'Both of you will have to come with me to Agra.'

The sisters were startled. The elder sister ventured to ask, 'When are we to start from here?'

'Tomorrow morning,' Akbar informed them.

'Then both of us will present ourselves before you in the morning. Permit us to go home till then.'

Akbar nodded his assent and the two sisters Tome and Tani went home.

The stars shone in the sky. The moon was hidden behind the clouds. Tome and Tani could not sleep that night. They sat before the idol of Ranchhodji, singing *bhajans.* After they returned from the temple at five in the morning, they bathed and put some *tulsi* leaves in their mouths. Then, standing in front of the mirror they put on their best clothes and jewels.

The two sisters then sat in the palanquin which was already at their doorstep. They were carried to the bank of the Sabarmati where the Mughal army was camping. Tansen was already there, waiting for them. When the palanquin was lowered to the ground he lifted the curtain. What he saw made him shrink back in horror. Both the sisters had stabbed themselves and the cushions of the palanquin were soaked with the blood of those innocent girls.

Tansen rushed to Akbar to inform him about that tragedy. Akbar was very upset because, although a powerful Emperor, he had a delicate heart. He said with remorse, 'Tansen, I'm the real culprit. Let two memorials be erected for these sisters right here on the banks of the Sabarmati. And from now on, the names of these two sisters should be mentioned in whatever you sing. They were so pure-hearted!'

Tansen's eyes were filled with tears. He told himself, 'This is terrible! How many such deaths am I destined to witness?' Soon, the marble-cutters were at work and in a short time they carved two lovely, marble memorials for the sisters. But while the memorials were still being carved, the enraged Nagar Brahmins of the area attacked the Mughal army. There was a bloody fight in which a large number of Brahmins lost their lives.

Unhappy, on account of the two girls Akbar decided, 'I shall visit some holy places. . . .'

He was walking at the head of the army, in a general's costume carrying a small dagger from the South. Many nobles had already gone ahead to welcome him on his return to the capital.

When Akbar neared Fatehpur Sikri, Fhaizi sang a *ghazal* for him which meant: 'The pleasant breeze comes from Fatehpur (Sikri) because my Emperor is coming after a long journey. . .'

So Akbar arrived at Fatehpur Sikri. His victory over Gujarat was celebrated with great fanfare, music and dance. There were demonstrations of martial arts—sword fights, horse-riding and other items. At the end of all those celebrations, Muzaffar Shah was presented in the *darbar*. He was ordered, 'Fight with a living lion. You would be set free if you emerge alive from that fight. But if you are defeated, the lion will kill you in any case.'

There was a particular spot in the Agra Fort where such fights used to be arranged. Akbar went and sat there accompanied by his flunkeys. A hungry lion was let loose. Muzaffar Shah fought with the lion for a long time. But finally, a powerful blow of the lion, made Muzaffar Shah fall flat on the ground. The starving lion, satisfied its hunger by feasting on human flesh. Then after the show, the evening air was filled with the notes of music and the jingle of anklets.

# 27

Tansen was particularly attached to two places—Gwalior and Vrindavan. He visited Vrindavan pretty often. At the feet of Swami Haridas, he learnt the way of self-liberation and sang *bhajans.* His mind was that of a fakir's, although physically he lived amidst comfort and luxury. Now, he was also advancing in age and ideas of renunciation were beginning to dominate his mind. Any worldly attachment seemed meaningless to him. The company of generous-minded Raja Birbal and Rahim Khan Khana had a beneficial effect on him. Tansen now indulged in giving much charity. He bore the marriage expenses of the daughters of poor parents, built water kiosks and whatever else he could.

Once, while at Vrindavan, Surdas came to meet Swami Haridas. Tansen promptly rose and embraced him. They had long discussions about God and Tansen sang his compositions with great feeling.

Once Tansen sang a couplet in praise of Surdas.

When Surdas came to know about it, he himself went to Agra and sang at Tansen's doorstep:

> It is good fortune that God gave Sheshnag no ears. Otherwise, hearing Tansen sing, the earth and the mountain would have trembled!

Hearing Surdas at his door, Tansen came out rushing. He found Surdas there singing the couplet to the accompaniment of his *ektara.* Overwhelmed with emotion, Tansen hugged Surdas. It was a unique union of music, devotion and poetry. Surdas stayed with Tansen for a few days and then went to Parsauli. After Surdas left, Tansen was overcome with the idea of renunciation. He said to himself, 'This world is an illusion that ensnares you!' And he started composing verses in praise of God and singing them with abandon.

However, he still enjoyed the same honour and respect in Akbar's *darbar*. No other singer dared to come forward to compete with Tansen.

But one day, as Tansen sat in Akbar's *darbar*, Misri Singh appeared with his *veena*. He had been a singer in Akbar's *darbar*. Akbar was also there in a happy mood. He commanded, 'Let there be a competition between Tansen and Misri Singh.'

> Where did Sur's arrow strike and whom did Sur's pain affect.
> Whom did Sur's *padas* touch, so that the mind and the body swayed!

Abiding by his orders, the two musicians prepared to compete. Misri Singh was actually a very competent musician, but Tansen gave such a turn to the *raga* he had begun, that Misri Singh could not play that tune on his *veena*. Tansen cried out triumphantly, 'He is defeated!!'

Misri Singh could not stomach that insult. In a fury, he picked up the broad sword lying by his side and struck Tansen with it. Tansen started bleeding profusely. Akbar was furious. He glared at Misri Singh with red hot eyes and ordered that he should be hanged. Abul Fazl got up to carry out the order. He took Misri Singh with him and after some thought, instead of arranging for his execution, put him in an underground cellar. The royal physicians treated Tansen and he recovered in a few days. . .

A few days after that incident, a musical session was arranged in the *darbar* for which a *veena*-player was required. Akbar remembered Misri Singh and he regretted that he had ordered his execution. He said, 'I wish instead of hanging Misri Singh, I had only sent him to life-imprisonment!'

Abul Fazl was a very shrewd person. Seizing that opportunity he said, '*Huzoor*, Misri Singh is alive. I would present him if you wish.'

Akbar was startled, 'You say Misri Singh is alive? How is that possible? I had ordered that he should be hanged!'

Abul Fazl replied, 'He's alive, that's all. He was taken to the gallows twice, but didn't die. So, taking it as *Allah*'s wish, we made no further attempt to hang him. Instead, we put him in an underground cellar!'

'You did well, Abul Fazl.'

Misri Singh was brought from his prison-cell. He played his *veena* so wonderfully that people listened in breathless wonder.

But Akbar noticed that Tansen and Misri Singh were avoiding each other and were reluctant to exchange any words. Akbar was not happy about it. He asked both of them to come to him and ordered them to shake hands and then made an announcement, 'I declare that Misri Singh's daughter would be married to Tansen's son. I will personally attend the wedding and the expenses would be disbursed from the royal treasury.'

Hearing that announcement, cries of *Allah-O-Akbar* were raised in the *darbar*. Everyone was happy and excited. . .

While preparations for the marriage were afoot, an unexpected incident took place in Agra. The Emperor had ordered that no singer could sing in Agra in public, and if he did, he would have to compete with Tansen. One day, a group of men passed by the Agra Fort singing *bhajans* to the accompaniment of *mridanga* and cymbals. When the Emperor's sentries heard their singing, they were on the alert. Some of them rushed to the scene and hauled them up and presented them in the *darbar*. They were told, 'Are you not aware of the order which forbids anyone from singing in public without competing with Tansen?'

The men pleaded innocence. But they were told, 'Since you've disobeyed the order, you'll have to compete with Tansen.' They agreed. Tansen sang a *raga*, which the deer from the nearby forest heard and came running. Tansen put a garland around the neck of a deer and said to the *sadhus*, 'Now you sing and get the garland back from the neck of the deer.'

The men sang with great concentration, but the deer did not come. They were sentenced to life-imprisonment for disobeying the Emperor's orders. There was a young man called

Baiju in that group who was set free, though his father was put in jail.

Baiju started walking from Agra to Mathura. He continued walking all through the night. Stumbling and bleeding all over he reached Vrindavan. It was still dark and so, he fell asleep on the sands of the Yamuna.

In the morning, when Swami Haridas was on his way to bathe in the Yamuna, he saw Baiju lying on the sands with his feet still bleeding. Swami Haridas stopped in amazement and woke him up. He cleaned Baiju's wounds with water from the Yamuna and asked him who he was and from where he had come.

Baiju introduced himself and narrated the whole incident in Agra to him. Swami Haridas was very disturbed, that success had gone to the head of Tansen and he had become conceited. He felt so sad that he almost wept.

After bathing in the Yamuna, Swami Haridas came back to his ashram with Baiju. He gave him thorough training in music for ten years. At the end of the training he said, 'Baiju, now you're fully trained. Wherever you go, your wish would be fulfilled.'

Baiju was overwhelmed. He touched the feet of Swami Haridas and left for Agra.

Baiju was fair and handsome. Youth emanated from every pore of his body. One evening on his way to Agra, he stopped in a village. He ate some roasted grams which he had brought in his bag from Mathura and went to drink water at a well, where village women were filling their pots. They stood still when they noticed an unknown man coming towards them. A charming young woman took courage to ask, 'Who are you? From where are you coming and where do you want to go?'

Baiju replied very courteously, 'I'm coming from Vrindavan. I'm new to this place. I'm on my way to Agra.'

'Agra? Why are you going Agra.'

'You're asking why I want to go to Agra? I'm going there to sing.'

That young woman looked at Baiju in amazement. She asked, 'You must be out of your senses. Don't you know that no outsider can sing in Agra unless he defeats Tansen in singing? And anyone who is defeated is put in jail for life or is killed?'

Baiju said with fire in his eyes, 'I know it. Ten years ago my own father was jailed along with a group of men, when they were heard singing *bhajans.*'

The woman, who was in the prime of youth, looked at Baiju with disbelief.

'You'll go to Agra to sing and get arrested or killed, is it?'

'Yes, I'll go,' Baiju said, lifting his head high and his chest swelled with pride.

'Don't go, please,' the young woman entreated.

'Why shouldn't I? I'll go, whatever happens. I don't love my life so much!'

On hearing Baiju's words, the woman's thoughts travelled back into the past. Ten years ago, her own father who had gone to Agra with a group of sadhus, had also been put in jail. She had no brother or sister. And her mother too had died some time ago, pining for her husband.

Then she suddenly looked at Baiju and asked, 'Do you think you'll win in your competition with Tansen?'

'I will surely win. Swami Haridas has blessed me!'

The young woman thought for a while. Then she said, 'Well, if you're going, I'll also come with you. Will you take me along with you?'

Baiju was startled. He said with a smile, 'I've no objection. But you must first consult your family.'

'I've no family. My father was put in jail in Agra ten years ago. I don't know whether he is alive or not. And there is no one left in the family. I am all alone.'

'Very well, you may join me if you wish,' Baiju said. 'We can go to Agra together. But tell me your name at least?'

'I am Chanchala. You?'

'My name is Baiju.'

'Fine, Baiju, wait here for me. I'll tie my things in a bundle, and bid farewell to the people I know in the village. I won't be long.'

Chanchala went to her hut and tied a few things in a bundle. She hid a dagger inside her blouse as a precaution. She told the people of the village that she was going to Agra to make inquiries about her father and returned to Baiju who was waiting under a tree near the well.

They started at once and after walking for long, reached the Agra Fort. At the foot of the Fort, Baiju sang the *bhajan*. 'You are best protected at the feet of the Lord.' Soon the soldiers came rushing and dragged Baiju and Chanchala into Akbar's *darbar*.

'What is their crime?' the Emperor asked.

'*Huzoor*, this man was singing on the road! He had disobeyed your order.'

'Very well, singer!' said Akbar, 'Do you know you will have to compete with Tansen? You will be punished if you are defeated.'

Baiju said in a gentle, yet firm voice, 'But *Huzoor*, what if I win?'

'If you win, you will punish Tansen.'

'Very well, *Huzoor*. I am ready.'

Soon Tansen entered. He began singing and soon a herd of deer came running and Tansen garlanded one of them. The deer immediately ran back to the forest. Tansen said, 'Now call back that deer which had ran into the forest.'

Baiju tuned up the *tanpura* and started singing. Tansen was stunned to hear Baiju's deep and resonant voice. Soon that deer came back running. Baiju took off the garland from his neck and handed it over to Tansen. Tansen's adversaries were very happy. Then Tansen sang the *Malhar raga*. In no time the sky was dark with the clouds and it started raining. Akbar looked at Baiju who took the hint and also sang the *Malhar raga*. Again the sky turned dark and it started raining. Tansen was completely nonplussed. Baiju said, 'I am putting this garland round the neck of this idol. Tansen, now you sing and see if it comes to you.'

Tansen sang but the garland remained where it was. Then Baiju sang and with that the garland lifted from the idol and descended on Baiju. Tansen was defeated.

Akbar said, 'Baiju, you have won. What punishment would you give to Tansen?'

'*Huzoor*, I have already punished him.'

'How?' Akbar was amazed.

'His pride has been humbled. There can be no greater punishment. Kindly forgive him.'

Akbar was gratified by Baiju's generosity. He said, 'In that case, Baiju, ask for something.'

'*Huzoor*, ten years ago, Chanchala's father and mine, were put in jail along with a group of sadhus who were singing *bhajans* near your Fort. Kindly set them free.'

Akbar immediately ordered the release of all those prisoners. After ten years, Baiju and Chanchala were united with their fathers. That very day the marriage of Baiju and Chanchala was performed in a Shiva temple.

When Baiju was about to leave, Tansen asked, 'Under which guru did you learn music, my dear friend?'

'I am the disciple of Swami Haridas who lives in Vrindavan.'

'That explains why there is so much depth in your music.'

'Yes, by the grace of my guru.' And with a courteous bow, Baiju left with Chanchala and Tansen kept thinking about Baiju for a long time.

# 28

There was great hustle-bustle inside the Red Fort, although it appeared quiet from outside. At first, the heavy artillery and ammunition were brought out, followed by the gunners, who came down fluttering the Mughal flag. After the infantry men, elephants, horses, tents, rations, drums filled with water and huge utensils, came the generals riding the elephants. Among the 'nine-jewels' were Rahim Khan Khana, Abul Fazl, Raja Todarmal, Raja Birbal and Tansen in military costume, riding on their carriages. Finally, Emperor Akbar emerged from the fort. A military operation was being undertaken to conquer Chittor, without which Mughal power could not be fully consolidated in Hindustan.

The Rajputs of Chittor were not prepared to accept Akbar's suzerainty on any account. Dying for the sake of honour was child's play for the Rajputs. Raja Udai Singh of Chittor had refused to come to Agra even when he had been summoned. Hence, the Emperor himself had set out, with his large army, to combat the Rajput's arrogance.

The Mughal army laid siege to the fort of Shivpur of Ranthambore. The Rajputs could not stand upto the might of the Mughal army. Hence, they went to Mada Surjan of Bundi. Akbar left one of his generals Nazar Bahadur behind and proceeded to Kota. After a victorious battle he handed over the charge of the fort to Shah Muhammed Kandhari and he surrounded the Fort of Gagron. From there, he sent some contingents to Malwa and he himself marched towards Chittor, fluttering his flag of victory.

Udai Singh's son, Shakti Singh, had returned from Dhaulpur and given advance information to his father about Akbar's planned invasion. Maharaja Udai Singh sent instructions to all the princes and generals. Jaimal Rathod, Rawat Sain Das, Chudavat, Rawat Sahib Khan Chauhan, Rana Sultan, Isar Das Chauhan, Chaudavat Fatta, Rao Ballu Solanki and others joined them in the assembly. Among the princes who were present were also Pratap Singh and Shakti Singh.

It was decided that Maharana Udai Singh should go into the jungles along with all the women in the harem, while all the young men and the princes would fight the battle. Maharana Udai Singh was not willing at first, but subsequently came round and leaving eight thousand soldiers in the Chittor fort, went into the jungles in the hill regions of south Mewar. The Rajputs intended to fight from the fort.

When the sky cleared and Akbar had the fort surveyed, it was found that the mountain ridge extended upto two *kos* and the circumference was five *kos*. Akbar could lay the siege to the fort in about a month's time. He arranged his forces facing the Lakhota Gate which was inside the fort. Inside the fort, Medatia Rathod Jaimal Viram Devat arranged his forces. Raja Todarmal and Kasim Khan took charge of another front, and Rawat Saidas took charge of the front inside the fort too. At the foot of the turret, Asif Khan and Vazir Khan stood in readiness.

But the Chittor fort was invincible, like steel. Akbar got tired of the siege. He felt like enjoying music. He sent for Tansen who arrived promptly and began the *raga Mian Ki Malhar*. For a long time the generals listened to him. When darkness descended, Akbar took a walk at the foot of the fort, along with his trusted generals. During the walk, he ordered two mines to be laid facing the turret of the fort. Thousands of hands got busy digging earth and collecting stones. Akbar, lavishly rewarded the workers. However, many of them were killed, by the cannons fired at them by the Rajput soldiers.

One day, the Rajput generals inside the fort decided to send a message of truce to the Emperor. They thought it would be good if the Emperor Akbar accepted the truce, but if he did not agree, then war was inevitable.

Accordingly, Rawat Sahib Chauhan and Dodia Takur Sanda approached Emperor Akbar with a message of truce. They pleaded with Akbar '*Shahenshah* Akbar, we are not at fault in any way. The Maharana has gone away to the jungles in the hills. We agree to pay you in money and give other gifts as well.'

Everyone advised Akbar to accept the proposal, because it was difficult to conquer the fort, situated at that height. Tansen also said, 'Intoxicating notes of music are far better than the anguished cries of bloodshed. Accept the truce, *Huzoor*!'

But Akbar was not willing to relent. At last he said after some thought, 'Nothing can be done unless Rana Udai Singh comes to me.'

Dodia Sanda said, 'Rana Udai Singh cannot come. Who knows where he is living inside these jungles!'

Akbar said, 'We cannot stop fighting. Ask for anything else and it would be granted.'

'No, we want nothing else. *Eklingji Bhagwan* has given us everything,' said the Rajputs generals and returned to the fort.

War trumpets were sounded. Swords, lances, daggers, cannons, arrows, and all weapons were kept ready. The Rajput blood was beginning to boil. The stage was set for battle.

So, the call was given and the battle began. Up on the fort fluttered the saffron flags of the Rajputs and down below the green flags of the Mughals. At the foot of the fort, the two mines ordered by Akbar were ready. The mine facing the Chittor fort was split into two, with 120 maunds of ammunition in one and 80 maunds in the other.

The generals in the fort also came to know about the mine and prepared themselves for the fight to the finish. Akbar's army was just awaiting the moment when the wall of the fort would blow up so that they could rush inside. The mine exploded on Wednesday. One of the turrets of the fort was blown up and fifty soldiers died. The Mughal soldiers were under the impression that the way had opened for them and they rushed in large numbers. But in the meantime the other mine exploded and countless Mughal soldiers died. However, overnight the Rajputs repaired the damaged portions of the fort. In the morning, the battle started again.

Inside the fort, a bullet hit the knee of Jaimal, the son of Viramdev Rathod of Medta. At that moment, Jaimal called all the soldiers to him and said, 'We are left without any food provisions. Let us burn our women and children and open the gates of the fort! And then, let all the Rajputs pick up their swords and whatever other weapons they have handy and fight the enemy and die with glory and dignity which would entitle them to go to heaven.'

Without a second thought, the soldiers piled up of logs of wood to make pyres and burnt their women and children. Thousands of women including Rani Padmavati and Isar Das, daughter, Bhagwatibai jumped into the flames to save their honour. The Rajput soldiers smeared their ashes on their foreheads.

The leaping flames were noticed by the Mughal soldiers. Raja Bhagwandas of Amber said, 'It is the fire of Rajput women immolating themselves. Now the Rajputs will fight desperately without any fear of death.'

That was enough provocation for Akbar. He commanded that the Mughal army should force their way into the fort next morning. But Tansen, who was standing nearby was very unhappy and sad. He said to himself, 'Man stoops to such depths and destroys life and sheds blood for the sake of his own happiness and prosperity! But when he has to depart from this world, he can take nothing with him!'

He felt like withdrawing from the scene and going away somewhere. But he was under the Emperor's command to remain where he was. Such was his sadness, that he wished he could be freed from his obligations to the Emperor. But the thought of Akbar's kindness and favours constrained him and he resigned, however, unwittingly, to his situation. . . .

The day had hardly dawned, when the Rajputs threw open the gates of the fort. Kalla carried Jaimal with his wounded leg on his shoulder and both of them fought a ferocious battle with their swords. But despite the resistance put up by the Rajput soldiers, the Mughal army rushed inside the fort. Many soldiers died on both sides and the earth was soaked with blood. Even common people jumped into the fray and died in large numbers.

By afternoon, Akbar conquered the fort. He stayed there for three days after which he handed charge of the fort to Asif Khan and left on a pilgrimage to Ajmer Sharif. On the way he received information about an uprising in Nagarkot.

Akbar commanded Raja Birbal and Hussain Kuli Khan to march to Nagarkot with an army contingent and to bring the Rajput king Jaichand to him as a prisoner. Raja Birbal marched with the army to Nagarkot to put down the revolt. In the meantime, Akbar came back after his pilgrimage to Ajmer. Soon after his return to Agra the Mughal victory over Chittor was celebrated with Tansen's music, dances and a ***mushaira***. Akbar sat on the throne and the poet Gang sang a poem, full of adulation for Akbar. The ***Diwan-e-Aam*** reverberated with applause. Akbar's smiling lips expressed his extreme happiness. Then Fhaizi became impatient to recite a poem.

While cries of praise for the poets singing Akbar's glory were still in the air, a messenger came to the *darbar*. He looked tense and distraught. He *salaamed* Akbar by bowing thrice and kept staring at Akbar vacantly. Surprised by his unexpected appearance, Akbar asked, 'What is the matter? Why are you staring like that?'

The messenger could not reply immediately. When Akbar repeated the question, he said in broken words, 'There is bad news, *Shahenshah-e-Alam*. Raja Birbal has been killed in the battle of Nagarkot.'

Akbar could not believe his ears. One of his 'nine-jewels' gone forever! Tears glided down Akbar's cheeks. It was the same Akbar who had seen thousands of soldiers in pools of blood on the battlefield. And there was no count of the soldiers whose chests had been pierced with his sword! That same Akbar had now broken down. Birbal's death completely shattered him. He was overcome with sorrow. As for Tansen, he started crying inconsolably. And Rahim Khan Khana lamented, resting his head on Tansen's shoulder. Raja Todarmal, Raja Man Singh, Fhaizi and others had also broken into tears instantly. Akbar was lost in memories of the past. He muttered in a gentle voice which everybody heard:

> You gave everything to everyone
> But gave misery to none,
> You gave us misery
> Only after you died.

The city of Agra was drowned in sorrow. The joyous celebrations on the conquest of Chittor suddenly ceased. The *darbar* dispersed amidst flowing tears.

Tansen had now reached a stage when he no longer felt at ease in the employ of the Emperor. Bloodshed, death cries, tears and the death of innocent people had rudely shaken the artist. He had abhorred the battlefield all along. He loved not the sword but the flute. The fakir in him was once again moved to sorrow. He said to himself, '*Yah Allah*, what is this world you have created!'

# 29

Now, Tansen had grown quite old. His health was also deteriorating. And Birbal's death had broken his heart. Then one day, he received the news of his daughter Saraswati's death, during childbirth. Tansen's delicate heart could not withstand all these blows.

Saraswati was buried in Ajmer, at a little distance from the tomb of Khwaja Moinuddin Chishti. Tansen often went to Ajmer where he sat for hours together before the grave of his dear daughter, thinking about the real meaning of life. To him, life and death appeared the same.

At times, Tansen was lost in his memories of the past. Behat village, his parents, the Shiva temple, his first meeting with Tani, Mohammad Gaus, Swami Haridas all came alive. The enchanting scenery of Bandhavgarh, the kind favours of Raja Ram Chandra Waghela, as well as the graces showered on him by *Shahenshah-e-Hindustan* Akbar became vivid. At last he would get up. Then casting a last look at Saraswati's grave, he would mount his horse and return to Agra.

Tansen was deeply attached to Saraswati. All along the way from Ajmer to Agra, he would remember incidents from her childhood to the time of her marriage. Like this, one day he returned to Agra with a sorrowful heart and a heavy step. All the wealth, position and honours that had been bestowed on him seemed meaningless. He thought to himself, 'What is this world? Why are we born after all? We indulge in all kinds of activities during our lifetime, but in the end, we depart, leaving everything behind! With passage of time, even the dear ones forget their dead.' He philosophized about life and with those thoughts crowding his mind, he slept off. . .

The current of the river at the Ganga *ghat* in Varanasi was very strong, that day. Waves covered the water's surface. The sun was about to rise and its early light had turned the river into a golden sheet. Small boats plied on the river, swaying like swans. The sweet singing of *bhajans* filled the air. An old woman at the Ganga *ghat* was guarding the clothes of visiting pilgrims. She applied sandalpaste on the foreheads of those who returned after bathing in the Ganga. That woman, though aged, was still remarkably beautiful. Inspite of her grey hair, broken teeth, wrinkled face and her body stooping with age, she looked lovely.

Suddenly, there was a commotion on the *ghat*. That old woman inquired, from one of the men hurrying past her, 'What is happening, my son? Why are so many people rushing around?'

The man replied, 'Tulsidasji has come to bathe in the Ganga. People are excited to see him here.'

'Would Tulsidasji come to my *ghat* too?' she asked eagerly.

'How do I know?' said the man and went towards the river for his bath.

After some time, Tulsidasji came to that old woman's *ghat*. She had been listening to the recitation of the Tulsi *Ramayana* all along. When Tulsidasji came to her for the sandalpaste she asked him, 'Baba, how is it that one feels at peace after listening to the recitation of the *Ramayana*?'

Tulsidas replied, 'That is because all our evil thoughts are dispelled at the feet of Rama. His feet have that power, *Mai*!'

'Then why doesn't man think of these things *Baba*!'

'That is because of his attachment to this worldly life! Man gets deeper and deeper into it. He is rarely able to free himself from it.'

'*Baba*,' the old woman said, 'I have lived in Varanasi for sixty years. But today after meeting you, I have found peace of mind for the first time. I think I won't live long now. I would like to die in the earth where I was born.'

'It can happen only when one has earned great merit by doing good deeds in life.' With that Tulsidas took leave of the old woman.

The old woman, with her failing health, had been living all by herself. After spending so many years at Varanasi she was now possessed with the desire to go back to her village and die there. She got up from the *ghat* and went to her hut. She tied her things in a bundle and set out in a bullock-cart which was going towards the village.

But once the bullock-cart started moving, she had second thoughts. 'People come to Kashi to die, whereas I am going back to my village! I have left that village long ago. Who is there in the village, who would know me? No one would even know that I was born there, I had played and grown in its earth. People say that one gets *moksha* by dying in Kashi.' But again she thought that the earth of her village was in no way less sacred then the lap of the Ganga. So, the bullock-cart moved on and its constant, jerky movements sent her to sleep. After a whole night's journey, the old woman moved to another cart which was going to Gwalior.

Tansen had reached the ripe old age of eighty. His voice had become very feeble with old age, the death of dear ones and illness. He did go to the *darbar* whenever called, but he always took his sons with him. They acted as his supporting singers.

A little later, Tansen contracted a serious illness. He withdrew from everything and devoted himself only to singing the praises of God. He composed a couplet which meant, 'Oh God, I feel miserable at the thought of my sins. I see only darkness all around. Abandoning my dear ones, wealth and property, I am surrendering myself at your feet. Protect me.' Lying on his bed, Tansen hummed such couplets.

Now everyone in Agra knew that Tansen would not live long. There was a stream of visitors from morning to night. One day, Emperor Akbar himself came to see him. Expressing his last wish Tansen said, 'Kindly bury me by the side of my *Ustad*, Muhammad Gaus at Gwalior.' Akbar sadly nodded his head.

Royal physicians treated Tansen but his illness was getting worse day by day. He was finding it hard to breathe. Then on 16 April, 1589. . . Tansen's condition was causing anxiety right from the morning. The physicians were giving him different kinds of potions to drink. He was unconscious. His wife and sons were by his side, sorrow and anxiety in their eyes. Tansen was unable to breathe because of congestion in his chest. In the afternoon, he had a mild hiccup, his head dropped to one side. Cries of lamentation filled the air of the chamber. All those present wept copiously. The body of that king of musicians lay there lifeless.

Akbar was duly informed about Tansen's sad demise. Raising his blank eyes to the sky, Akbar mumbled '*Yah Allah*!' And then he ordered that Tansen's bier be taken out like those of fakirs and *ouliyas*. He should be taken to Gwalior with full honours and be buried by the side of Muhammad Gaus. Thousands joined Tansen's funeral procession, as his coffin was carried towards Gwalior. . .

The morning sun had already appeared in the sky. The sun rays were spreading their light, cutting through the early morning haze. When the funeral procession reached Gwalior, the whole city turned up to witness the scene. As they reached the tomb of Muhammad Gaus, Tansen's body was lowered on the ground, near the dug out grave. A little later, an old woman, carrying a bundle and walking with the help of her staff, cut through the crowd and went up to Tansen's body. She stood motionless for some time and then sat at his headside. Very gently, she lifted the shroud and for a long time stared at Tansen's face with tearful eyes. Then she got up and herself dropped on Tansen's feet. There was great commotion in the crowd. They sprinkled water on her face. They shook her. But she showed no signs of life. Looking at her motionless body they said, '*Yah Allah*! She is dead! Who is she?' Not knowing who she was, people began moving away from her.

Just at that moment, an old man from Behat village who was in the crowd, recognised the old woman. He cried, 'I'll tell you. This is Tani from Behat village. She was madly in love with Tansen. She had gone away from the village many years ago. Nobody knew where she had gone! But see her dedication!

In the last moment she somehow reached this place and breathed her last at Tansen's feet!'

Soon after, Tansen was buried and Tani's body was consigned to the flames. Tansen and Tani thus died together. And Tansen's music and the legend of their love lived ever after!

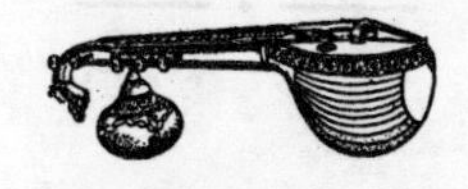

# Glossary

*Alap*: The contemplative unfolding and development of the raga to reveal its form and spirit.

*Arati*: A hymn of praise, sung at the hour of lighting the lamps.

*Bahar* (Raga): A raga celebrating the spring.

*Bhajan*: A devotional song; a song of *bhakti*.

*Dhruvapad, Dhrupad*: A musical form of Hindustani classical music of great dignity and sombreness, older than the *khayal*. It has four components. Raja Mansingh of Gwalior (1486-1517) is considered the father of the *dhrupad*.

*Geet*: Any piece of poetry which can be set to music.

*Machan*: A hunting platform.

*Maharasa*: The divine dance of Radha and Krishna with the adoring *gopis* and cowherds.

*Megh Malhar* (Raga): A raga celebrating the monsoon.

*Mohar*: A gold coin or sovereign weighing 8 gms.

*Nayika-bhed*: Classification of *nayikas* (heroines) in classical Sanskrit literature.

*Pada*: A poetic composition with verses of lyrics. Each verse is scored to music.

*Paan*: A betel leaf.

*Phaag*: Songs of the Holi festival which comes in March or *Phalgun*.

*Prasad*: A sacred offering.

*Qavali*: A musical composition, usually sung in a group. In the 13th century, this form was used by followers of Sufi saints to spread the message of Sufism. *Qavals* are *qavali* singers.

*Sarangi*: A string instrument played with a bow.

*Sarpada*: A raga.

*Saajgiri*: Virtuosity in playing an instrument.

*Sohar*: A song to celebrate the birth of a child.

*Shairi*: Musical recitation of Urdu poetry.

*Shiva Linga*: A symbol of Shiva.

*Tarana*: A composition where meaningless syllables like *nom*, *tom* and *tana* are used to extrapolate the raga and produce rhythmic delights.

*Varag*: Silver leaf.

—— ✼ ——

# *Some Famous Compositions of Tansen*

—— ✼ ——

## *Raga Basant*

Oh, my friend! Let us go to the bowers
Where Krishna plays with Radha in the bloom of spring.
Radha the embodiment of beauty and virtue wears a necklace
And a lovely garland adorns her.
Bees are humming in the garden
And Radha-Krishna come to the *Saal-Vana* today.
The *koels*, parrots, and pigeons coo,
Bees hover above *Manmohan* (Krishna),
The Lord of Tansen frolics there, singing the *raga Basant.*
Blessed is one to witness such a sight.

❖

## राग बसन्त

चलो सखि कुँज धाम, खेलत बसन्त स्याम,
संग लिए राधो नाम रूप गुन जागरी,
मुक्तहार रूमाल माल केतका के सुक.
जल औरन प्रकटवन फूलवन बागरी,
बोलत कोकिल कीर कपोत गुँजत भँवर समीर
धीर उड़त मनमोहन आमेरी
तान सेन के प्रभु प्रितमिलि केल करत गावत बसन्त राग धन्य दरस भागरी,

| 1 | 2 | 3 | 4 | 5 | 6 | 7 | 8 | 9 | 10 | 11 | 12 | 13 | 14 | 15 | 16 |
|---|---|---|---|---|---|---|---|---|---|---|---|---|---|---|---|
| म | ध | न | सं | रें | सां | न | सं | मधन | संरें | नध | गम | मग | रे | स | स |
| च | लो | स | खी | कुं | ज | धा | म | खेऽऽ | ऽऽ | लत | ऽऽ | बसं | त | स्या | म |
| स | स | म | मग | म | म | ग | ग | मध | नसं | सं | स | नध | न | म | ग |
| सं | ग | लि | एऽ | रा | धे | ना | म | रूऽ | पऽ | गु | न | जाऽ | ऽ | ग | री |
| मध | न | सं | सं | संरें | सं | न | सं | नध | नि | म | ग | म | ग | रे | स |
| मुऽ | क्ता | हा | र | रुमा | ल | मा | ल | केऽ | त | का | के | सु | क | ज | ल |

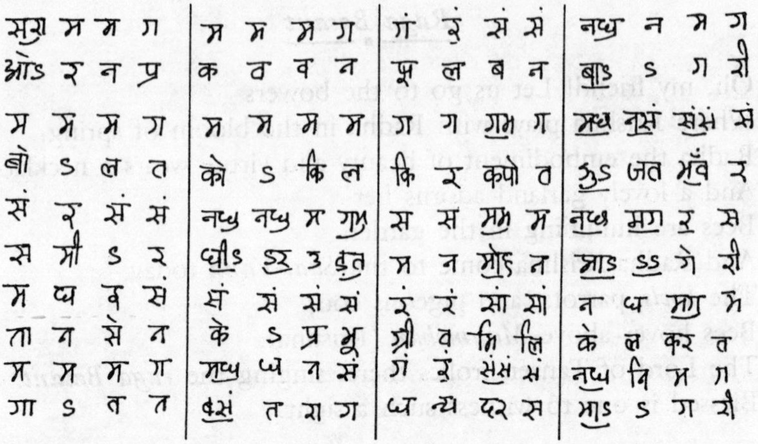

| | | | | | | | | | | | | | | | |
|---|---|---|---|---|---|---|---|---|---|---|---|---|---|---|---|
| सग | म | म | ग | म | म | म | ग | गं | रें | सं | सं | नध | न | म | ग |
| ओऽ | र | न | प्र | क | व | व | न | फू | ल | ब | न | बाऽ | ऽ | ग | री |
| म | म | म | ग | म | म | म | म | ग | ग | गम | ग | मध | नसं | संसं | सं |
| बो | ऽ | ल | त | को | ऽ | कि | ल | कि | र | कपो | त | गुऽ | जत | भँव | र |
| सं | र | सं | सं | नध | नध | म | गम | स | स | मम | म | नध | मग | र | स |
| स | मी | ऽ | र | धीऽ | ऽऽ | उ | हुत | म | न | मोऽ | न | भाऽ | ऽऽ | गे | री |
| म | ध | ध | सं | सं | सं | सं | सं | रं | रं | सां | सां | न | ध | मग | म |
| ता | न | से | न | के | ऽ | प्र | भू | ग्री | व | मि | लि | के | ल | कर | त |
| म | म | म | ग | मध | ध | न | सं | गं | रें | संसं | सं | नध | नि | म | ग |
| गा | ऽ | त | त | धसं | त | रा | ग | ध | न्य | दर | स | भाऽ | ऽ | ग | री |

## ***Raga Tilak Kamod***

Murari is the Lord of the Three Worlds,
Indra the Lord of Gods,
Kuber, the Lord of Wealth and
Sheshnag, the Lord of animals.
Vishnu is the Lord of Milk and Wind,
And of the Sun which dons the jewel of Kaustubh.
The Lord of all good deeds is Ganapati,
The Lord of strength and physical prowess is Hanuman.
Narada, the prime devotee, excels at the *veena* and *mridanga*.
With folded hands, Shripati Kavi prays that you,
Master of all men, Akbar Badshah, and Tansen live forever.

## राग तिलक कामोद

मुरारे त्रिभुवनपति, इन्द्र सुरनपति, धनेश धनपति, शेषनाग पानपति॥
क्षीर औ दधि सलिलपति कौस्तुभमणि रत्नपति, दिनकर दिनपति नारायण कमलापति
शशिउर गनपति, हनुमन्त बलनपति, नारद भक्तनपति वीण मृदंग बाजनपति॥
कर मिनति कहे श्रीपति, चिरन्जीव रहो, क्षत्रपति, अकबरशाहे नरनपति,
तानसेन ताननपति।

| × ग | ग | म | म | म | पप | पप | ध | मप | मग |
|---|---|---|---|---|---|---|---|---|---|
| मु | रा | रे | ऽ | ऽ | त्रिभु | वन | प | तिऽ | ऽऽ |
| स | न | प | प | ध | म | प | ग | म | ग |
| इन | ऽ | द्र | ऽ | सु | र | न | प | ति | ऽ |
| र | ग | म | प | प | न | सां | रें | न | सं |
| ध | ने | ऽ | ऽ | श | ध | न | प | ति | ऽ |
| सं | सं | न | प | प | ध | म | प | गम | गस |
| शे | ष | न | ऽ | ग | प | न | प | तिऽ | ऽऽ |
| म | पं | न | न | न | सं | संसं | सं | सं | — |
| क्षी | ऽ | रौ | द | धि | स | लिल | प | ति | ऽ |

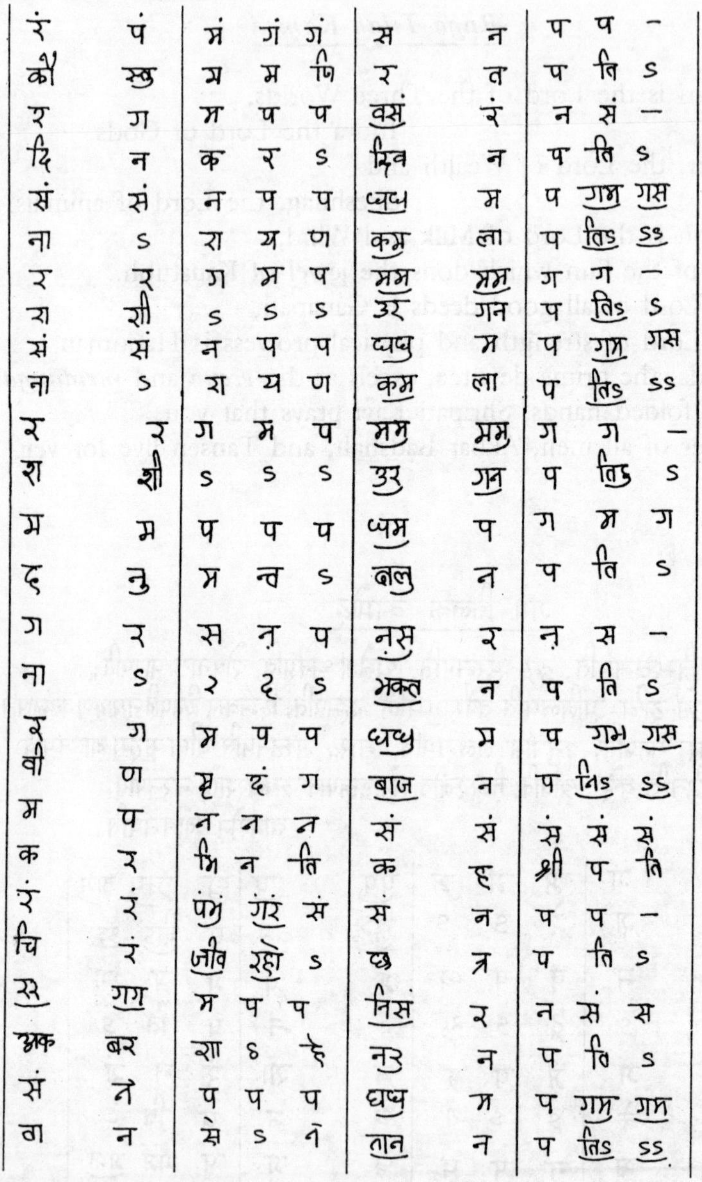

| रं | पं | मं | गं | गं | स | न | प | प | — |
|---|---|---|---|---|---|---|---|---|---|
| कौ | स्तु | म | म | णि | र | त | प | ति | ऽ |
| र | ग | म | प | प | वसं | रं | न | सं | — |
| दि | न | क | र | ऽ | दिव | न | प | ति | ऽ |
| सं | सं | न | प | प | ध्यध | म | प | गम | गस |
| ना | ऽ | रा | य | ण | कम | ला | प | तिऽ | ऽऽ |
| र | र | ग | म | प | मम | मम | ग | ग | — |
| रा | शी | ऽ | ऽ | ऽ | उर | गन | प | तिऽ | ऽ |
| सं | सं | न | प | प | ध्यध | म | प | गम | गस |
| ना | ऽ | रा | य | ण | कम | ला | प | तिऽ | ऽऽ |
| र | र | ग | म | प | मम | मम | ग | ग | — |
| श | शी | ऽ | ऽ | ऽ | उर | गन | प | तिऽ | ऽ |
| म | म | प | प | प | ध्पम | प | ग | म | ग |
| द | नु | म | न्व | ऽ | कलु | न | प | ति | ऽ |
| ग | र | स | ऩ | प | ऩस | र | ऩ | स | — |
| ना | ऽ | र | द | ऽ | भक्त | न | प | ति | ऽ |
| र | ग | म | प | प | धध | म | प | गम | गस |
| वी | ण | सू | दं | ग | बाज | न | प | निऽ | ऽऽ |
| म | प | न | न | न | सं | सं | सं | सं | सं |
| क | र | मि | न | ति | क | ह | श्री | प | ति |
| रं | रं | पमं | गरं | सं | सं | न | प | प | — |
| चि | रं | जीव | रहो | ऽ | छ | त्र | प | ति | ऽ |
| सर | गग | म | प | प | निसं | र | न | सं | स |
| अक | बर | शा | ऽ | हे | नउ | न | प | ति | ऽ |
| सं | ने | प | प | प | धध | म | प | गम | गम |
| वा | न | से | ऽ | नें | तान | न | प | तिऽ | ऽऽ |

## *Raga Yaman Kalyan*

Oh, Madhava!
Let the happiness of being at your feet last forever.
May you joyfully dwell in my heart.
The flute rests on your lips.
You bear the crown of dharma.
Myriads of your images appear when your name is uttered.
Says Mian Tansen, by your *darshan*,
He gains bliss of body, mind and wealth.

❖

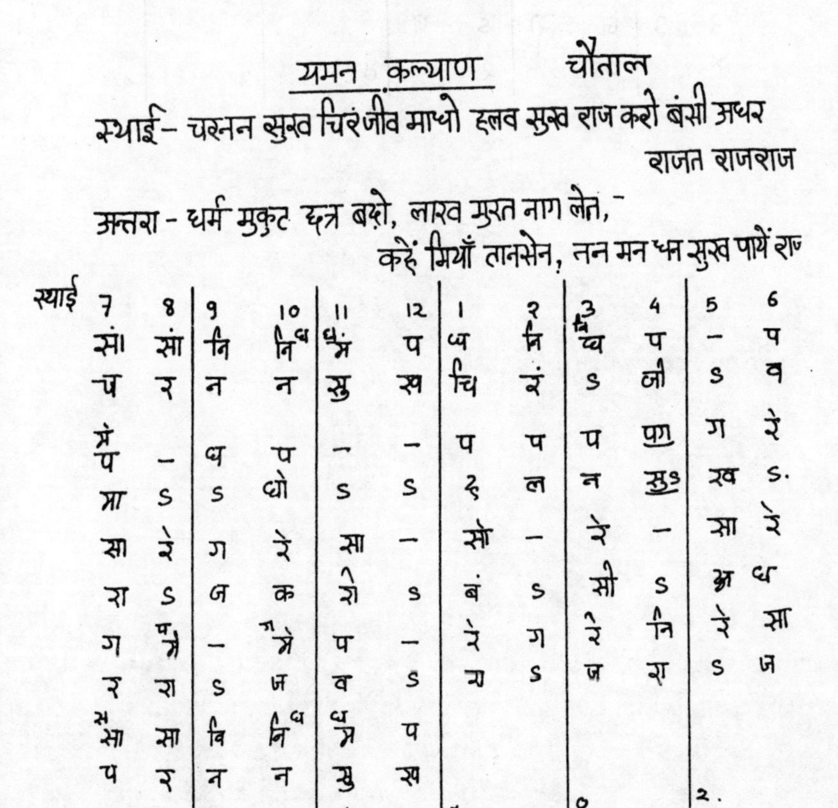

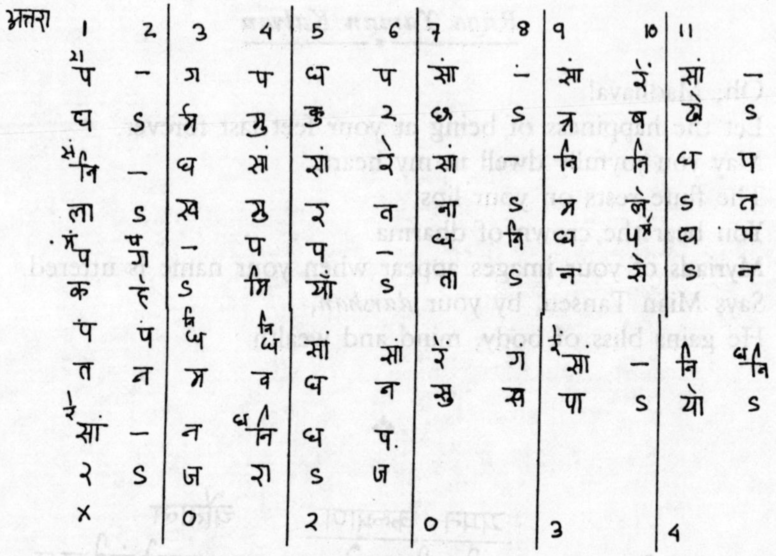

| अन्तरा | 1 | 2 | 3 | 4 | 5 | 6 | 7 | 8 | 9 | 10 | 11 | |
|---|---|---|---|---|---|---|---|---|---|---|---|---|
| | (सा)प | — | ग | प | ध | प | सां | — | सां | रें | सां | — |
| | ध | ऽ | मे | मु | कु | २ | छ | ऽ | ग | ब | ढे | ऽ |
| | (सं)नि | — | ध | सां | सां | रें | सां | — | नि | नि | ध | प |
| | ला | ऽ | ख | मु | र | त | ना | ऽ | म | ले | ऽ | त |
| | (मं)प | पग | — | प | प | — | ध | नि | ध | (म)प | ध | प |
| | क | हे | ऽ | मि | याँ | ऽ | ता | ऽ | न | से | ऽ | न |
| | पं | पं | (नि)ध | (नि)ध | सां | सां | रें | गं | (रें)सां | — | नि | धनि |
| | त | न | म | व | ध | न | सु | स | पा | ऽ | यो | ऽ |
| | (रें)सां | — | न | धनि | ध | प. | | | | | | |
| | र | ऽ | ज | रा | ऽ | ज | | | | | | |
| | x | | 0 | | 2 | | 0 | | 3 | | 4 | |

## *Raga Jai Jaivanti*

Oh Queen! You the one worthy of respect,
You are the symbol of *Vaikunth* and learning.
You are both, latent and manifest.
In water or on earth, you prevail everywhere.
You are the universal, supreme goddess.
You are Tansen's mother.
How can I describe your intensity?
You have made my speech,
That is my singing well-known to all.

❖

## राग . जयजयवन्ती

जयमाल रानी, तू मान गाजी.
विद्या सरस्वती, बैंकुण्ठ की निशानी.
तू ही गुप्त तू ही प्रगट, तू ही जल थल में
सकल श्रेष्ठ मानि तू, आदि भवानी॥
तानसेन की माई, कहा कहूँ प्रभुताई.
जगत विदित कर दीनो, मेरी बानी तैं ने।

| स्थाई- | 1 | 2 | 3 | 4 | 5 | 6 | 7 | 8 | 9 | 10 | 11 | 12 |
|---|---|---|---|---|---|---|---|---|---|---|---|---|
| | (ग)रे | (ग)रे | – | (ग)रे | ग | (रे)गप | म | – | ग | मरे | ग | सा |
| | ज | य | ऽ | मा | ऽ | लऽ | रा | ऽ | ऽ | ऽऽ | ऽ | नी |
| | (सा)नि़ | – | सा | रे | रेग | रेस | सा | – | रे | नि़ | ध़ | प |
| | तू | ऽ | ऽ | मा | ऽऽ | नऽ | गा | ऽ | ऽ | ऽ | ऽ | जी |
| | – | सा | – | रे | म | प | (प)नि | (नि)म | प | नि | सां | सां |
| | ऽ | वि | ऽ | द्या | ऽ | स | र | ऽ | ऽ | स्व | ऽ | ती |
| | – | सां | नि | धप | ध | म | (ध)प | ध | म | गरे | ग | सा |
| | ऽ | बैं | ऽ | कुंऽ | ऽ | ठ | की | ऽ | नि | शा | ऽ | नी |

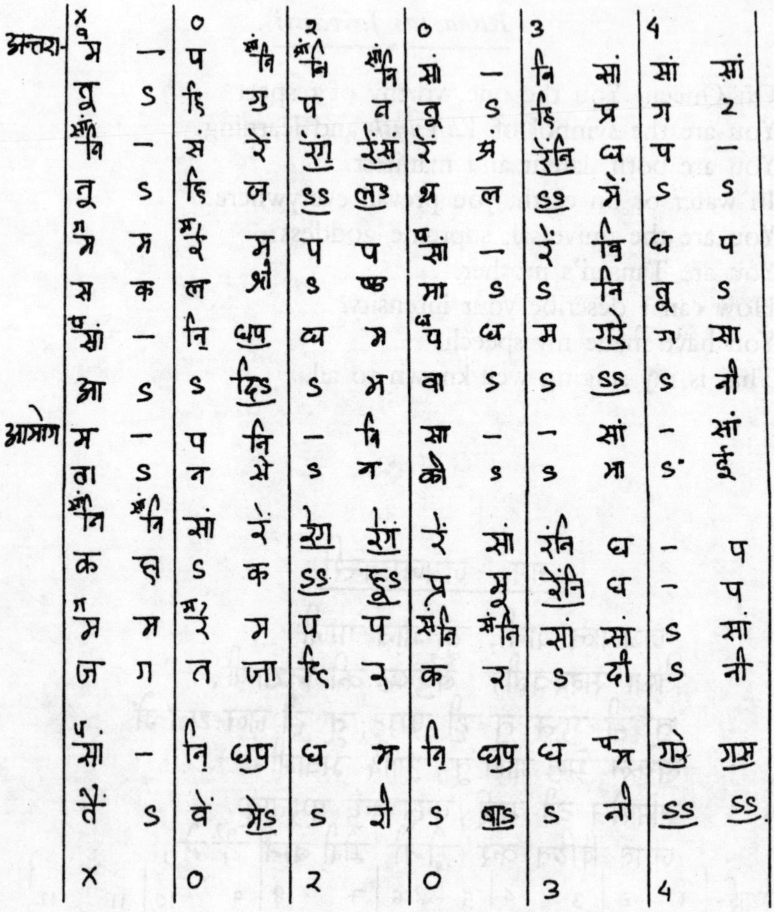

| | x | | 0 | | 2 | | 0 | | 3 | | 4 | |
|---|---|---|---|---|---|---|---|---|---|---|---|---|
| अन्तरा | [ग]म | — | प | [सां]नि | [सां]नि | [सां]नि | सां | — | नि | सां | सां | सां |
| | तू | S | हि | गु | प | न | तू | S | हि | प्र | ग | ट |
| | [सां]नि | — | सं | रें | रेंगं | रेंसं | रें | सं | रेंनि | ध | प | — |
| | तू | S | हि | ज | SS | लS | थ | ल | SS | में | S | S |
| | [ग]म | म | [म]रे | म | प | प | [प]सां | — | रें | नि | ध | प |
| | स | क | ल | श्री | S | ष्ट | मा | S | S | नि | तू | S |
| | [प]सां | — | नि | धप | ध | म | [ध]प | ध | म | गरे | ग | सा |
| | आ | S | S | दिS | S | म | वा | S | S | SS | S | नी |
| आभोग | म | — | प | नि | — | नि | सा | — | — | सां | — | सां |
| | ता | S | न | से | S | न | को | S | S | मा | S | ई |
| | [सां]नि | [सां]नि | सां | रें | रेंगं | रेंगं | रें | सां | रेंनि | ध | — | प |
| | क | रू | S | क | SS | हुS | प्र | भु | रेंनि | ध | — | प |
| | [ग]म | म | [म]रे | म | प | प | [सं]नि | [सं]नि | सां | सां | S | सां |
| | ज | ग | त | जा | हि | र | क | र | S | दी | S | नी |
| | [प]सां | — | नि | धप | ध | म | नि | धप | ध | [प]म | गरे | गसा |
| | तैं | S | वें | मेंS | S | री | S | बाS | S | नी | SS | SS |
| | x | | 0 | | 2 | | 0 | | 3 | | 4 | |

## *Raga Shankara (Dhrupad)*

Come, oh Lord!
How did You grace my house by Your sacred feet!
You have done well by coming, my *Navala Lal*, Krishna!

You are wise, learned and are familiar with all qualities *(gunas)*.
You are the embodiment of the Great Knowledge.
Wandering elsewhere, you took long to come to me.
Oh, kindly One, you should not do this.

Oh, Lord of Tansen, You, the Omnipresent.
Reveal yourself to me so that I feel blessed!

❖

ध्रुपद शंकरा चौताल

स्थायी - आयो कैसे आवन पाये, भले हो आये. मेरे नवल लाल
अन्तरा- तुम हो चतुर सुजान, बूझत सब गुन-विधान.
महारान मूरत हो अति रसाल.
सञ्चारी- हम सों अवधि बदी, अन्त बिरम रहे, ऐसो न कीजे दीनदयाल.
आभोग - "तानसेन" के प्रभु तुम हो बहुनायक दीजे दरश कीजे निहाल.

स्थाई

| 0 | | 3 | | 4 | | x | | 0 | | 2 | |
|---|---|---|---|---|---|---|---|---|---|---|---|
| सां | - | न | प | न | ध | सं | - | न | प | ग | - |
| आ | S | यो | S | जी | S | कैं | S | S | S | से | S |
| ग | प | ग | सा | स | ऩ | - | मऩ | स | स | स | - |
| आ | S | व | S | न | पा | S | य | S | भ | ले | S |
| न | प़ | ऩ | ध़ | स | स | - | ग | - | प | न | प |
| ही | S | आ | S | S | ये | S | मे | S | S | S | S |
| ग | प | न | ध | सां | - | सं | गं | सं | न | प | प. |
| रे | S | S | S | S | S | न | व | ल | ला | S | ल |

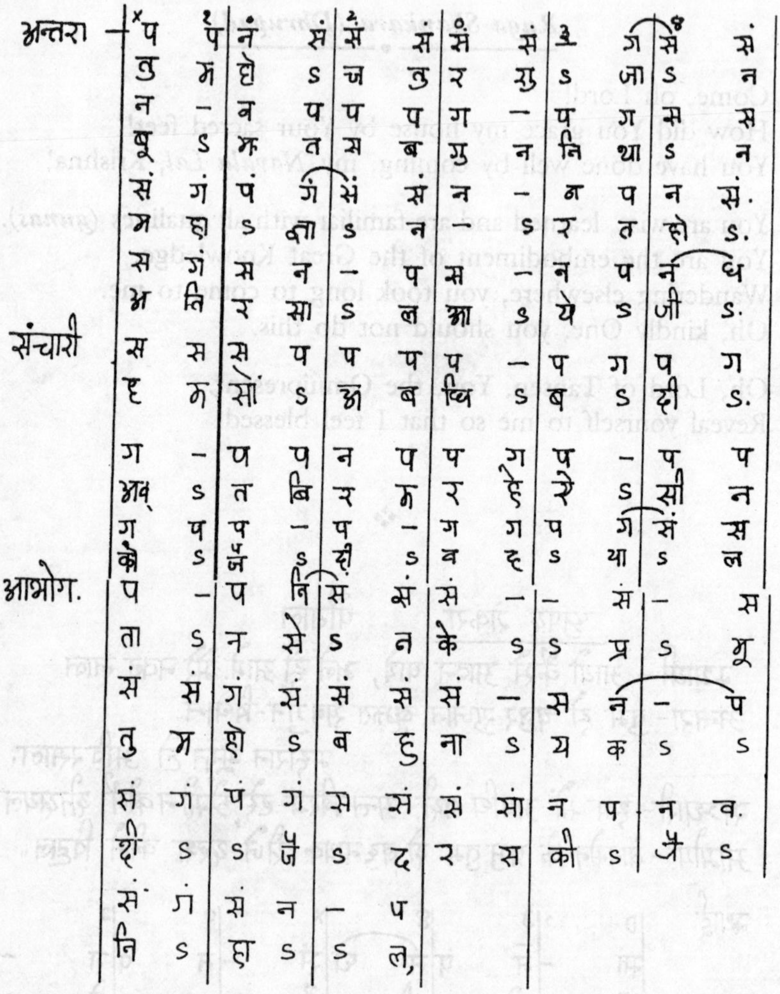

| | | | | | | | | | | | | |
|---|---|---|---|---|---|---|---|---|---|---|---|---|
| अन्तरा | प | पं | नं | सं | सं | सं | सं | सं | — | ग | सं | सं |
| | तु | म | हो | ऽ | ज | तु | र | गु | ऽ | जा | ऽ | न |
| | न | — | न | प | प | प | ग | — | प | ग | म | स |
| | बू | ऽ | झ | त | स | ब | गु | न | नि | था | ऽ | न |
| | सं | गं | पं | गं | सं | सं | न | — | न | प | न | सं. |
| | म | हा | ऽ | ता | ऽ | न | — | ऽ | र | त | हो | ऽ. |
| | स | गं | म | न | — | प | म | — | न | प | न | ध |
| | अ | ति | र | सा | ऽ | ल | आ | ऽ | ये | ऽ | जी | ऽ. |
| संचारी | स | स | स | प | प | प | प | — | प | ग | प | ग |
| | ह | म | सो | ऽ | अ | ब | वि | ऽ | ब | ऽ | दी | ऽ. |
| | ग | — | प | प | न | प | प | ग | प | — | प | प |
| | अव् | ऽ | त | बि | र | म | र | हे | रे | ऽ | सी | न |
| | ग | प | प | — | प | — | ग | ग | प | ग | सं | स |
| | को | ऽ | जन | ऽ | ही | ऽ | व | ह | ऽ | या | ऽ | ल |
| आभोग. | प | — | प | नि | स | सं | सं | — | — | सं | — | स |
| | ता | ऽ | न | से | ऽ | न | के | ऽ | ऽ | प्र | ऽ | भु |
| | सं | सं | गं | सं | सं | सं | सं | — | स | न | — | प |
| | तु | म | हो | ऽ | ब | हु | ना | ऽ | य | क | ऽ | ऽ |
| | सं | गं | पं | गं | स | सं | सं | सां | न | प | न | व. |
| | ही | ऽ | ऽ | जै | ऽ | द | र | स | की | ऽ | जै | ऽ |
| | सं | गं | सं | न | — | प | | | | | | |
| | नि | ऽ | हा | ऽ | ऽ | ल, | | | | | | |

## *Raga Komala Rishabha Asavari (Dhamar)*

You have come home so late, my *Lal*!
Where had you been all night?
With collyrium on your lips and *mahavar* on your forehead,
You are swaying on your feet.
You had promised me you would come, but you went elsewhere.
Who has enticed you, oh *Lal*?

Oh Lord of Tansen! Now stay with him,
For you find no ease away from him.

❖

## राग – कोमल रिषभ आसवरी (धमार)

भोर हिं आये मेरे आँगन सगरि श्यन तुम कहाँ जागे ललव?
अधर अँजन, भाले महावर, डगमगात पग धरत धरन॥
आवन बदि मोसे अन्त सिधारेहु कवन रस बस कर लिए ललव,
तानसेन के प्रभु वहीं सिधारो, जाही के घर रहे बिन कल न॥

| 1 | 2 | 3 | 4 | 5 | 6 | 7 | 8 | 9 | 10 | 11 | 12 | 13 | 14 |
|---|---|---|---|---|---|---|---|---|---|---|---|---|---|
| नि॒ | नि॒ | ध॒ | प | प | म | प | म | ग॒ | रे॒सा | रे॒ | म | प | प |
| मो | ऽ | ऽ | र | हिं | ऽ | ऽ | आ | ऽ | ऽये | मे | ऽ | रे | ऽ |
| प | प | प | प | प | प | प | नि॒ | नि॒ | नि॒ | ध॒ | ध | प | प |
| आँ | ऽ | ऽ | ग | ऽ | न | ऽ | स | ग | रि | र | ऽ | य | न |
| म | प | म | प | नि | ध | प | मप | ग | रेसा | रे | म | प | प |
| तु | ऽ | म | क | हाँ | ऽ | ऽ | जाऽ | ऽ | गेऽ | ला | ऽ | ल | व |
| म | ष | प | न॒ | ध॒ | सं | सं | सं | सं | सं | स | रें | सरे | गरे |
| अ | ध | ऽ | र | ऽ | ऽ | ऽ | अँ | ज | न | भा | ऽ | [illegible] | लेऽ |
| सं | रें | नि॒ | सं | सं | सां | सां | म | प | प | ध॒ | ध | सां | सां |

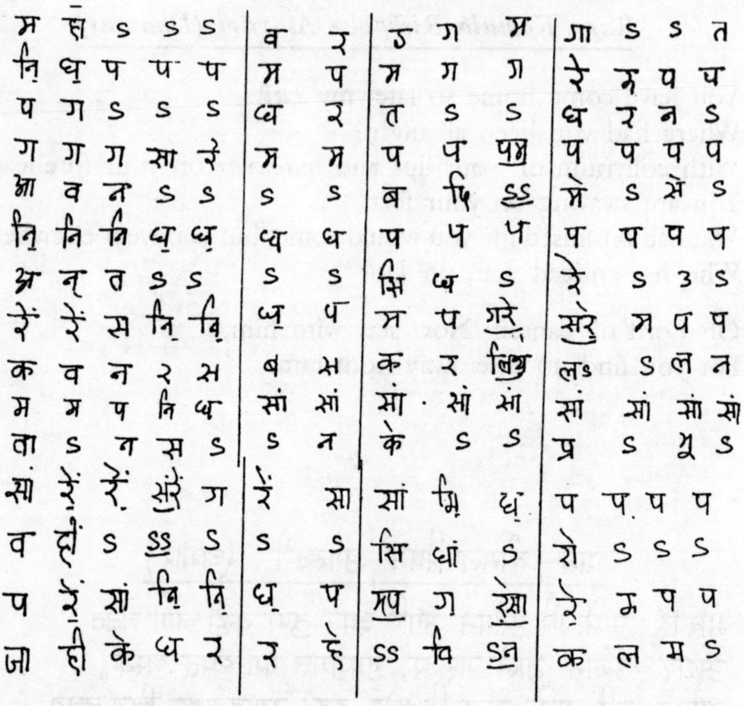

| म | हा | ऽ | ऽ | ऽ | व | र | ऽ | ग | म | गा | ऽ | ऽ | त |
|---|---|---|---|---|---|---|---|---|---|---|---|---|---|
| नि | ध | प | प | प | म | प | म | ग | ग | रे | म | प | प |
| प | ग | ऽ | ऽ | ऽ | ध | र | त | ऽ | ऽ | ध | र | न | ऽ |
| ग | ग | ग | सा | रे | म | म | प | प | पम | प | प | प | प |
| आ | व | न | ऽ | ऽ | ऽ | ऽ | ब | दि | ऽऽ | मे | ऽ | से | ऽ |
| नि | नि | नि | ध | ध | ध | ध | प | प | प | प | प | प | प |
| अ | न | त | ऽ | ऽ | ऽ | ऽ | सि | ध | ऽ | रे | ऽ | 3 | ऽ |
| रें | रें | स | नि | नि | ध | प | म | प | गरे | सरे | म | प | प |
| क | व | न | र | स | ब | स | क | र | लिख | लऽ | ऽ | ल | न |
| म | म | प | नि | ध | सां | सां | सां | सां | सां | सां | सां | सां | सां |
| ता | ऽ | न | स | ऽ | ऽ | न | के | ऽ | ऽ | प्र | ऽ | गु | ऽ |
| सां | रें | रें | सारें | ग | रें | सा | सां | मि | ध | प | प | प | प |
| व | हीं | ऽ | ऽऽ | ऽ | ऽ | ऽ | सि | धां | ऽ | रो | ऽ | ऽ | ऽ |
| प | रें | सां | नि | नि | ध | प | मप | ग | रेसा | रे | म | प | प |
| जा | ही | के | ध | र | र | है | ऽऽ | वि | ऽन | क | ल | म | ऽ |